AFRICAN PURSUIT

DAVID ALRIC

To Amy
Happy Christmas
from David Alric
December, 2014

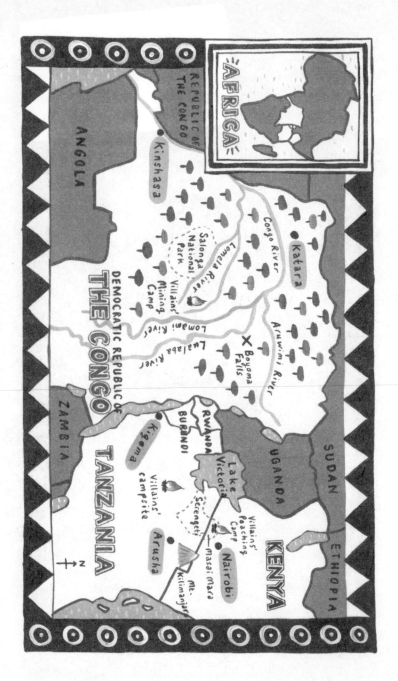

AFRICAN PURSUIT

DAVID ALRIC

Illustrated by
David Dean

Acme Press

First published in 2011
by Acme Press Limited
PO Box 65725, London, N21 9AY

Printed and bound by CPI Group (UK) Ltd, Croydon, CR0 4YY

British Library Cataloguing in Publication Data. A catalogue record for this book is
available from the British Library.

ISBN 978-0-9568356-0-4

To Pauline

Acknowledgements

The author wishes to thank his wife, children and grandchildren for their help and patient support during the writing of this book, Catherine and Pauline for their editorial and secretarial contributions and Toby Clements for his constant encouragement.

He greatly valued the advice he received from his five young advisers, Clare McEvoy, Lucy McEvoy, Georgie Hill, Martha Clements and Sadhbha Cockburn, all of whom made comments that influenced the final text.

Finally, his grateful thanks are due to David Dean for his wonderful illustrations, Stephen Page of Faber & Faber for his kindness and generosity, Clive Martin for his help in creating Acme Press and John Nicholson and Steve Millar of Design Online for their expert and patient assistance.

Contents

Preface

The first two books in this series recounted the extraordinary adventures of the Bonaventure and Fossfinder families in the remote jungles of the Amazon river. This book completes the trilogy of stories, and for the benefit of those readers who have not yet had the opportunity to read *The Promised One* and *The Valley of the Ancients,* a brief synopsis of those stories is included below as a prologue.

As in the first two books of the trilogy, I have tried in this tale to combine an adventure story with a style of writing that is fairly demanding in its use of grammar and vocabulary, and to incorporate a great deal of factual information about geography, science and natural history. Although the book is primarily intended as a story for children I have endeavoured to write it in a style that will appeal to all ages and hope that it will be enjoyed as much by adults as by younger people. I make no apologies for the somewhat challenging level of English that I have employed but, as in the previous books, I have included a glossary of unusual and difficult words to help the young reader with vocabulary. I have also included new versions of '*Lucy's Lexicon*' and '*Notes on the names in the book*' so that readers can again have some fun guessing the meanings of neologisms and names and, perhaps, learn something at the same time.

With regard to units of measurement I have used the same compromise as in the previous books in the trilogy. Heights and distances are usually expressed in imperial units, particularly when referred to by the older characters in the book for whom such usage would be everyday speech. I have used metric units or SI units for specific anatomical dimensions and scientific measurements. These 'rules' have not been rigidly applied and I have endeavoured to use those units that would come most naturally to an English-speaking person in the particular situation being described. I have included a short unit conversion table at the end of the glossary.

Happy reading!

David Alric, London, 2009

Prologue

This story is set in the present day and starts as the Bonaventure family return to England after spending an eventful fortnight in Brazil with their close friends, the Fossfinders. The families share an extraordinary secret. Thirteen-year-old Lucy Bonaventure is the Promised One, somebody whom animals throughout the world have been expecting since time immemorial to come and restore harmony between mankind and the animal kingdom. Lucy has an elder sister Clare who is nineteen and a younger sister Sarah who is ten. The Fossfinders have two boys, Clive who is twenty and Mark who is seventeen.

The first book in the trilogy, *The Promised One*, describes how Lucy regains consciousness after a road accident and finds that she has acquired the power to speak to animals. Following the discovery of her apparently unique ability, Lucy and her family have some extraordinary adventures. Shortly after her accident Lucy, with the help of various animals, rescues her explorer father, Richard, from a remote jungle valley in the Amazon containing prehistoric animals from the Pleistocene era where he has been trapped for several months with two other scientists, Helen and Julian Fossfinder. The Fossfinders, inevitably, learn of Lucy's power, but the two families

1

agree to keep this knowledge secret from outsiders to protect her from those who might wish to exploit her special ability.

In the second book of the trilogy, *The Valley of the Ancients*, the two families return to South America eighteen months after their first adventure to investigate a valley adjacent to the one they had previously explored, which they suspect might contain creatures surviving from an even more remote era. The explorers narrowly escape with their lives for not only does their plane crash into a crater inhabited by dinosaurs, but they come into conflict with an avaricious professor and his criminal gang who are making invisibility robes from a special ore found only in that crater. Before coming to the crater the professor had stolen the secret of making the invisibility material from his research assistant, Lucinda, whom he had tried to murder but, unknown to him, she had survived the attempt.

All the villains except the professor are eventually killed by prehistoric animals and he is seriously injured while trying to hijack Julian's plane with the intention of leaving the explorers to die in the crater.

This final story in the trilogy begins with the Bonaventures returning home to England from their second Amazon adventure and the evil professor fighting for his life in a Brazilian hospital.

1

A Nightmare Recalled

Thirty-five thousand feet above the Atlantic, the plane flew steadily towards Heathrow in brilliant late-afternoon sunshine above the ocean clouds. During the long flight Richard was making some scientific notes about the flora and fauna of the new valley they had discovered and Joanna was sitting next to him reading the newspaper. Suddenly she nudged him and pointed to an article she had just read. He glanced over, then seeing the heading to the article, dropped his work, took the paper from her and started to read.

Second sighting of 'monkey' girl

from our correspondent in the Democratic Republic of Congo

Two weeks ago in this column I reported that villagers in a remote area close to the Salonga National Park claimed to have seen a white girl of about thirteen foraging with a small group of bonobos (pygmy chimpanzees). On being approached the group had disappeared immediately into the forest, accompanied by the girl who seemed to move through the undergrowth with extraordinary agility. As there had been no reports of missing children in the area no further action was taken. Wildlife experts are anxious that the few remaining groups of this threatened species should be left as undisturbed as possible and, as the sighting occurred shortly after a somewhat boisterous tribal wedding party, no further credence was given to the villagers' tale.

Yesterday, however, the story took an intriguing turn. Two (alleged) poachers arrested in the reserve said that they had not been after bush meat but had seen a child in the forest and had gone into the reserve to rescue her. When they called to her she climbed a tree at an astonishing speed, joined several small apes and then made off with them in the trees through forest so dense that the men were unable to follow.

These sightings inevitably raise the question as to whether this is a feral child – one who, by being lost or abandoned, has become separated from human society and has been reared by wild animals. Stories of such children have been around for thousands of years and many of them are clearly the stuff of myth or legend. Famous fictional feral children include Romulus and Remus, the founders of Rome; Mowgli, from The Jungle Book *by Rudyard Kipling; and Edgar Rice Burroughs' Tarzan. There are, however, approximately one hundred reports in the literature of real feral children. Some of the most famous of these include the Hessian wolf children (1341); Wild Peter of Hamelin (1724); Victor of Aveyron (1797), portrayed in the film* L'Enfant Sauvage *by Francois Truffaut; Kaspar Hauser (1828), found near Nuremberg in Germany; and the Indian Wolf Girls (1920) aged eight and eighteen months, who were discovered in the care of a she-wolf in Godamuri, India.*

Researching these cases has proved to be one of the most fascinating assignments I have ever undertaken but it has also been, it has to be said, a somewhat depressing one. Most of these children, isolated from all human contact from a very early age, never become satisfactorily reintegrated into society. They rarely learn to speak properly, and many die at an early age. It is to be hoped that, if the present stories turn out to be true, and this 'monkey' girl is restored to the community, modern

4

psychological rehabilitation techniques will prove to be more successful than those attempted in previous cases.

Richard lowered the paper, frowning. He looked at Joanna, then turned to see what the others were doing. Clare was studying a medical book, Clive was listening to his iPod, and Lucy and Sarah were watching the in-flight movie. His three young nephews were all asleep. They had come with the family to South America for a holiday and had spent their time sightseeing with Joanna while the others explored the remote Amazon valley. He looked back to Joanna. Her eyes were moist.

'Is it possible?' His voice came out in a whisper.

'I don't know,' said Joanna, her voice trembling. 'I just... don't... know.'

Richard picked up the paper and together they read the article again.

'It's the right place... and the girl's the right age... but how could she possibly have survived that hell?' said Richard.

'It would have been a miracle,' Joanna agreed. She paused. 'But we've got to go and check. Otherwise we'll never sleep easy again for the rest of our lives.'

They both lay back, held hands and wrestled with their tormented thoughts as the plane thundered on towards the evening sky.

Richard woke from a fitful sleep. The plane was in darkness apart from a few subdued reading lights here and there, and silent but for the continuous drone of the engines. He turned to check on Joanna but she was fast asleep. A passing stewardess noticed he was awake and he gratefully accepted her whispered offer of a drink of chocolate. As he sipped the steaming cup his thoughts turned, inevitably, to the 'monkey girl' article which had recalled for them both the terrible events surrounding Lucy's birth. Richard and Joanna had met and married while working in the same university botany department. Their work on tropical species of trees involved them in field trips to faraway places but after their first daughter Clare was born Joanna no longer accompanied Richard on these expeditions as they involved trekking and camping in remote, wild places under conditions unsuitable for a young baby.

When Clare was six, however, they were invited to undertake a particularly interesting one-year project in the Democratic Republic of Congo, then called Zaire. The research opportunity focused on a species of fig that had been one of Joanna's major research interests and so they decided to go together, leaving Clare back in England in the care of Joanna's parents.

When, five months into the project, Joanna discovered with delight that she was pregnant, she and Richard were pleased when they realised that she would have just enough time to complete her work and return to England before the actual birth. This was a relief because their studies were being conducted in an exceedingly remote area with only limited medical facilities, and political upheavals in the region were leading to increasing civil unrest.

The project went well: they were lucky enough to discover a large stand of the trees they were studying very close to the village they were using as a base. This meant that they had to make only relatively few camping trips into the bush. As the months passed Richard noticed Joanna's rapidly growing size and began to wonder if she was expecting twins. Although he had qualified in medicine before becoming a botanist he had never prac

had virtually no obstetric experience. Fortunately

in the village who worked for the World Health

had been there for years and was known throughout

as 'Big Mama'. Her daughter Mzuri was a kind girl o͟   who

had been halfway through nursing training when her hospital had

been burned down in a recent riot and she was now back living at

home. Until she could resume her training she was helping Joanna in

the house and she cooked local dishes that Richard was particularly

fond of. Richard asked Big Mama for her advice about Joanna and

she agreed with him that Joanna was probably going to have twins,

though without any ultrasound equipment she couldn't be absolutely

certain. Richard and Joanna were concerned about this for they were

not due to return to England for another month and knew that twins

often arrived early. They were now at a crucial stage of their work,

however, and Joanna was very keen not to shorten their stay.

'It'll probably be fine,' she said, 'but if I do go into labour I'm sure

you and Big Mama can cope between you – she must have delivered

hundreds of babies over the years.' Richard wasn't so sure about

coping, but reluctantly agreed to stick to their original travel plans.

During the next fortnight, however, the civil unrest rapidly

became worse and when they heard reports of groups of rebel soldiers

marauding neighbouring towns and villages they both realised it was

time to go. The roads were now unsafe – many had been mined and

others were under guerrilla control and the only safe route back to the

airport was an armoured train that ran once a day. A few hours before

they were due to leave Richard heard a gasp and ran through to where

Joanna was doing some final packing. She sat on the edge of the bed

clutching her swollen abdomen.

'you all right?' asked Richard.

'Well, yes and no,' Joanna replied with a nervous smile. 'I've had a few twinges in the last few days that I haven't worried you with. They turned out to be false alarms, but now I think I may be going into labour. We'd better wait and ...' but before she could finish Richard had gone to find Mzuri. 'Quick,' he said, 'get your Mum. I think Joanna's started!'

By the time Big Mama appeared Joanna had had another contraction and had decided that this time she really was in labour. Just at that moment there was the sound of distant rifle fire and, going out into the street, Richard saw that many of the villagers were leaving, some with hastily packed possessions on carts and bicycles, others leading goats and sheep. People were shouting and screaming and there was a general air of panic. Richard rushed back inside but saw at once that the labour was now well in progress and that it was too late to try and escape. The next few hours were the worst he had ever experienced. He was overcome with guilt and remorse at having got them into this awful situation and bitterly regretted that he hadn't insisted on their returning to England earlier. Big Mama remained calm and efficient throughout, comforting and helping Joanna and reassuring Richard.

Eventually the first baby was born.

'It's a girl!' Mama announced. 'A beautiful girl.' She showed her to Joanna then gave her to Mzuri, telling her daughter to take the infant across to the clinic and clean her and wrap her up. Big Mama's clinic was across the road and was stocked with dressings, nappies and baby clothes. When Mzuri had left with her precious bundle Mama turned back to Joanna. 'Now for number two,' she said briskly. Sure enough within five minutes the second child was born. 'It's another girl,' said Mama excitedly. 'I can't be sure, but I think they're identical twins.'

A few moments later, however, their feelings of elation, were deflated by a series of events that they would all remember in vivid detail for the rest of their lives. There had been sporadic gunfire throughout the whole time she had been in labour, but now, terrifyingly near, came the sound of automatic weapons. Mama ran to look out of the window facing the clinic, then turned and thrust the baby and a handful of towels into Richard's arms.

'Quick – take Joanna and the baby. The truck is out the back. The keys are in the ignition.You'll have to risk the roads. Go! Now!'

'But the first baby,' cried Joanna. 'What about my other baby!'

Mama turned, tears streaming down her face.

'I fear we have both just lost a daughter, Memsahib. The rebels have taken the clinic and will invade here shortly. I will stay and do what I can, but you must go.' Even as she spoke they heard the sound of voices outside the door. Richard grabbed Joanna with his free hand and pulled her out to the pick-up truck outside. Frantically he wrenched open the car door, helped Joanna into the back seat and bundled the screaming baby into her arms. He dashed round to the driver's door, jumped in, and prayed the engine would start. To his heartfelt relief it did so even as a burst of machine-gun fire came from within the room they had just left and as the truck roared off with a squeal of tyres a group of young men in camouflage gear ran out into the road and started firing. As the truck disappeared in a cloud of dust the firing petered out and soon they had escaped. As the truck bounced over the uneven road Richard prayed they wouldn't hit a mine or a road block. The baby was now silent and he glanced back to see that Joanna was now feeding her, weeping bitterly as she did so.

'We had to save this one,' was all Richard could think to say. Joanna nodded through her tears. By some miracle they reached the airport

'We had to save this one...'

unscathed. A British consular official dealing with the crisis issued them with emergency passports and they flew back to London with their new baby, torn between relief at having escaped with their own lives and that of this little infant, and desperate sorrow at their loss.

On the flight home Joanna and Richard had decided not to tell Clare what had happened. She was overjoyed to see her parents again with her new baby sister Lucy, and there seemed nothing to gain from telling her all the tragic circumstances surrounding the loss of Lucy's twin.

Over the years they had never quite got round to telling Lucy either. They had vaguely imagined they would tell her when she was older but, somehow, the time had never seemed quite right.

And now? Richard dragged his thoughts back to the present. As he and Joanna had read the newspaper article a few hours earlier, the same incredible thought had come into both their minds. Was it conceivable that Lucy's twin sister had survived? The child mentioned in the article was the same age as Lucy, and lived in the very area where the twins had been born.

Suddenly Richard was struck by an overwhelming thought. The feral child described in the new article was apparently living with animals. If she was Lucy's identical twin she had an identical genetic make-up to Lucy, and an identical brain structure, and an identical ability to... Richard's mind was spinning with the possible implications. *That* was why this feral child could live among the animals. Suddenly he was seized with the conviction that this feral child must indeed be Lucy's twin. He recalled Joanna's words: '... *we've got to go and check. Otherwise we'll never sleep easy again for the rest of our lives.*'

She was right. They would have to go to Africa – and as soon as possible. If the child *was* his daughter he couldn't bear the thought of what might happen to her. His blood ran cold at the thought of the scores of journalists and sensation-seekers already heading for the jungle as a result of the article. Would she be hunted down and kept captive or killed, or, perhaps even worse, captured and smuggled away to appear in freak shows or circuses?

The stewardess started to pull up the blinds in the cabin. It was time for breakfast. Richard waited impatiently for Joanna to wake up. They had a lot to talk about.

2

Rescued from Rebels on the Rampage

Mzuri-Mlezi Hakimu had been born in Kenya in 1976 where her father worked as a game warden in the Tsavo National Park. When she was five he had been offered a post as a ranger in the Salonga National Park in the Congo where his brother already worked as chief ranger. Her father had felt honoured to be offered a position at the famous game reserve, the largest tropical rainforest reserve in Africa, which had become a UNESCO World Heritage Site in 1984. Despite the upheaval of moving to a new country with a young child, he and Mzuri's mother had both realised that the job was one that he had to accept, and so they had set up home in the heart of the Congo.

Her mother, known to everyone as 'Big Mama', was a midwife who ran a small maternity clinic, funded by the WHO, in the tiny village where they lived. Opposite the clinic was a house owned by the United Nations Organization where various scientists stayed when conducting studies at the nearby game reserve. Petrol generators maintained the electricity supply to both the clinic and the UN house during the frequent local power cuts. Throughout Mzuri's childhood there was an undercurrent of political unrest and her mother, aware from her own childhood during the Mau Mau uprising in Kenya of the intense passions that could be aroused by tribal loyalties and jealousies, decided to build an underground storeroom in her clinic which could, in a crisis, act as a temporary refuge or hidey-hole. She was a large, strong, practical woman and over a period of months she excavated a large chamber under the floor of a back room in her clinic and covered it with timber, which became the restored floor of the original room.

A trapdoor and a few steps led down into the chamber and when the trapdoor was shut, and the boards covered with rush matting, no casual observer would ever guess that a secret chamber existed below the floor. In this cool chamber lined with shelves she kept some clinic supplies, tinned food and bottled water, and a chemical toilet, a refrigerator and a freezer. The only other people who knew of the existence of this extra storage space were her daughter and her husband, Mlinzi.

From an early age Mzuri had decided that she would like to train as a nurse and eventually take over her mother's clinic. In 1996 rebel groups started the campaign of insurgencies that would eventually culminate in the first Congo war and, in an early incident in this unrest, the hospital at which Mzuri was training was burnt down. She returned home to help her mother at the clinic and was delighted to earn some money by doing some housework and cooking for the current tenants at the UN house opposite – a Dr and Mrs Bonaventure.

Mrs Bonaventure was pregnant with twins and just before she was due to return to England she went into premature labour. By a malignant stroke of fate this happened on the very day that a violent insurrection occurred in a nearby village and during the labour Mzuri was terrified by the sound of repeated gunfire drawing ever nearer.

When the first baby was delivered Big Mama was concerned that its airways were obstructed by mucus. 'Take the baby to the clinic,' she told Mzuri quietly, not wishing to alarm the Bonaventures. 'Quickly, there is a sucker there and you can extract the mucus. Then,' she added more loudly, 'clean the baby, wrap her and bring her back here so you can help me with the next one.'

Mzuri hurried across the road with her precious bundle and was horrified to see a band of armed guerrillas moving up the road towards her down the street, firing randomly into the air over the houses they passed. Some drank beer from a bottle held in one hand while firing a rifle with the other. One of her neighbours, a kind man she had known for years, ran out into the street to protest and she saw him fall in the gutter riddled with bullets. She hurried into the clinic, praying she had not been seen. She cleaned out the baby's nose and mouth with the sucker, switched off the machine, opened the back door to make it look as though the clinic occupants had fled, then opened the trapdoor into the hidden storeroom. She took the baby down, closing the door behind her. Big Mama had nailed a square of rush mat to the top of the door, so once it was closed it was invisible amongst the other squares of matting. The baby, stimulated by being cleaned, was now crying lustily and Mzuri hurriedly made up a bottle of feed from the supplies in the chamber. No sooner had the infant started sucking at her bottle than Mzuri heard the front door crash open, the clump of boots across the floor above her and coarse shouting and laughter from the soldiers. Mzuri sat terrified as she fed the child and prayed that she wouldn't start crying again; her initial fear subsided when there was no sign of the trapdoor's being discovered, only to be replaced by a fresh horror: from the shouted instructions she could hear she realised that the officer in charge had decided to make the clinic their base in the village. How on earth could she keep the baby quiet for days on end? She cuddled the baby close and to her relief the infant eventually fell asleep. Mzuri had never felt so lonely or frightened. She was desperately worried about what might have happened to her mother and the Bonaventures, and if the soldiers above her settled in for several days, she couldn't imagine how she could avoid detection. She was in no doubt as to what the outcome would be for her and the baby if they were discovered.

In the morning, after a night spent sick with fear – she didn't dare even to doze in case the baby woke and started crying – Mzuri was surprised at the absence of noise above. She gently laid the baby down, and treading carefully went up the steps and listened at the trapdoor. To her disappointment she could hear heavy breathing – they must still be there. Then she heard what sounded like a groan and someone retching. They were obviously all in a drunken stupor. She crept back to the baby and used the temporary respite to have something to eat herself and to prepare some more feeds for the baby. She then sat down to wait and eventually, as all remained quiet above, she fell into a fitful sleep. She awoke with a shock to hear the baby crying and hurried to calm her, but all remained quiet above. She looked at her watch and saw that it was already six in the evening; she had been in hiding for almost thirty hours. By midnight she had still heard nothing from above and wondered if she dare peep out, but decided that she would play safe and wait until early the next morning when any soldiers still present might be asleep or still drunk. At five o'clock the following morning she cautiously pushed the trapdoor but to her horror it did not move. She pushed harder and suddenly it gave way and swung open much faster than she had intended. There was a thump as something fell off it. She froze but there was no further sound.

Eventually she put her head out and looked around. An extraordinary sight met her eyes. The bodies of three soldiers lay in the clinic; the leg of one had been sprawled across the trapdoor which is why she had at first been unable to open it. She climbed out and looked around. The room stank of beer and smoke but there was also another smell: a chemical odour. Guns and beer bottles littered the floor. The shelves of the clinic were practically empty and Mzuri now saw that among the discarded bottles strewn about the room were the clinic's entire stock of chemicals and reagents. Looking out of the window she saw the body of another soldier in Big Mama's little vegetable garden and in the dawn light she could see smoke rising from the neighbouring plots and houses. The entire village had been ransacked and burnt. She and the baby had been saved from being hacked to death by Big Mama's secret chamber, but they had only escaped being burnt because the soldiers had chosen to make the clinic their own base. But what had happened to the soldiers? She looked around the devastated clinic and the truth dawned on her. The soldiers had drunk everything in the clinic that smelt of alcohol. The clinic had supplies of ethyl alcohol for medicinal purposes but other alcoholic substances were used as solvents and cleaners and chemical reagents. At her feet a young soldier was clutching a large flask with an English label. She bent down and read:

Danger !
Methyl alcohol. Use only as instructed.
Poisonous substance. Ingestion may cause blindness or death.

The flask was empty.

Despite the devastation wrought in her village Mzuri felt a spasm of sympathy and sorrow for the young rebels – conscripted probably against their will into an uprising that had led them to a ghastly end because of their inability to read a label. The front door was open and she ran out to see the smoking remnants of the Bonaventure house. She picked her way gingerly through the charred rubble and there, in the garden behind the house, lay Big Mama. The body of her father, Mlinzi, who had died trying to protect his wife, was lying nearby. Of the Bonaventures there was no sign. Mzuri knelt and rocked her mother's body in her arms and wept. She was there until the sun was flooding the garden with the light and heat of a new day, when she heard the baby crying and remembered that she now had a new responsibility. She covered her parents as best she could with bricks and stones and then hurried back to see to the baby.

Later that day, praying that she would not meet further rebels, she put the baby and some supplies into the basket of her bicycle and set off along the dusty road, strewn with cartridge cases, to her uncle's village. She had only cycled a hundred yards or so when a thought struck her. She stopped, torn between what she had just remembered and her desire to escape from the dreadful scene behind her as soon as possible. Soon, she had made her decision and reluctantly turned and cycled back to the Bonaventures' house; it was to be a decision with far-reaching consequences. Mercifully, the baby was fast asleep. She propped the bike against the blackened trunk of a tree and, averting her eyes from her parents' little cairn, dashed back into the ruined dwelling. She ran into the room that had been Dr Bonaventure's study and looked anxiously about her. The desk and all the filing cabinets had been destroyed, but the fireproof wall safe was intact. Its feet were cemented to the floor and its back screwed into the wall. Its solid steel door was pockmarked by bullets and the lock bore the scratchmarks of knives and bayonets, but the rebels had failed to open it. They had intended to return later with explosives but their plans, as Mzuri well knew, had come to an abrupt end in her own clinic. She knelt down and felt for the piece of Blu-Tack stuck behind the back foot of the safe. To her relief the key was there, embedded in the adhesive. She had never opened the safe but had been told where the key was, so that she could leave it undisturbed when cleaning the room. She hurriedly found what she sought: the passports that would prove the parentage of the baby now in her care. She also removed as many research files as she could manage: one day, she was sure, the child would be proud of her parents' discoveries. Soon she was back on her bike and cycling away as fast as she could.

As was the case in many such insurrections the fighting had been sporadic – at least in this area – and though her uncle's village was only a few miles away it was further from the main road, had no strategic importance, and had been completely unaffected by the fighting. Her uncle and aunt were horrified to hear her story and immediately took her and the baby in.

Mzuri wanted to report the baby to the authorities so that she could be reunited with her parents if they were still alive, but after some thought her aunt and uncle advised her against it.

'In these troubled times,' her uncle said, 'we can trust no-one. The fact that you worked for the English scientists may upset some of those in authority who are not friends with the UN. Others may be upset because you survived the massacre when others didn't, meaning you may be in sympathy with the rebels. If you talk to anyone you will put yourself and the baby in danger – and maybe us as well. Remember,' he added, 'from what you have told us the parents of this child can be in no doubt that she did not survive and they are fortunate to have escaped with her twin. We must pretend that the baby is yours – if anyone asks, we'll pretend you had a white husband who had to return urgently to Europe without ever knowing about his daughter – and your aunt and I will help you to teach her and bring her up. One day perhaps, when things have changed, we can tell her the truth.'

And so it was that Mzuri came to have a child. She called the baby Neema because she represented good fortune and grace, and grew to love her as her own. Her uncle Ulindaji who was now chief ranger at the reserve was very busy because the National Park had become a prime target for animal poachers during the civil war, but her aunt, who was a teacher, made sure that Neema received the best possible education under the circumstances. She was a happy child who was good at her school work, loved music and dancing, and excelled at all kinds of sports. The most striking thing about her, however, was her passion for animals and the degree to which they responded to her. Even the fiercest village dog would lick her hand and wag its tail for her and she was always surrounded by a variety of pets, some domestic, others half-wild who had come in from the bush and adopted her as their mistress.

Then one dreadful day in the aftermath of the second Congo war, when Neema was eleven years old, Mzuri's worst fears were realised.

Neema, as she had done frequently in recent months, had gone with Mzuri's uncle to the reserve where she seemed to be fascinated by the bonobo chimpanzees. A group of militia had turned up at the house and arrested Mzuri and her aunt. They then took them to the reserve where they arrested her uncle. Fortunately Neema was not with her uncle at the park office, but out in a forest research cabin watching the bonobos. She was not listed in any records and the army unit were completely unaware of her existence.

Mzuri was taken away in an army truck with her aunt and uncle. As they were driven away to an unknown destination Mzuri dreaded what might lie in store for them but most of all she feared for the fate of her precious Neema, alone in the forest and ignorant of what had happened to her family.

3

A Special Child

Neema's earliest memories were of happy times spent playing with her pets in the house and garden where she lived with Mzuri, her mother, and her great-aunt and great-uncle, whom she knew simply as 'grandma' and 'grandpa'.

As she grew older she was thrilled by Mzuri's stories of the faraway land where she had been born – a land of endless plains where giraffe and antelope grazed; where rhinos and elephants lived; and where lions, cheetahs and hyenas roamed in search of prey. Grandma was very kind but also very firm; she made sure that Neema learnt all her lessons, and taught her many things more than she learnt at the village school. Grandpa worked in the immense national park called Salonga which, he proudly told her, was the largest forest reserve in the whole of Africa and contained some of the rarest and most exciting animals in the world. After school he would take her with him on his expeditions along the enthralling jungle waterways and paths and she came to know the forest and its animals as well as any of the rangers who worked there.

Neema had discussed her pale skin with Mzuri and her 'grandparents' many times and knew that her father had been an Englishman who had returned to his own country long ago as the result of the troubles. There was not a single child in her school and village who had not been affected in some way by the two Congo wars that had occurred in their short lifetimes, and to have a missing, unknown or foreign parent was sufficiently commonplace as to arouse no curiosity whatsoever. Neema had always assumed Mzuri to be her mother and while Mzuri always intended one day to tell her the whole story and to answer truthfully any questions, those questions were never asked. Then, when Neema was eleven, something happened that was to change her life for ever. It was morning and Neema wasn't feeling well and had decided not to go to school. Grandpa and Mzuri had gone to work and Grandma had gone shopping.

At about half-past nine she suddenly developed a bad headache. One day in the future she would come to realise that, at that very moment, her identical twin sister was being knocked down by a car in a London suburb. For the moment, however, she knew of nothing but her headache, and she rang her grandfather at work in his office at Anga in the reserve.

'I expect it's just this virus that's going round,' he said. 'Have you taken anything? I think there's some paracetamol in Grandma's bedside cupboard. She shouldn't be out too long but if she isn't back by lunchtime, give me another ring and I'll try to pop back to see you.'

Neema carried a glass of water into her grandparents' bedroom and looked in the bedside cupboard, but there were no tablets there. As she turned back towards the door, she saw that Grandpa's desk, usually locked, was open. She looked inside and to her relief saw the tablets and took two immediately. As she did so she splashed a few drops of water onto some papers which she hurriedly mopped dry with a tissue. As she did so her attention was caught by a box file on which a label had been pasted. It said:

"In the event of the simultaneous death or disappearance of myself and my wife please deliver to the UNESCO heritage site office at Salonga or the British Embassy in Kinshasa."

Intrigued, Neema opened the file which contained all the material that Mzuri had retrieved from the safe in the Bonaventures' burnt-out home. There were two British passports and a bundle of research notes and letters, but on the very top was a letter written by her grandfather. Her mouth ran dry as she read it:

"To whom it may concern. I, Ulindaji Hakimu, do solemnly declare that the information below is accurate to the best of my knowledge:

The infant girl known as Neema, who has been brought up in my house under the care of my wife, Shangazi, and niece, Mzuri-Mlezi, is not related by blood to this family. She is the twin child of two UN scientists called Bonaventure from the UK who lost touch with her during rebel activity at the start of the first Congo War. I do not know the fate of her parents and twin sibling. They apparently escaped unscathed from a local massacre that took place at the time of Neema's birth, but I fear it is extremely improbable that they ever managed to leave the country alive. In order to protect the child during the various political upheavals that have ravaged the country during her lifetime we have brought her up as our own. I implore the recipient of this file to ensure that, in the more settled times that we hope and pray the future will bring, she may one day be made aware of her origins and be assisted in any appropriate action she may take, to re-establish contact with her roots and any surviving relatives. Her parents' passports are enclosed in this file together with a copy of my will in which I leave my estate to be divided equally between my niece, Mzuri, and the aforementioned adopted great-niece, Neema Bonaventure."

With shaking hands Neema closed the file and replaced it in the desk. Stunned by what she had just learnt, she went and lay on her bed to try and gather her thoughts. Her initial feelings of resentment against her 'family' were soon replaced by those of love and gratitude at the sacrifices they had all made on her behalf. She could see that they had attempted always to act in her best interests during the strife-torn years of civil war when neighbours had found themselves on opposing sides and nobody could trust anybody except their closest relatives.

It dawned on her now how her grandmother had tried to link her to her heritage by focusing so many of her extra lessons on British and European history and on English poetry and literature. And she had had a twin, probably dead, whom she had never known. She wondered whether it had been a boy or a girl.

As she pondered she became aware of unusual noises. She shook her head, thinking it was an unpleasant symptom of her viral infection, but the noises persisted. Gradually she began to realise that the noises were like distant voices. Then her pet mongoose scurried into the room, its eyes bright.

'Greetings O Special One!'

Neema looked about her in bewilderment, then back at the mongoose. There was no doubt it had spoken, for it lifted its head and repeated the greeting.

'Greetings to you also, little one,' said Neema. She did not speak aloud. She intuitively realised that she and the little creature could communicate soundlessly. *'Why can I suddenly speak to you?'* she asked.

'To learn that, thou must speak to wiser ones than I,' replied the mongoose. *'I am but a malevobane and know not of these things. Thou must seek out the little hairy tailless ones known as the bonobokin.'*

Neema knew immediately that the mongoose wanted her to speak with the bonobo chimps, a rare species of pygmy chimpanzee that her

grandfather had pointed out to her in a remote part of the reserve –
an area that he was especially careful to protect from poachers.

She suddenly felt a curious sense of elation at this new world of
experience that had opened for her. She opened the door and the
sound of the voices she had heard earlier assaulted her from all sides,
now loud and distinct. She realised that they came from countless
forest creatures: squirrels, birds, monkeys, even chameleons and
lizards. She made a conscious effort to exclude them and to her great
relief found she could 'turn down the volume' at will. Her headache
remained (as it would until her twin's operation had been successfully
completed) but had improved since taking the tablets and now
seemed less intrusive since her mind had become occupied with the
excitement of her new power.

She went back inside and rang her grandfather.

'Are you OK? Isn't Grandma back yet?' He sounded concerned.
Hearing him now, knowing for the first time of her true relationship
to him and the sacrifices he had made, she felt a sudden rush of
affection for this kind and generous man who had risked so much for
the sake of a foreign foster-child.

'I'm fine, grandpa,' she said. 'My headache's much better. In fact,
I was wondering if I could come in to see you later. I think a jungle
walk would do me good.' Her grandpa was relieved.

'Of course. I've got a conference with some UNESCO officials all
afternoon, but I'm sure you can accompany one of the rangers on his
rounds.'

She told the mongoose of her plans but decided not to tell any
of the family what had happened. She was sure that her new-found
powers were somehow related to the emotional shock of reading her
grandpa's letter, and she didn't wish the family to feel she had been

prying. She was also worried that they might think her viral infection was affecting her brain if she started telling them about her ability to talk to animals. As for her discovery about her parents, she needed more time to decide how – or whether – she would tell her beloved adoptive family that she now knew the truth.

Later that day Neema sat in the ranger's boat as they passed down the river, a tributary that led deep into the area of the bonobo tribe. The National Park was criss-crossed with waterways and travelling by boat was by far the best way of moving about. Over vast areas, indeed, it was the only means of travel at ground level. She knew that the rare species of chimp was found only in certain parts of the reserve and had specifically requested that the ranger did a detour through their territory. Eventually they stopped and moored beside a forest glade. The scene was magical. Steam rose from the trees and bushes and, around the edges of the glade, the sunlight streamed through countless gaps and spaces in the surrounding canopy. Exotic butterflies and giant dragonflies fluttered before their eyes and birds with brilliantly hued feathers flew across the glade and though the trees.

The ranger pointed silently and Neema nodded. She had known long before he pointed that the bonobos were there for she could hear them chattering among themselves; the kind of chatter that she now knew would be completely inaudible to the ranger. Suddenly the ranger's radio-bleep vibrated. He had switched it to silent mode as soon as he had seen the shy bonobos. He pressed it to his ear and, bending down into the boat, spoke in a low voice. Eventually he switched it off and turned to Neema.

'Bad news,' he whispered, 'poachers on the south-eastern border! They're shooting hippos for tusks and bush meat. I have to go immediately but we've got a problem. You can't possibly come with me – it's far too risky.'

'Leave me here,' said Neema. 'The bonobos don't attack humans. I'll just sit quietly till you return.'

'What! leave you alone in the jungle! Your grandpa would sack me on the spot.'

His bleep vibrated again and he again conversed rapidly.

'It's urgent: the poachers have cornered two of my colleagues and are firing at them. I've got to go. Look, I'll leave you the spare gun and once I'm under way I'll ring base and they'll send someone out to pick you up. They should be here in about twenty minutes. Stay still in the glade and keep well away from the water — the crocs are the greatest danger.'

'OK,' said Neema simply. Secretly she was delighted. The ranger showed her how to cock and uncock the rifle, helped her out of the boat, then set off at full speed to help his colleagues, radioing the base camp as he did so.

As soon as the craft had disappeared Neema walked further into the glade. She had never been alone in the jungle before and would certainly never previously have dared to wander through an unknown clearing. Her grandpa had told her about all the dangers that existed: the snakes that could poison or crush her; the insects that could sting or bite; the forest elephants and chimpanzees that were normally calm but which could be dangerous when frightened or excited; the unpredictable wild pigs; the crocodiles in the swamps and rivers; and countless other dangerous and venomous creatures. But now Neema felt no fear. She felt at one with the world of the animals and confident that she could talk to any creature she met. It gave her an immense sense of liberation as she strolled confidently into the centre of the glade.

'*I seek ye O bonobokin,*' she called. For a few seconds the voices of the astonished forest creatures surrounding her fell silent, then there was a burst of excited chatter as Neema's presence among them was revealed. Soon the branches parted at the edge of the glade and a bonobo emerged. It was a full-grown female, but the pygmy chimpanzee, even when standing erect, only came up to Neema's chest.

'*So thou art the one who speaks!*' she said. Neema was immediately aware of the fact that this creature was vastly more intelligent than her pet mongoose at home. The chimp continued: '*We have observed thee now for many moons with thy male kin and have sensed thee to be special; it is well that now thou canst speak to us.*' Neema was thrilled at being able to speak to the chimpanzees. She explained that very soon she would have to go but that she would return because she had so

'*So thou art the one who speaks...*'

many questions to ask. She noticed, even during the short period she was in the glade that many different species of animals had gathered near to see and hear her, and she began to wonder if this was simply natural curiosity, or whether she had some special significance for the animals. Suddenly the chimp became alert.

'Hark!' she said, looking across to the river. *'One of thy kin approaches in the house that floats; I must return to the trees. Come again soon to see us – there is much to tell thee.'* Then she disappeared silently into the undergrowth. Neema was surprised and disappointed to be "rescued" so soon. As it happened, another ranger had been patrolling in his boat only a few hundred yards away and had come immediately on receiving urgent instructions and coordinates from the park office.

When Neema got back to the main park offices her grandpa was just emerging from his conference. He looked pleased, and explained to Neema that UNESCO had agreed to fund a new observation laboratory for study of the bonobos. This gave Neema an idea and that evening she asked her grandfather if the scientists studying the bonobos could use some extra help.

'I'm sure they could,' said grandpa. 'A lot of the work involves sitting for hours and silently observing and recording the chimps' behaviour. It can be very boring and isn't always the best use of a skilled scientist's time.'

Soon a secure observation hut was built near the favourite haunt of the apes and Neema started to spend time after school, and at the weekends and holidays, observing the bonobos. At first she always accompanied one of the scientists, but she soon learnt the observation and recording routines and eventually persuaded her grandfather that she could sit alone in the hut in perfect safety.

On her first day alone in the hut Neema was very excited. At last she could wander out into the glade to speak to the bonobos without interruption!

Jambo, the female she had first spoken to, turned out to be the senior female in the tribe and she too was eager to resume their conversation. She explained that Neema was a human being whom the chimps had been expecting to come for a very long time. The chimp found it difficult to express lengths of time, but Neema was astonished to learn that she seemed to be referring to a period of thousands of years, or even longer.

'But who has been expecting me?' she asked. *'Is it just your kin or is it other animals too?'*

'It is all the junglekin,' said Jambo simply. On further enquiry Neema learnt that "the junglekin" were all the animals inhabiting the forest – not just the Salonga reserve but the entire extent of the tropical rainforest.

Jambo then tried to explain to Neema how the legend of her being expected had come about:

'Long, long ago, before the time of my mother's mother and many other mothers back in time, it is said that some hairy tailless ones left the junglekin and joined those animals in the Lesser World. It seems that over many, many moons those Tailless Ones outside became as thyself, without fur, and our legend says that one such would some day return and speak our tongue, and reunite those outside with the junglekin they had deserted long ago. I understand not all that this means but it seems as though thou art the one who returns, and to thee we owe our homage.'

Neema was astonished by these words. She had learnt theories about the possible evolution of mankind on the plains of Africa, and here was a creature who seemed to be referring to a time in prehistory when *Homo sapiens* and fellow hominids were developing from remote primate ancestors. It seemed impossible that such knowledge could have persisted in chimpanzee folk-legend over untold millennia, yet there seemed no other explanation for Jambo's words.

The bonobos made frequent references to "the junglekin", and Neema soon realised that the junglekin regarded themselves as being separate from, and superior to, the animals of the swamps and deserts to the north, and the savannahs to the east and south. The great apes – the gorillas and chimpanzees – had become, through their intelligence, the natural leaders of the junglekin and jealously guarded the status of the forest over which they held sway. The junglekin saw the rainforest as being the centre of all things. They referred to it as the Greater World and remained aloof from the animals of the plains and the rest of the Lesser World with which they had little or no communication.

Over the next two years Neema spent more and more time with the animals, and the UNESCO scientists were astonished and thrilled at the detailed information with which she was able to provide them.

'It's almost as if she could *talk* to these animals,' one of them said to Ulindaji during one of their scientific discussions. 'On our own we could never have acquired a fraction of the information she has provided us with.'

Ulindaji, naturally, imagined that Neema spent her observation periods sitting safely in the hut with a notepad, camera and radio, looking out with a pair of binoculars. In reality, of course, she spent the time roaming free with the bonobos learning everything about the way they lived and becoming skilled at climbing and swinging her way with lianas and creepers along their favourite jungle routes.

4

Bonding with Bonobos

Jambo was keen that Neema should meet as many of the junglekin as possible, and contrived that many animals made special journeys across the rainforest, sometimes hundreds of miles from their regular haunts, to meet Neema whom she referred to as "the Special One". In this way Neema met most of the principal rainforest animals: the massive gorillas who journeyed from afar to see her; the common chimpanzees; leopards; red-river hogs; hippos; forest elephants; pygmy buffalos; many different kinds of monkey; the shy and rare okapi; the beautiful bongo; and countless other fascinating animals and birds such as the potto, the pangolin, the golden cat, the bustard and the Congo peafowl.

Neema was fascinated by the interaction between the pygmy chimpanzees – the bonobos – and their larger cousins, the common chimpanzees. The latter were larger and heavier than the bonobos, and much more aggressive. Jambo explained that the common chimpanzees lived mostly on the other side of the great river and, as neither species liked swimming very much, they hardly ever met. Neema thought the bonobos seemed a bit frightened of the big chimps, but both groups still felt themselves to be superior to the even larger and coarser gorillas, and all the other creatures of the rainforest.

Neema was interested to meet the larger species of chimpanzee but was secretly relieved that it was the bonobos by whom she had been "adopted". In later years she was to learn that these gentle creatures were the closest genetic relatives to human beings in the animal kingdom, having about 99% of their genetic material in common with *Homo sapiens.*

One exciting day Jambo told Neema she was going to see two very special creatures.

'They live in the densest jungle and swamp,' she explained, *'and are but rarely seen beyond where they dwell. But they have now heard tell of thee through the fledgiquills and the Dreadful Ones and desire to see thee. We must go as near to them as we can, for they never venture far.'* Neema was fascinated and wondered what on earth they were about to see. Jambo and her sons took Neema to the farthest corner of their usual territory and then along tree paths she had never traversed before into the heart of the densest jungle she had ever encountered. Eventually they came to the edge of a swamp and the bonobos moved cautiously along the bank, peering nervously ahead at frequent intervals.

'Hist!' said Jambo suddenly, taking Neema's arm and pointing through the undergrowth. There, rising above the swampside bushes, was an enormous nest. It appeared to be constructed of whitened branches but, as they drew nearer, Neema realised with amazement that it was composed entirely of interwoven elephant tusks. Beyond it, at the edge of the swamp, stood a huge creature the like of which she had never seen before, even in picture books. It was larger than an elephant and brownish-grey in colour. It had a long tail like a crocodile and a long neck like a dinosaur. As it slowly turned its head to inspect the visitors Neema was astonished to see that it had a single giant horn, larger by far than the horns she had seen in pictures of

rhinos. She detected a primitive and unformed greeting emanating from the animal, which she acknowledged with a bow, but it became apparent that the bonobos were completely unaware that the creature had communicated with her.

'The Greathorn uses not the common tongue,' Jambo said quietly to Neema. As far as she was concerned the creature had just made a meaningless grunt. *'It speaks only to the Dreadful Ones.'* The bonobos were clearly terrified of the great beast, and the entire group withdrew with Neema as soon as possible. Neema was disappointed: she wanted to see if she could speak back to the extraordinary creature, but felt she had to follow Jambo and her family. Soon they were making their way back along the side of the swamp, the bonobos occasionally casting nervous glances behind them. Whatever the animal was, thought Neema, it certainly had a fearsome reputation.

They had travelled about a mile from the Greathorn and the chimps were looking considerably more relaxed when Jambo pointed across the grey-green water.

'Lo!,' she said, *'the other who seeks thee comes nigh.'* Then, over the swamp came a harsh and eerie cry. Neema looked out across the forbidding quagmire to see a black creature like a giant bat come flapping slowly across the swamp. The amazing creature had membranous wings spanning about two metres and a long black beak containing rows of vicious-looking teeth. It passed close to the girl and the apes, muttering a raucous rasping sound as it passed by and disappeared across the swamp.

'It's a pterodactyl!' Neema gasped aloud. Once again she had clearly been aware of a primitive greeting being emitted.

'I think the Great Flitterkin pays thee homage,' said Jambo. *'I cannot be certain, for he speaks only in a strange and ancient tongue,'* she added

by way of explanation. Before Neema had recovered from the shock of seeing a creature supposed to have been extinct for millions of years, she had another surprise. This time so, apparently, did Jambo. The chimp suddenly pointed across the swamp and said:

'The Ancient Ones come. I knew not that they were aware of thee'.

Neema gazed in fascination as two massive, long-necked shapes emerged through the surface of the swamp. From her school books she knew they could only be plesiosaurs and realised that the swamp she had been brought to contained several species that had survived since prehistory. The creatures gazed in silence for a few minutes at Neema then sank below the surface once again. A massive swirl of the waters as they disappeared gave Neema some idea of the true bulk of the monsters.

'It is said they speak but slowly and often not at all,' said Jambo, *'but they came to see thee. I have heard tell of them but never before have I seen them.'*

As they made their way back to the hut Neema wondered what she should say to her grandfather. She knew he would be particularly interested in these creatures, but could hardly admit she had travelled through the depths of the jungle to a swamp when she was meant to be sitting quietly in her hut. In the end she decided to mention only two of the animals she had seen, on the grounds that they were both species she could conceivably have seen from her observation post.

That night she told him first about the giant horned creature. To her surprise he showed no scepticism whatsoever, only giving a smile of quiet satisfaction.

'So it *does* exist!' he said. 'The BaAka pygmies in the north speak in their legends of a giant unicorn who lives in the remote swamps of Ndoki. The creature is called mokèlé- mbèmbé, which means "The

'The Ancient Ones come. I knew not that they were aware of thee...'

one who stops the flow of rivers" in the Lingala language. I once thought I saw one in the reserve here but never told anyone for fear of being called a fool or of being accused of trying to attract tourists with a "Loch Ness Monster" type of story. Your sighting proves that the creature exists and that there is a population here as well as at Ndoki. They say that the unicorn lies on a bed of elephant tusks, but I suspect that that part of the story is an embellishment to the original legend.' Neema smiled to herself but said nothing; she could hardly admit to having seen the creature's nest from a seat in her little hut.

Encouraged by her grandfather's response she then told him of the pterodactyl.

'Good heavens!' he said, in great excitement.' In one day, sitting quietly in your cabin, you've solved two of the greatest mysteries of the Congo basin!'

'Why, what did I see this time?' Neema asked innocently.

'From your description this is almost certainly the "flying demon of the swamps" – known to tribes in Zambia as Kongamato. The creature is most probably a living relic from the Cretaceous Period and has been seen by several respected scientists over the last hundred years in Zambia, Tanzania, Kenya, West Africa and Zaire. I think we can now submit an official report about these creatures in your notes. What a pity about the camera!' Neema had already explained that her sightings of the unicorn and the pterodactyl had been so fleeting, and she had been so excited to see them, that she hadn't had time to photograph either creature. She felt the white lie was justified in the circumstances.

'It's quite amazing, your seeing these Cretaceous Period creatures,' her grandpa continued. 'There have always been reports of mysterious creatures in the deep interior of the continent. Nobody believed even in the existence of the gorilla at first and the other "unicorn", the okapi, was only identified with certainty comparatively recently. Many other explorers have reported Loch Ness-type monsters in the remote jungle swamps and I see no good reason why some of these accounts might not also turn out to be true.' Neema had to bite her tongue not to tell grandpa of her other experience that day, but decided that it would be better to go on a swamp expedition with him on a future occasion when they might "discover" the plesiosaurs together.

The worst day in Neema's life dawned bright and clear. She was thirteen years old. After school she went as usual to the reserve to do a couple of hours observation. She thought her grandpa looked thoughtful as she left him in the park office to set off with a ranger to go to her cabin. She recalled that he had had a series of phone calls in the last few days that had left him preoccupied and tense, and had led to long discussions into the night between him and grandma and Mzuri. It seemed as though some politicians were becoming jealous of his prominence in zoological circles and of his close relationship with UNESCO officials. They were accusing him of fomenting unrest and having allies in anti-governent circles.

She was chatting to the bonobos when suddenly a grey parrot flew into the group and spoke quietly to Jambo. The little chimp turned to Neema.

'There is trouble,' she said. *'Tailless Ones with thundersticks have taken thy kin. Even now they are in a house that moves and travel to where the Brilliant One rises.'*

'Are they all gone?' asked Neema.

'Yes,' said the ape. *'Your mother and the two old ones have all been taken. Only she with the ears of silver remains. Other Tailless Ones with thundersticks stand near the place you dwell and it is not safe for you to return.'*

'Have my kin been hurt?' asked Neema, desperately upset and frightened.

'No, they seem to be unharmed. The fledgiquills say they sit talking together in the back of the house that moves. They have water to drink.'

Neema sat down to think. Her grandpa's political enemies must have arrested the family and they were obviously in a lorry, heading east. Her grandpa had repeatedly said that they wouldn't dare to execute him because of his links with the UN, so perhaps the plan was to exile him to Rwanda or Burundi. There were obviously guards keeping watch over the house so she clearly couldn't return there. The problem was, where could she go? The rest of her schoolfriends' parents were friendly with grandpa and grandma and she didn't know who else might be targeted in this political move. There was no-one she could really trust or, at least, there was no-one with whom she could be sure she would be safe. She might even bring trouble to an innocent family by staying with them.

She decided without further thought what she must do. She pulled her notepad towards her and scribbled a note to Chakula, the girl who helped the family with cooking and housework. She was seventeen, loved bangles and brooches and was particularly proud of her large silver earrings. She had obviously been spared as being unimportant by whoever was targeting the family.

"Dear Chakula,

I know what has happened to the others but I am safe. Please can you put some bottles of water, some matches and some clothes in a small bag and leave it near my bedroom window. I may send you more notes when I know what I need.

Thank you,

Love from Neema

P.S. Destroy this note immediately and tell no-one about it.

P.P.S. Don't forget my spare glasses!"

She folded the note into a tight wad and turned to Jambo.

'Jambo. I wish to come and stay with thee and thy kin.'

'That will be a great honour and privilege for us, O Special One,' was the immediate reply. *'We shall be held in high esteem by all the junglekin. No harm shall befall thee whilst thou art in our care.'* Neema was relieved to hear this reply.

'There are things I shall need from the place I dwell.' She handed Jambo the note she had just scribbled. *'Canst thou take this to the one with the silver ears? Those with the thundersticks must not see thee.'*

'My kin cannot be seen in the village,' said Jambo, *'for we never leave our own place. The leaf thou hast scratched on is small. A mimicquill shall take it.'*

She turned and called up to the canopy and within a few seconds a grey parrot fluttered down. Jambo spoke to it and soon it grasped the note in a powerful claw and flew off towards the village.

'Another must also go,' said Neema. *'Maybe one of the arborikin? One who can carry a burden.'* She gestured with her hands to indicate the size of a small bag. Jambo turned again to the canopy and soon a black and white colobus monkey swung effortlessly to the ground. Neema explained what he must do and soon he scampered away on his journey to Neema's bedroom window.

The next few days were both stressful and enthralling for Neema. She was in a state of constant concern for her family and could not see a satisfactory way out of her current situation that would enable her to resume a normal life. On the other hand she found life in the rainforest intensely liberating. The bonobos were gentle and kind and did their utmost to help her in every way. They brought her all manner of food: things with which she was familiar such as pineapples, peaches, avocados, bananas, papayas and coconuts, but also many kinds of succulent fruits and vegetables that were unfamiliar to her. They were terrified when she first lit a fire, but after a while got used to it and brought her fish and crustaceans to cook, and she baked eggs, yams and plantains in the ashes. She roamed far and wide in the vast jungle and was taken to regions so remote and impenetrable that they had never before been visited by any human being. After some days, to her great relief, the animals reported to her that her family were now in a land far to the east, and were no longer under guard. Neema correctly assumed that they had been exiled, and as the animals said that there were gorillas in that land, she guessed that they were probably in Rwanda. After much thought she used the birds to send them a message assuring them that she was safe and that would one day join them. She knew that they would be utterly bewildered by getting a message apparently out of nowhere (a crumpled note on a table near an open window), but decided that this was better by far than having them constantly wondering whether or not she was alive.

One day she was playing with some baby bonobos near the edge of the reserve while the adults foraged for food. Suddenly she heard a shout and saw two men with rifles in a boat that had appeared round a bend in the river. She easily disappeared into the jungle with the bonobos as the men were scrambling on to the shore, and she heard a single shot from far behind as she clambered through the canopy. She assumed the men must be poachers – no ranger would have attempted to shoot at her or the chimps – but was still frightened that they might report what they had seen and initiate a search for her. She told Jambo her fears and the entire troop moved to the very furthest limits of their range in the hope that nothing further would come of it.

5

Preserving Prehistory

Julian and Helen Fossfinder and their son Mark gave a final wave to Clive as he passed through security control at Rio airport to return to London. Their older son, aged twenty, was returning with the Bonaventures, ostensibly to get back to his medical studies, but Julian suspected the real reason had more to do with Clare, the Bonaventure's nineteen-year-old daughter with whom Clive seemed to have become very friendly. Their younger son Mark had opted to stay with his parents in Rio while they had a holiday before returning to their university jobs in England. They certainly felt that they had earned a break. Julian, as the pilot for the party of adventurers from the two families, had flown thousands of miles in the previous fortnight, across the remote vastness of the Amazon jungle. He had managed to save the lives of his passengers when his plane had been hit by a giant pterosaur in a lost valley dating from the Cretaceous period sixty-five million years ago. He, Richard and Lucy had survived attacks by velociraptors in the lost valley and his wife, Helen, had been at the mercy of villains hidden in invisibility robes who had attempted to take her hostage. Finally, he had himself only narrowly escaped being killed by a brilliant but evil professor who, had he not walked backwards into Julian's propeller, would have kidnapped and eventually killed Julian and left the rest of the party to die, marooned in the remote crater without a radio.

As they now bade farewell to those heading home Julian turned to Helen and Mark with a grin.

'Phew! What a fortnight! And now I think we've earned some time doing nothing but sightseeing.' The others heartily agreed and that evening they made plans for their holiday. The next day Julian apologized to the others.

'I know I said we were now going to chill out, but there's just one thing I *must* do before we start our break'.

Helen looked across at Mark with a resigned smile.

'How did I guess there'd be something?' she said. 'Nothing changes! Well, hurry up and do it and then we can all relax.'

'Actually, it's not just me. You should come too! I'm sure Mark can occupy himself sunbathing by the pool and chatting up some of the local talent.'

Mark was only too happy to do this and after breakfast Julian and Helen went to the UN offices. They were both by now highly respected scientists who had benefited from UN support for a number of projects, including the one they had just completed. Up until now, the prehistoric crater that they had discovered with the Bonaventures had remained a secret because they had been terrified of its being exploited for commerce or tourism. They now realised, however, that it was only a matter of time before the crater was discovered by others and they had agreed with the Bonaventures that the UN should be told, with a request that the information should be restricted to a few senior officials until the future management of the site could be properly planned.

Helen and Julian insisted on speaking only to the most senior official at the Rio office, who listened in astonishment to their story about the prehistoric crater with its two extraordinary valleys. As they showed him dozens of photographs and videos of giant ground sloths, sabretooth tigers and dinosaurs of every size and shape, his attitude turned from an initial one of deep scepticism to one of wonder and admiration.

Helen and Julian also told him about the villains but did not mention the invisibility robes. They mentioned the visit to the crater by the policeman investigating the deaths of the villains, Inspector Colarinho, but explained that he knew nothing of the prehistoric nature of the site. At one point the official rang the detective, without disclosing the secret, and the inspector was able to confirm the details that Helen and Julian had given concerning the position and inaccessibility of the crater. When they had finally finished their story and requested that the information they had given him should remain confidential to all but the most senior people, he sat in deep thought for several minutes. He then asked an assistant to download all the photographic material he had been shown on to his computer and turned back to Helen and Julian.

'They're just not going to believe this,' he said with a wry smile, 'but let's give it a go.' Over the next hour he spoke to UN officials in New York, London and Paris, and then to the Brazilian Minister for the Environment. Every call followed the same pattern. First, frank disbelief at the other end, then the emailing of the photographic evidence, then an excited discussion about what to do next. The Rio officer proved to be a strong and eloquent advocate for Helen and Julian and they were relieved to have had the good fortune to be dealing with such an intelligent and sympathetic person.

Finally he turned back to Helen and Julian.

'We will obviously need you to come to a top-level conference in the near future to discuss this in detail and to formally present your evidence,' he said. 'My colleagues point out that, before that meeting, it will be essential for our experts to verify that the photographs and videos are genuine. In the meantime I think I've managed to convince the appropriate authorities that the site should be put completely out of bounds. The Brazilian authorities are, with immediate effect, banning all flights within an area of fifty square miles centred on the crater on the grounds of national security. This won't raise any eyebrows; there are lots of military sites that are restricted and everybody will just assume it's just another defence project.'

Helen and Julian thanked him. They exchanged contact details and it was agreed that a strategy meeting would be arranged in the next month or so, to which both the Fossfinders and the Bonaventures would be invited.

As they left Helen and Julian were delighted with the outcome of their interview.

'The crater is now safe, but is still effectively secret as far as the public are concerned,' said Helen. 'I can't wait to tell the others but we'll wait till they've recovered from their flight.'

Two weeks later, relaxed after their holiday, it was time to return to England. Before they left Rio, Julian arranged a meeting with Inspector Colarinho's colleague in Rio, Inspector Poirot, to enquire about the professor. Poirot was the detective who had originally investigated an attempt by the professor to murder his research assistant, Lucinda, and steal her research.

'I'm afraid I've got some bad news,' said the detective after they had exchanged greetings. 'The blighter's escaped'.

'What do you mean *escaped?*' asked Julian with a frown. 'I thought he was desperately ill under armed guard in hospital.'

'He was,' said the policeman uncomfortably. 'He had a brain operation – that was about three weeks ago now – then made an amazingly good recovery; he's a tough character all right. Then he suddenly disappeared under the very noses of the guards.'

On hearing the word "disappeared" Helen and Julian immediately looked at each other in horror. Not only was the professor at large once again but it sounded very much as though he had recovered an invisibility robe that he must have kept concealed in Rio. They were frustrated at not being able to explain about the invisibility factor to the policeman, especially as it would reassure him that his arrangements for guarding the professor had not been as inadequate as they now seemed. They both knew, however, that the invisibility robe must remain secret until Lucinda was ready to present it as a scientific development to the world of physics.

'What about Lucinda Angstrom, the girl he tried to kill?' asked Helen.

'Well, that's really confidential police business, but between ourselves we've told her to remain in hiding with her sister. The only other person who knows she's still alive, apart from the university authorities, is her boyfriend, Peter Flint. He sends her work from the university. If the professor learns she's still alive I'm sure he'll have another go at her.'

Julian and Helen thanked the detective for his help, wished him luck in re-capturing the professor (though privately they knew that it would be almost impossible) and headed back to the hotel to pick up Mark and their baggage to head for the airport. Later, on the plane, they discussed the professor's escape.

'The first thing he's going to do,' said Julian, 'is try and get some more ore to extract that special stuff – what was it – photogymnospar?'

'Photogyraspar,' corrected Helen with a smile.

'Well, whatever it is, he'll need more of it. He'll probably try to return to the crater to pick up that crate of the stuff he left behind. He doesn't know we brought it out with us and sent it to Peter Flint at the university.' Julian was referring to the fact that the professor had tried to force Julian to transport a crate of ore out of the crater and had only been prevented from doing so by his near-fatal collision with the plane's propeller.

'It doesn't matter now, either way,' said Helen with a grin. ' After our chat with the UN the crater is now a complete no-go area. He can't get anywhere near it.'

'Gosh you're right!' exclaimed Julian, 'I hadn't thought of that. 'And that means ...'

'Yes,' Helen finished for him. 'If and when his present robe fades, or stops working, or whatever, he's done for as far as making himself invisible is concerned. It's probably just a question of time. How long nobody knows, except perhaps Lucinda. We'll just have to hope he doesn't get up to too much mischief in the meantime!'

And on that note they settled down to sleep as the plane headed east into the night sky.

6

Serengeti Safari

After arriving home in London Joanna and Richard lost no time in putting their plans into action. They had decided on the plane that they would have to return to the Congo to try and establish the truth about the feral child they had read about.

They didn't want the rest of the family to know why they were going, as they still both thought in their heart of hearts that their quest would end in disappointment. Luckily, their interest in botany provided the perfect excuse for visiting the African rainforest – the need to make some scientific comparisons with the South American rainforest they had just visited. The children, still on holiday, were eager to accompany them, but they felt that the presence of the family would hinder their investigations so they had arrived at a compromise plan. On the entirely valid grounds that the political situation was still unstable in the Congo the family would fly to Tanzania for a holiday. After some days spent together Joanna and Richard would then leave Clare in charge of further sightseeing with Lucy and Sarah while they flew to the Congo for a few days, purportedly to undertake their botanical studies, but really to check out the feral child story. They would then return to Tanzania to rejoin the rest of the family before returning to England.

While they were discussing these plans, the children's cousin Ben who was ten, the same age as Sarah, pleaded to come with them; he had done a school project on the Serengeti and the prospect of actually visiting the place he knew so much about seemed too good an opportunity to miss.

Joanna and Richard were doubtful.

'It means that Clare would be in charge of Lucy, Sarah *and* Ben in Tanzania when you and I are in the Congo,' Joanna said to Richard. 'It's too big a responsibility to place on Clare'. Richard agreed, but Clare broke in.

'I've got a great idea!' she exclaimed. 'Why don't we ask Clive to come along as well? The two of us can easily look after the others for a few days and you can relax and enjoy your study trip without worrying about me.'

Richard and Joanna looked at each other. They knew there was more than one reason Clare wanted Clive to come along. They had, however, both formed a very high opinion of Clive during their recent adventures in South America and what Clare said made perfect sense.

'Well, if Clive wants to come and can get more time off from medical school I suppose that would solve the problem,' said Richard.

'And the trip would be much more fun for Sarah if Ben comes along,' added Joanna.

And so it was agreed. Clive was delighted to join the party and rang his parents who were still in Rio to let them know. Just one week later the party of seven landed at Kilimanjaro International Airport in Tanzania on the start of what would prove to be another momentous adventure.

For the first part of the holiday they were all together. Using a hotel in Arusha as a base they visited the great natural features of that amazing area. They stood spellbound at the sight of Kilimanjaro, the highest mountain in Africa, which provided the stunning and extraordinary spectacle of a mountain capped in snow rising from the plains of the equator. They visited the famous Ngorongoro crater, the world's largest unflooded volcanic caldera, with a floor covering over 100 square miles containing an amazing variety of wildlife. Lucy was enthralled to speak to the African animals, all of whom had been eagerly awaiting her arrival after learning of her visit through the animanet.*

After Richard and Joanna left to fly to the Congo, Clive and Clare planned to take the younger ones on a one-week safari in the Serengeti National Park, but soon after her parents had left for the airport, Lucy became ill with food-poisoning. Sarah and Ben were so excited about the safari trip that Clare and Clive felt they couldn't disappoint them, so Clare stayed behind to keep Lucy company in the hotel in Arusha while Clive took Sarah and Ben to the offices of the tour company that would take them out to the safari lodges in the bush. Clare and Lucy planned to join them when Lucy had recovered. Sarah and Ben were bursting with excitement as they reached the first of the lodges where they were due to stay. After unpacking their things they set off in an open truck in the afternoon to see the wild animals. The truck had zebra stripes on the side just as they had seen in documentaries and films about Africa. There was a driver and a ranger in the front and about eight passengers behind on raised seats. As they bounced along the dusty roads Ben and Sarah were thrilled to see herds of zebra and wildebeeste. Gazelles could be seen grazing at every turn, and now and then they saw bigger antelopes, buffaloes, giraffes, and elephants.

The "animanet" is the name given by Lucy to a worldwide animal communication network that reminds her of the internet.

After a while the truck stopped near some rocks and they all got out and sat on folding bush chairs under the shade of some trees for a picnic.

'This is usually a quiet spot where it is safe to sit out,' said the ranger. 'We'll stop for an hour or so. If you need to go behind a bush or a rock for a wee it's safe as long as you don't go too far away. Just watch out for snakes and insects.'

Just then an elderly man in the group groaned and clutched his chest. Clive, now in his third year of medical school, went over to him, then turned to the driver.

'I think he may be having a heart attack. He seems OK just now but I think we should get him back immediately.'

After some discussion it was decided the driver should take the patient and Clive back as quickly as possible to the lodge while the ranger, who had a rifle, would wait with the party until the driver returned to continue the tour. Clive asked one of the other tourists to keep an eye on Sarah and Ben, then hurried off to help the driver get the sick man into the truck.

It was a little daunting for the tourists seeing the truck drive away. For the first time they felt they really were out in the African bush and somewhat vulnerable. The ranger seemed completely relaxed, however, and soon everybody settled down to enjoy their picnic. After lunch the guide took one or two interested tourists to examine some dung beetles which were busily disposing of a pile of elephant dung nearby and the woman looking after Ben and Sarah started to doze under the combined effects of jet lag, the afternoon heat and the large glass of wine she had just drunk.

'Come on,' said Ben to Sarah. 'Let's see what's on the other side of the rocks.'

'Do you think we should?' asked Sarah.

'He said it was OK to go a little way, and we'll just be very careful,' replied Ben confidently. They scrambled over the nearby rocks and found themselves looking out over an open area dotted with bushes and occasional trees. They wandered here and there, fascinated by the giant millipedes, the beetles and the lizards. They had gone about a hundred yards from the rocks when Sarah suddenly realised how far they had strayed and said they should go back. Just then they saw something move. In the bushes ahead of them three lion cubs were playing tag with each other.

'We'd better run back,' said Ben, turning pale, 'their mum may be around.'

'No,' said Sarah. 'Cats like to chase things that run. I think we'd better move back very slowly and keep watching all the time.'

'We'd better run back...'

53

They held hands and started slowly to step backwards. At that moment one of the cubs saw them and bounded up to them with a little yelp. Then, beyond the cubs there was another slight movement and magically, as though conjured up in a kaleidoscope, the bushes transformed themselves into the outline of a crouching lioness. Sarah and Ben clutched each other in terror as the great cat gave a low growl and slowly began to edge towards them, belly flattened to the ground in an unmistakable stalking movement.

After his conversation about dung beetles the ranger strolled back to the group under the trees. He frowned as he saw the dozing tourist.

'Excuse me, Ma'am,' he said, 'where are the two children?'

She woke with a start, then looked round in horror as she remembered where she was.

'I don't know. I must... must have nodded off for a few seconds.'

The ranger grabbed his rifle and scrambled over the rocks. The children were nowhere to be seen. He slowly scrutinised the entire area and then his heart stopped as he saw a child's sunhat lying on the ground.

'Oh my God ...' he muttered. He ran over and then saw more clothing. Then, in some sandy earth nearby, he saw the unmistakable pugmark of a lioness. He immediately called for help on his radio, then turned and ran back to the group.

At that moment the driver returned to the tour group. Clive jumped down from the truck, little realizing he was about to receive the worst news he had ever heard in his life.

7

Oresome Developments

Peter Flint, Senior Lecturer in Geology at Sabedoria University, looked in dismay at the e-mail he had just opened. It was from Detective Inspector Colarinho of the Manaus department in the Amazon. The news it contained threatened to bring an end to the most promising research project of his career and would, he knew, come as a bitter disappointment to his fiancée Lucinda. He dreaded the thought of telling her.

Hi Peter Flint,

Thanks for your query about the location of the crater which we recently visited in an attempt to locate the data stolen from your department by Professor Strahlung (currently in hospital awaiting interrogation). I'm afraid that we have been informed that the crater has been declared a site of exceptional national interest under the auspices of the UN and its location must remain secret. We have, furthermore, been informed that, at the request of the UN, the crater is under continuous satellite surveillance and we are to investigate immediately any attempt to land an aircraft in or near the site. These instructions have been conveyed to us from the highest government levels and I can only conclude that the crater must contain something of great importance relating to national security. I am aware of the fact that the rocks in the crater are of great interest to your scientific endeavours but regret to say that there is nothing further I can do to help you. If the cloak of secrecy surrounding this place is ever lifted I will, of course, let you know immediately.

With kind regards

Manuel Colarinho

Detective Inspector.

P.S. I hope you are managing to cope with the situation concerning Lucinda Angstrom.

Peter leaned back in his chair with his hands behind his head and wondered how to break the news to Lucinda. His mind inevitably, went back over the events of the last few months. For years the geology department had been a quiet and uneventful corner of the university. As the vice-chancellor had once remarked, with completely unconscious irony,

'We never expect anything ground-breaking to happen in Geology.'

That had all changed earlier that year, however, when a charter pilot had asked Peter to look at some rock samples he had found in a remote crater, deep in the Amazon jungle. He had flown to the crater to rescue some stranded explorers and picked up the rocks as ballast for his small plane. After noticing that the rocks appeared at times to glow he thought they might contain a valuable radioactive ore such as uranium and had taken them to the university for analysis. Peter had discovered that the rocks were not radioactive but that they contained a previously unknown metamaterial which seemed to have the power to distort beams of light. He had given the rocks to his then girlfriend (now fiancée), an expert on light, who worked in the physics department, and she had given the name "photogyraspar" to the ore. The new metamaterial had proved to be of crucial scientific importance for it had enabled her to create the world's first invisibility robe. When her head of department, Professor Lucius Strahlung, learned of her amazing breakthrough he had immediately recognized the criminal potential of her discovery, stolen her research data and attempted to murder her. He was, however, unaware of the fact that Lucinda had actually survived and the police inspector who had investigated her case had advised her to remain in hiding in case the professor discovered she was alive and made another attempt on her life.

Lucinda, staying in secret with her sister, had continued her invisibility research at her sister's home, in collaboration with Peter who was her contact at the university. They had by now used up all the original samples of ore given to Peter by the pilot. Their breakthrough discovery about invisibility was still known only to the Fossfinders, the Bonaventures and of course, the professor, and they now urgently required further supplies of ore so that they could complete their research and formally present their findings to the scientific community and the public. Peter had e-mailed Inspector Colarinho for help in locating the secret crater where the ore had originated and he now looked dejectedly at the reply he had just received as he forwarded it to his own laptop. The inspector had advised him not to use his office computer to contact Lucinda in case somebody in Peter's office should realise she was still alive, so all their e-mails were conducted through Peter's laptop. He then forwarded the inspector's reply from his laptop to Lucinda and within a few moments she replied.

Hi Pete,

Disappointing news but nil desperandum. *We'll just have to find some similar ore somewhere else – talking of which, any news yet from London?*

Love L. XXXX

PS If we have to go somewhere nice to get the the ore we could bring the wedding forward and make the trip our honeymoon!

Peter brightened up a bit. Lucinda's optimism was infectious and in the shock of receiving the inspector's e-mail he had completely forgotten that he had sent one of their final specimens of ore to an expert who possessed a large library of rock samples from all over the world. If they could find some similar rocks at another location they would never need to revisit the crater in the Amazon.

Two days later an e-mail arrived from England.

Dear Peter (if I may),

It was a pleasure meeting you at the international convention in Chicago last month. I have now had a chance to investigate the fascinating sample you sent me. I agree with you that it is a precambrian deposit of a form of kimberlite but its exact composition is most unusual. As you know, the museum here receives samples from all over the world and we keep detailed scientific records because of the crucial economic importance of mineral deposits. In our entire database, however, we have only a single sample that corresponds precisely with the one you sent. This came from a test sample obtained by a mining company exploring potential diamond deposits in the Democratic Republic of Congo. They surmised (correctly) that the well-known diamond seam, the Kasai Craton in Mbuji-Mayi, might extend much further north than was previously appreciated and the sample they sent us was extracted from a precambrian terrain in a river gorge on the Lomela river. The exact map reference of this site is attached. The site was never developed because this lode extension is actually situated in the heart of the rainforest and its remoteness and inaccessibility meant that commercially it was a complete non-starter.

The lode they located is apparently visible above the surface, as the rock stratum within which it is contained emerges in an exposed river cliff. If you were ever to make the formidable journey to the site I have little doubt, from the company explorers' descriptions, that you would be able to obtain further samples of the ore without the necessity of any sophisticated mining equipment.

I hope this information is helpful. Thanks again for sharing this exciting sample with me and I look forward to seeing you again at the Sydney Conference next year.

Yours sincerely,

Alan Cutcliff, Curator of Minerals

Peter forwarded it to Lucinda, then rang her to discuss the good news. They decided that, whatever the difficulties and cost, they would have to go on an expedition to Africa to obtain the ore, though Lucinda wasn't sure the Congo was quite the right spot for their honeymoon.

The next morning Peter was sitting at his desk making a start on planning the Congo expedition when there was a knock and a porter put his head round the door:

'Your package has arrived, sir. Where do you want it?' Peter looked up.

'What package?' He was not expecting any rock samples. The porter opened the door wider, revealing two other porters who were struggling to get a heavy crate out of the lift opposite.

'Arrived from the airport in a taxi this morning, sir. It came from Manaus several days ago, but has been stuck in customs. They're checking everything from the Amazon for drugs.'

Peter hurried over to look. A letter was stapled to the top of the crate.

Dr Peter Flint, Faculty of Geology, Sabedoria University, Rio de Janeiro

Peter tore the envelope open and read the scribbled note inside.

Dear Peter Flint,

Inspector Poirot (the Rio policeman who investigated Lucinda Angstrom's attempted murder by Professor Strahlung) gave us your name and contact address. We thought you and Lucinda could use this collection of ore in your research. Professor Strahlung collected it for his own use but is now, we are happy to say, indisposed.

Good luck to you both in your amazing work.

Kind regards,

Julian and Helen Fossfinder.

Peter couldn't believe his luck as he reread the note in excitement. The porter coughed politely.

'The box, sir?'

'Oh, sorry! Stick it in my lab please.' He pointed to the next door down the corridor and thanked the men. Then he picked up the phone. 'Lucinda, you're just *not* going to believe this. Julian Fossfinder has sent us a box of ore that the professor collected in the crater. Julian obviously guessed it must be important for the invisibility research and brought it back when they all left the crater.'

'She paused. 'So what about the honeymoon?'

'Sorry about missing the trip to Africa,' said Peter, pretending he hadn't heard the final question, 'but to tell the truth it would have been an incredible hassle to arrange, very expensive and possibly dangerous. And we know for certain that the ore in this box is photogyraspar – there was always a possibility that the African ore might not have been quite right. Now we can get to work straightaway on these samples—I think we'll just have time to assemble the data in time for the Sydney congress.'

'Sounds cool,' said Lucinda.

'Then off to Stockholm,' he added.

'Stockholm?'

'That's where they dish out the Nobel prizes isn't it? You can pick yours up at the same time.'

'Same time as what?'

'The honeymoon of course!'

'So you did hear,' she laughed, 'OK, but if they offer me a Nobel prize I'll only take it if they let me share it with you!'

'If you insist!.'

8

A Perfidious Professor

Professor Lucius Strahlung finally became fully awake. For several days he had been drifting in and out of a confused state of consciousness; a mixture of moments of comparative lucidity and long periods of outlandish dreams and nightmares. Now, though, he was really awake. He was lying in a hospital bed. An intravenous drip was fixed to his left arm and above his head he could see a monitor recording regular events that he assumed were to do with his heart rate and breathing. His head and throat were sore and when he gingerly explored them with his right hand he could feel dressings protecting the parts that were hurting. Later he was to learn that he had had two operations: one to remove a blood clot from his brain and the other to insert a breathing tube into his throat to keep him on artificial respiration in the intensive therapy unit where he had lain unconscious for several days. He had in fact, been moved back to his present room only a few hours earlier. As he became more aware of his surroundings he realised that a regular sighing noise which he had at first assumed to be emanating from some medical equipment was, in fact, the sound of someone snoring. Slowly and painfully he turned his head to one side and there in the corner of the room he saw a muscular figure slumped in a chair. The man was young and darkly handsome and was dressed in a uniform, but it was not a medical uniform – and doctors and nurses did not normally have handcuffs dangling from their belt and machine pistols resting on their knees. The professor began to analyse his situation. He was obviously recovering from some operation but why was he being guarded! And from whom? Slowly, fragmented memories began to piece themselves together as his mind attempted to reconstruct his life and situation. The most distant memories came back first and most easily. His repressive childhood in South America with his over-protective mother and his arrogant father; both had been immigrants from war-torn Europe, his father fleeing from retribution for suspected war crimes. Luke's childhood memories were dominated by recollections of his father's sneering comments and sardonic wit, and by the dread of incurring his wrath and the cruel and unusual punishments that would inevitably follow.

At university Luke had excelled in his chosen subjects of physics and mathematics and he had followed an illustrious academic career, his researches into the physics of light culminating in his being appointed professor at one of the most prestigious departments in Brazil. He had, however, inherited many of his father's unpleasant qualities and his academic progress was marked by ruthless ambition and complete disregard for the rights and concerns of his fellow workers. When eventually he was appointed Chairman of his department after the unexpected death of his principal rival under somewhat mysterious circumstances, the predominant emotions among his colleagues were those of fear and apprehension rather than respect and admiration. As his mind moved on to his time running the department more recent memories began to return. He could now vividly recall the day he first found his brilliant young researcher, Lucinda Angstrom, experimenting with an invisibility robe that she had invented using materials found only – where was it? – yes, found only in a remote crater deep in the jungle.

Luke's recollections were interrupted by the sound of the door opening and a nurse entering. The snoring ended abruptly. Luke was determined to continue with his thoughts, however, so he quietly closed his eyes and pretended still to be asleep. The nurse glanced at the ever-flickering monitor above the professor's bed.

'He's improved,' she said to the policeman in Portuguese, the principal language of Brazil. 'I think he'll be coming round soon.' The policeman gave a vague grunt in reply. In the dream she had so rudely interrupted he had just been about to score the only goal in the match in the last minute of extra time to win the world cup for Brazil and he found football a great deal more interesting than nurses, especially this one.

'I'm so glad you're here,' she continued coyly. 'If he wakes up I'd hate to be alone. A beast like that ...'

Luke forgot all about his reminiscences. The policeman wasn't here to guard him from others. He was obviously here to guard others from *him*. He listened intently as the nurse continued.

'Funny that – his heart rate suddenly changed when I just spoke – he's definitely coming round. Please don't leave me alone with him. When I think of that poor girl – and all those others he was going to maroon to die in that remote place ...'

'Just a minute,' said the guard who realised he was going to have to postpone winning the world cup until this chatterbox was silenced. 'He hasn't even been tried yet. For all you know he could be innocent. I'm just here to make sure he doesn't escape before standing trial. And should you be speaking like that in front of a patient? He might be able to hear you.' The nurse was affronted by this dig at her professional competence.

'I think I'm better qualified than you to decide what he can and can't hear,' she retorted huffily. 'And you must be the only person in Brazil who thinks he isn't a cold-blooded murderer. Oh, and don't think I don't know you were fast asleep when I came in. Some guard!' She swept out, throwing back a final shaft across her shoulder. 'And, by the way, you snore like a pig!'

Luke's mind was racing as the nurse's comments caused memories to come flooding back. 'That poor girl' was of course Lucinda Angstrom. A pity he had had to kill her; she'd been a nice kid, but if he was to succeed in taking the credit for her incredible scientific discovery and making himself the richest man on earth by abusing the power of making himself invisible at will, there had really been no other realistic option. After pushing Lucinda off the cliff into the depths of the Atlantic Ocean he had stolen her invisibility robe and all her research data, only to discover that he could not make any more invisibility clothes without obtaining supplies of the raw material, photogyraspar, from which they were made. This was vital, for the stolen research data gave no indication as to how long the original invisibility robe would retain its power. He had discovered that the ore from which photogyraspar was obtained came from a remote prehistoric crater deep in the Amazon jungle and had used a gang of criminals to get him to the crater and assist him in mining supplies of ore. His plan had gone well up to the point at which a group of explorers, including a young girl of thirteen, had landed their plane in the crater where the ore was being mined. A series of adventures had ended in all his fellow criminals being killed by animals and he had become dependent on using the explorers' help to escape from the crater. He had pretended to befriend them with the intention of taking their pilot hostage and leaving them marooned in the crater. The pilot he had intended to kill once he reached civilization and then he would be free to make unlimited use of his knowledge and the ore he had acquired... Luke stopped short in his thoughts as he desperately attempted to recall the final moments of his stay in the crater. He was aware that a head injury (and that, it was now obvious to him, is what he must have sustained) could cause loss of memory of previous events, and particularly those immediately preceding the injury. He also knew that this memory loss could be permanent. In his case, however, it was vital that he should remember as much as possible of his final moments of consciousness or he might never know the results of his studies in the crater. As he struggled to recall the events of that day he gradually became drowsier and eventually fell asleep to the monotonous sound of the policeman snoring.

The next morning Luke woke early and immediately started once again to try and remember the events preceding his accident. He tried to be logical. The two things he would have needed to take from the crater were his research data on invisibility – the original material he had stolen from Lucinda and the results of the additional research he had conducted in the crater – and the actual ore from which new robes could be made. He recalled loading all his data onto a USB memory stick from his computer but where had he concealed it? Of course! He suddenly remembered that he had hidden it in a false cavity in the heel of his shoe. It was vital that he regained his clothing. But what about the ore? He remembered that in the crater he had filled a box with highly concentrated ore that had turned out to be so heavy that he had found it impossible to move on his own. Whatever had happened to it?

Just then he heard voices. Opening one eye he saw that a new nurse had come in to change his intravenous fluids and was chatting to the guard – a different one from yesterday.

'So what happened to him?' the guard was saying.

'Apparently he walked backwards into a propeller,' the nurse replied. 'He was lucky not to have had his head cut off.'

'Must have given him quite a turn just the same,' joked the guard as he turned back to his newspaper.

Luke, who had hurriedly closed his eye again, listened to this exchange with interest. That was it! The nurse's remark had triggered a hidden memory. He had held Julian, the pilot, hostage at gunpoint and was about to force him to help load the crate full of ore onto the plane when all had gone black. But that meant... with dawning horror Luke realised that he must have failed in his attempt to obtain ore from the crater. Without fresh ore all his research data were useless and his dreams of power and riches would come to nothing. He obviously needed to work out a very careful plan.

A fortnight later Luke sat in his room waiting for his first visitor. He was now feeling much better but he found the continuous presence of the guards intensely irksome and couldn't wait to escape. With any luck that would be very soon, especially as the detective in charge of his case was due to come and interrogate him the next day and he told himself he had better things to do than to waste time telling a pack of lies to some half-witted local plod. His request for his clothes and shoes to be returned had been politely refused – even the police seemed to have worked out that it would make it easier for him to escape if he were dressed – but he had at least established that his possessions had been kept and were in a locker outside his room. His request to telephone his housekeeper for some personal items such as a toothbrush and dressing gown had been approved, though the call had been carefully monitored. His housekeeper, Frau Schadenfreude, was an elderly German widow who had worked loyally for the professor for years and, despite her name, she had refused to believe any of the scandal she had read about him in the newspapers. She seemed delighted to hear his voice and listened carefully as he told her where his spare washbag and new dressing gown were to be found. She was very impressed when he told her that he had bought the gown in London's Savile Row. She would have been even more impressed to know that the 'dressing gown' was, in fact, the very first invisibility robe that the professor had stolen from Lucinda on the day he had pushed her off the cliff. After using it to assist some criminals to escape from jail and then create a second robe, he had concealed it in his flat against just such an eventuality as this one.

When his housekeeper arrived at the hospital the guard searched the bag she had brought with her and after confiscating some nail scissors and tweezers from the washbag allowed her to see the professor. The soft invisibility helmet, an essential part of the kit, was masquerading as a shower cap in his washbag but the guard didn't seem to appreciate that the Professor's thinning wisps of grey hardly necessitated such an item.

During his period of convalescence Luke had perused the newspapers and read the accounts of his capture. Apparently the family he had intended to maroon in the crater, including Julian the pilot he had intended to murder, had returned safely to civilization. None of the accounts he had read referred to the exact location of the crater, simply using phrases such as "a remote jungle valley" or suchlike. There was no mention anywhere of invisibility robes or of prehistoric animals and the professor rightly concluded that the family had decided to keep these secret. He himself was described as "recovering in hospital from a serious injury, under constant police supervision." Because of the severity of his injury he had, apparently, been transferred from the Amazon hospital where he was first taken to a top neurosurgical centre in Rio. According to the news articles he would, when fit, be questioned concerning the murder of Dr Lucinda Angstrom, the attempted theft of a plane, the taking of a pilot hostage and the intent to leave a family abandoned in a remote location where they were unlikely to survive.

His chat with his housekeeper confirmed all he had gleaned from the newspapers and he thanked her for her loyalty while reassuring her that the vicious slander to which he had been subjected had originated from what he described as "eco-nuts and anti-German pressure groups".

After she had left Luke put his carefully thought-out plan into action. He took his dressing gown into his small bathroom, put it on and then let out a cry of anguish as though he had suffered some serious injury. The guard rushed in (the door had no lock) to find the room empty. The tiny barred window, a few inches wide and large enough only to admit a cat, was open. The guard ran out and unlocked the main door to Luke's room in order to call for assistance. He did not feel Luke brush past him. As the guard spoke frantically into his mobile and sounded a general alarm Luke casually removed an axe from the fire cuboard and split open his locker door. With trembling fingers he opened the secret compartment in the false heel of his shoe. To his unspeakable relief the little memory stick that contained everything he had ever stolen or discovered about invisibility still nestled securely in its hiding place. He slipped the precious gadget into his pocket, retrieved his house keys, wallet and other possessions, put on his shoes, then walked round the corner, past the guard frantically phoning for help at the nurses' station, out of the ward through a door fortunately propped open for ventilation, down the stairs and out of the hospital.

The professor had to get back to the crater if he wanted to be sure of future supplies of photogyraspar. The problem was that, as far as he knew, only two people knew where the crater was: the criminal pilot Biggles who had first taken Luke and his gang there, and Julian Fossfinder, the amateur pilot from the family Luke had tried to take hostage.

Biggles was now dead, killed in the crater, and Julian was obviously not somebody who was going to tell the professor how to get back to the scene of his crimes. Luke knew, however, that Biggles had given some samples of ore to Lucinda's boyfriend, Peter Flint, a geologist at the university, and hoped that Flint might have established where the crater was, to obtain further samples for his own research. Luke had spent a great deal of time in hospital considering this problem and had decided that his best – possibly his only– chance of finding out the location of the crater was to explore Flint's office for information. After leaving the hospital he returned to his flat which was, as he had suspected, under constant police surveillance. Still invisible, he smashed a window at the end of the corridor leading to his apartment and when the policeman went to investigate he slipped through his front door and quickly retrieved the keys to his university department. He then went to the university and from a concealed compartment in his desk removed the keys to Flint's research laboratory and the password to his computer which he had stolen from Lucinda. The password wasn't really necessary – the professor was an IT wizard who could hack his way into almost any computer system – but it would certainly save him time.

Soon he was sitting, invisible, at Flint's computer searching for any reference to the pilot and the crater. Within moments he found found Inspector Colarinho's e-mail to Flint informing him that the crater was now a prohibited zone.

Luke slammed his fist on the desk and swore in frustration. Now he could never get back to the crater. He felt all his dreams and aspirations ebbing away. As for the postscript asking how Peter was coping with the situation concerning Lucinda – well personally he couldn't care less about the effect Lucinda's death had had on Peter Flint. As he scrolled down further through Flint's correspondence, however, he read, with a flood of relief, the letter that Flint had received from London concerning a possible alternative source of the ore in Africa.

No sooner had Luke printed off this page with its vital map reference than his attention was caught by a final outgoing e-mail to Julian Fossfinder, copied to the Bonaventures:

Hi Julian,

Thanks a million. You've saved me a great deal of time, money and trouble.

Peter Flint.

What in heaven's name was Flint thanking Julian for, Luke wondered. If he had happened to walk ten yards along the corridor into Flint's lab he would have found out and saved himself a great deal of trouble for there, in the middle of the floor, stood the very box of concentrated ore samples that Luke had himself laboriously collected and saved back in the crater. With those samples, and the priceless information he already possessed in his USB stick, the professor could have fulfilled all his evil ambitions and the world would have been a very different place. But the course of history turns on the most trivial of circumstances and the professor didn't go into the next-door laboratory simply because he was unaware of any reason to do so.

He closed down the computer, put his hands behind his head and sat back to think over what he had learnt. The Congo. Of all the places on earth. What an extraordinary stroke of luck for the location to be the one place where his cousin could help him – a cousin, moreover, who owed him a favour. Well, he told himself, he was certainly due a lucky break. He looked at his watch and did a rapid calculation of time zones. It was early evening in Central Africa. Perfect. He picked up Flint's phone and rang international directory enquiries. A few minutes later he was through to a number in the Democratic Republic of Congo.

'Hello,' he said. 'Please may I speak to Mr Moriarty; you can tell him it's Luke calling.' There was a short pause, then Moriarty came on line.

'Hi Luke.'

'Hi Hans.'

'What news?'

'Good – for both of us, I think,' said Luke. 'Do you remember the favour you asked of me some time ago?'

'I certainly do,' came the reply.

'Well, as you know, I was unable to help at the time because of my accident. Can I assume that you still need a great deal of money to solve your little problem?'

'Yes, I...I need it more than ever.' Luke was pleased to hear the note of desperation in the man's voice; it would ensure his full cooperation.

'Well, by a curious chance my money-making operation has been switched to your part of the world. I should be able to give you what you need within a couple of months. Oh, and just to remind you – we're talking millions here.'

'That's fantastic,' said Hans.

'There's just one problem,' Luke continued. 'I'm going to need your help. I need you to bend a few rules and bribe a few officials. I'll need some mining and extraction permits and some mineral export licences. Oh, and I may need some visas if I use helpers. All these documents will have to be fake because we'd never get approval for real ones – even if we had the time to wait for them. Are you OK with that?'

There was no hesitation on his cousin's part.

'That won't be a problem,' came the quiet reply. 'I'll fix anything you need, whatever it takes, as long as you can give me the dough as quickly as possible.'

'Good' said Luke, 'We've got a deal. I've got a few arrangements to make and I'll ring you back as soon as I know what I need.'

' Luke...' Luke thought he heard a stifled sob on the other end of the line. '...Luke. Thanks. You've really saved my bacon.'

'Auf Wiedersehen, Hans!' came the brief reply.

After he put the phone down Hans (or John as he was known to his local associates in the Congo) poured himself a large drink from a cabinet on his office wall and sat back in his chair. Maybe, at last, this miraculous phone call would bring an end to the nightmare that had haunted him for the last six months. John held a very responsible position but had one secret weakness which was gambling, a vice which had recently put him into a position from which only a large sum of money could retrieve him. Although he and Luke had only met on a few occasions, the cousins were linked by an indissoluble family bond. Towards the end of the second world war Hans' father, a senior German naval officer, had managed to arrange a passage to Brazil on a naval ship for his sister, Luke's mother, and her husband who was anxious to leave Europe before the allies charged him with war crimes. Over the years the families had kept secretly in touch and the young cousins, though not knowing the details, were always acutely aware that Luke and his family owed Hans' family a great deal.

When Hans had faced ruin through his gambling habit he had rung Luke in Rio and pleaded for his help. As it happened he had rung at a most propitious time, for it was just after Luke had stolen Lucinda's invisibility robe with the intention of making himself a fortune from her discovery. To bail out his cousin and repay the family debt of gratitude using a tiny part of the prodigious wealth he expected to possess was no issue and Luke had readily agreed.

Reading of Luke's crater accident in the news had been disastrous for Hans who saw his hopes of escaping ruin shattered. Now, however, it seemed as if Luke was still on track for saving him: and this time he could return the favour. Bribing some corrupt local officials to fiddle a few mining concessions, and issuing some fake export licences were all in a day's work for Hans.

He finished his drink and returned to work with renewed vigour. He couldn't wait for the next communication from his cousin.

9

Planning a Rendezvous with Renegades

Back in Peter Flint's office the professor was already planning his next move. Now he had cleared the way to obtaining the necessary documentation from his cousin for mining the photogyraspar he faced the problem of actually extracting and processing the substance; the last time he did this, in the Amazon, he had enlisted the services of a bunch of greedy criminals to help him. As he pondered, the thought struck him that he might do exactly the same thing again. He suddenly remembered that Chopper and Sam Sawyer, his erstwhile companions in crime, had mentioned that their twin brothers Sid and Fred, on release from jail, had gone to Kenya to start up a poaching business. No sooner had the thought entered his head than Luke went into action. First he removed any evidence of his visit from Flint's office, locked the door and, still invisible, slipped out of the university building. Outside, as luck would have it, a cab driver had left his taxi with the engine running while he helped an ageing lecturer up the steps with her suitcase. Hearing his cab suddenly roar off down the street the driver ran into the road and was astonished to see that nobody was driving it. Twenty minutes later Luke arrived at the city prison. This was the jail from which Chopper and the criminal pilot Biggles had escaped to help Luke on his previous mission. He knew it well, for it was here that he had first made contact with Biggles, concealed in the same prototype invisibility robe that he was now wearing. In the robe he slipped easily through the security guards at the prison entrance and made his way to the records department. He soon located Chopper's file and there, under "next of kin" were listed his brother Sam of "no known address," and his twin brothers, Sid and Fred. Their last known address was Manaus prison in the Amazon. Luke returned to his taxi and drove back to a street near his flat where he dumped the car. Returning home to his own computer he then hacked into the Manaus jail records and within moments had located the files on Sid and Fred Sawyer and noted their release date. He then established which airlines flew from South America to East Africa and an hour later had hacked into the computer system of the largest operator. He scanned through the passenger lists for the dates following the twins' release from jail and there, just two weeks after their discharge, he found Fred and Sid Sawyer, destination Nairobi. He now had enough to go on to plan his own expedition to Africa. His first act was to hack into the airline booking system and within moments a bewildered airline clerk seemed unable to fix a computer glitch that insisted on a first class seat to Nairobi the following day remaining empty and unreservable. The next morning, invisible, the professor went to a large department store and stole all he needed for his journey. In a nearby bank a clerk spent the rest of the day trying to explain to his manager how an immense pile of banknotes had disappeared from under his nose, and a clerk at the passport office failed to notice that the new passport for a Senhor Luz was missing from a pile of passports due to be posted to their owners. Two hours later, at the airport, a check-in computer seemed magically to switch itself on, and the glitch that had been blocking a first-class seat suddenly corrected itself. A few moments later a distinguished-looking gentleman carrying an expensive new suitcase emerged from a nearby toilet, asked if any first-class seats were still available and was, apparently, pleasantly surprised to find that there was just one left. An interested observer (there was none) would have then been perplexed to see that the immaculate Senhor Luz, having paid for his ticket in cash and checked in his main luggage, returned to the toilet with a small hand bag but never came out again. Another observer, on the other side of security control, would have been equally perplexed to see a Senhor Luz carrying a small bag emerging from an apparently empty nearby toilet.

After a relaxing flight and another uninterrupted passage through security control in Nairobi, the professor checked in to a posh hotel, then headed for the Kenya Wildlife Service Offices. There, once again invisible and unaccosted, he perused the files on poaching. Soon he found what he sought:

"Mara, 12 October 2008. A further report came in today concerning the murder of Mushina Jangili, a well known poaching baron whose remains were found last week on the border of the Masai Mara Game Reserve. The torso of the man had been partially consumed by hyenas, but was still readily identified by his widow who was accompanied to the mortuary by a younger associate of Jangili and who seemed to be bearing her sudden loss with remarkable fortitude. The lower half of the body was intact and the words "Sid and Fred" had been branded onto the buttocks with a red-hot iron; an injury almost certainly inflicted, according to the police doctor, before death. The chief suspects are two white men, apparently identical twins. It is believed that the men, known locally as "the twins from hell," have established a rival poaching business and are

responsible for the recent massive increase in the loss of valuable wildlife species in this locality. They were described by the police as being stupid and vicious, and possibly called Sid and Fred.

Luke smiled to himself and walked back to his hotel. Soon he emerged from his room in bush kit carrying a small bag and went over to the concierge. 'Can you find a taxi that wants to go two hundred miles?' he asked. The concierge glanced at the professor's hand resting casually on a thick wad of notes.

'There's one waiting outside, sir,' he replied.

10

A Pestilential Pair

The crash of a heavy rifle shattered the still afternoon and was followed by the alarm calls of myriad birds and animals in the surrounding bush. The rhino sank to her knees then, following a second shot, rolled over onto her side. Her calf trotted round her, perplexed at his mother's behaviour.

'Nice shootin' Sid,' said Fred to his brother.

'Pity it's a female though,' Sid replied.

'Yeah – the horn's so much smaller,' agreed Fred. 'Never mind though. It's better than nothin' an' it all goes in the booze and fags fund.' He raised his rifle and casually shot the calf which collapsed beside its mother's lifeless corpse. 'Talkin' of which, you owe me a beer – I got the kid in one shot.' They both laughed as they watched their gang of African helpers hack off the mother rhino's horn with axes. The 'helpers' were virtually slaves as they were all criminals wanted by the police on various charges and Fred and Sid had acquired them by the simple expedient of murdering their previous leader.

Sid, older than Fred by five minutes, was the natural leader of the two and also marginally brighter. More accurately, perhaps, he was slightly less stupid. As they strolled back to their camp he decided that they should move on. He and Fred had spent a great deal of their lives in prisons in Europe, Asia and South America and Sid had no particular wish to repeat the experience in Africa. Their last jail spell had been for capturing and killing protected species in the Amazon jungle and on being released from jail over a year ago they had moved to Africa, where they were unknown to the authorities, to resume their poaching skills on a new set of animals, principally rhinos and elephants for their ivory. In recent weeks Sid had been aware of increasing activity on the part of the anti-poaching wardens and reports were circulating among the poaching fraternity of plans for a major crackdown on their activities. Though he was not overburdened with brains, Sid's criminal antennae were beginning to twitch and his animal cunning warned him that the police were beginning to close in on their prey.

At the camp fire that night he shared his thoughts with Fred over roasted impala and beer.

'It's only a matter of time before they get us,' he explained, 'an' with all these new 'viromental laws it's gettin' harder and harder to flog the ivory.'

'Wot else can we do?' asked Fred. 'Killin' an'mals is our professhun, innit?'

'We just gotta move our operation,' said Sid. 'They say you can get a fortune killin' chimps an' gorillas for their meat and skins.'

'Where are these g'rillas?' asked Fred.

'Out west in the Congo,' said Sid. 'It's all a bit dodgy out there with rebels an' such like but I expec' we'll survive – we usually do, eh?' They both laughed. 'There's also talk of diamon's in them parts,' Sid went on, 'so we could move in on a bit of that action if we need to top up the funds.' As he spoke two of the gang appeared with a young boy between them. He looked terrified. His nose was bleeding and a large bruise was rapidly developing around his right eye.

'Found this kid creeping round the camp, boss. Shall we waste him?'

'No,' said Sid. 'Not before we know what he's doing.' He turned to the boy.

'Whaddya want?'

'I seek,' he faltered, 'the... the Ndugu Shetani. The villagers said they were near here.'

Sid turned to one of those clutching the boy.

'What's he saying, Mgosa? What's this "unduggy shite" rubbish?'

The henchman looked embarrassed. 'He seeks the devil brothers,' he said. He paused, then decided he had to explain. 'That's what they call you and Fred in the village. It's like saying "the twins from hell".' Sid frowned and then, much to Mgosa's relief, burst out laughing.

'I like it! The twins from hell – we'll have that carved on our gravestones eh, Fred?'

Meanwhile Mgosa was speaking to the boy who then held out a note. Sid opened it and read it slowly, pointing at each word with his finger as he did so.

I'm looking for Sid and Fred. I have news of Chopper and Sam and a proposition to put to you. If you agree to meet me send this note back with a tick (the professor had guessed, correctly, that Sid's reading skills probably exceeded his writing ability) *and the boy will return with me tomorrow.*

Professor Kuficha.

P.S. Lots of money involved

Sid handed the note to Fred, then decided it would probably be quicker to tell him what it said, especially as Fred was holding it upside down. When he had finished he looked at Fred.

'Wotcha think?'

'Could be a trap by the cops,' said Fred.

'Yeah, but how would they know about Chopper and Sam – 'specially as Sam got eaten by them 'gators?' Fred thought about this and then nodded. Sid turned back to Mgosa.

'What do you guys think?'

'Well, the name is probably false, boss – it means 'unseen one' in Swahili. The boy swears it's nothing to do with the police and the guy who sent him is splashing money around the village like there's no tomorrow. I'd say it's worth a chance. We'll set an ambush and if it's the cops we'll wipe them out.'

'OK,' said Sid. 'Give the kid some food.' He ticked the note and the boy, looking greatly relieved, trotted off with Mgosa to have some supper before his hazardous journey back through the African night.

'On second thoughts,' Sid called after them, 'send him in the morning – he's probably more likely to make it.'

At the crack of dawn the boy disappeared, to return three hours later with the Professor who had by now acquired an automatic pistol.

He shook hands with Sid and Fred and they sat down with bottles of beer. The Professor started by telling them how he had formed a close working relationship with Chopper and Sam to make a great deal of money from diamonds.

'But Sam's dead. He was eaten by 'gators in the jungle,' said Sid.

'No, apparently he escaped,' said Luke, 'and he managed to spring Chopper and me from jail. I was in jail for murdering a university colleague who was becoming something of a nuisance, and Chopper and I hit it off immediately'.

Sid and Fred leaned forward. They were getting more interested by the moment. The Professor had risen enormously in their estimation by being a murderer and a jailbird.

'Where d'you find these diamon's?' asked Sid. The professor gave a little smile.

'Oh, we don't find them — we *make* them!' The twins' eyes bulged. 'The science is immensely complex,' he explained, 'but, basically I have invented a technique for creating genuine diamonds of any size from low-grade diamond ore thought to be commercially useless. Unfortunately...' He paused for dramatic effect, then continued, putting on a suitably grave expression, '...I have some very bad news for you both. Your poor brothers died in a shoot-out with the police. I nursed Chopper on his death bed and his dying wish was that I should contact you two and share with you the benefits of my invention; the benefits that Chopper would never himself be able to enjoy.' He paused once more, and wiped a tear from his eye. Then he cleared his throat and continued.

'I have good information that the kind of ore that yields the best diamonds using my process is found in Africa. Obviously the process is illegal as it will make us into millionaires while undercutting the official world market in diamonds. I will need your help in extracting the ore and in protecting me from, let's say, unfriendly authorities and greedy neighbours. In return I will split the proceeds of the operation with you fifty–fifty.' He caught the avaricious glance that the brothers exchanged and knew he was succeeding in his plan.

'There's just one snag,' he said. He knew already that it wasn't a snag, for the large banknote which he had pressed on the henchman who had first greeted him that morning had yielded valuable information about the brothers' conversation of the previous night.

'This snag is that you, gentlemen, will need to move your camp to a different location. One that's some way distant. Actually, about a thousand miles away, for that's where the diamond-bearing shale exists.' He paused and took a long draught of beer. 'Well, there it is boys. Are you on board for a few million or not?'

The brothers almost fell over in their eagerness to be the first to shake Luke by the hand.

'OK, now I'm going to return to Nairobi and hire a couple of big trucks. I'll be back to pick you up and any of your...,' he looked across at the motley group of ruffians eating breakfast, '... hmm, 'gentleman associates that you wish to accompany us. Then I'll kill the driver of the second truck – we don't want to leave any loose ends.'

Sid looked at him with renewed respect. This man had the same ruthless streak that he had so admired in his elder brother Chopper.

'We'll take the ones we trust,' he said quietly, ' – there'll be about eight of us in all. The other four can share a spot in the bushes with your spare driver.'

They shook hands and the Professor left with the boy.

Two days later two ex-army trucks roared southwest towards Serengeti and the southern shores of Lake Victoria on the first stages of their long drive to the Congo. The lorries were ten-ton vehicles with military camouflage markings covering their metal front cabs and canvas-covered bodies. Moments after the vehicles had left the camp, vultures began to circle down to investigate something they obviously found very interesting in a hollow in the surrounding bush.

Back in Nairobi Inspector Kukamata of the Wild Life Service Office, examined the latest poaching reports. They were nothing short of appalling. Three more rhino corpses and five elephants had been found within a week, all with horns and tusks hacked out and their carcasses left for the hyenas, vultures and jackals. And every report seemed to implicate the infamous *Ndugu Shetani* – the twins from hell. It was time to act. The World Wildlife Fund, various UN agencies and, most important of all, the Minister for Tourism, would all be breathing down his neck within days if he didn't do something. He picked up the phone.

'Get me aerial surveillance on the other line,' he snapped at an assistant as he started to dial the head ranger at the Masai Mara National Park.

After a dusty and bumpy ride the trucks eventually left Kenya and crossed into Tanzania.

'We're goin' through the Serengeti,' said Sid to the professor who was sitting next to him in the front cab of the leading truck. 'It's by far the quickest way. There's a chance of meetin' a park ranger, but if we do we'll just waste 'im.' He pointed to a well-worn map on his knees. 'Then we go south of Lake Victoria and into Burundi – or Rwanda – I ain't sure yet which route will give us the least aggro at the border. Then it's west into the middle of the Congo. It'll take days on these roads – weeks if it rains – so you got plenny of time to decide where our little diamond mine's goin' to be.' As they crossed the border into Tanzania along a disused forest track a small plane could be heard. It was clearly looking for something, for it circled as it gradually moved southwest and eventually disappeared. Sid had stopped the trucks in the forest where they were invisible from the air.

'Rangers call in a plane sometimes,' he said, 'when they think the poachin's gettin' out of hand. Good job we're movin' out.'

Soon the trucks were rolling across the great plains of the Serengeti. The immense herds of game and breathtaking views were of no interest whatsoever to the men in the trucks whose thoughts were only on the fortunes they intended to make. As they neared the western edge of the reserve Sid suddenly pointed ahead.

'Look!' Luke peered in the direction he indicated and there, beside a large scree of boulders, were two children, a boy and a girl of about ten. They were standing stock still and at first Luke thought they were playing some kind of game. Then he saw what held the children transfixed. Directly in front of them, about thirty yards away, a pride of lions lay dozing under some bushes. Even as Luke watched, the children began to walk slowly backwards towards the bank of rocks, never taking their gaze off the predators. Then, a lion cub which had been playing with its litter-mates suddenly saw the children and bounded towards them with a yelp. The lioness nearest to them lazily opened one eye then immediately opened both wide and sprang into the crouching position so familiar to anyone who has watched a domestic cat stalking a bird. The children clutched each other in terror. Sid immediately put the truck in gear and drove it between the lioness and the children. The cub ran back to its mother as the truck approached and Luke opened his door and pulled the children in.

'Thank you, thank you!' said the children, sobbing with fear and relief.

'There, you'll be safe now,' said the Professor who, when it suited him, could be all kindness and charm. 'Now, where are your parents?' he continued. The boy simply gesticulated back across the rocky hill; he seemed speechless from shock.

'The other side of that little hill,' said the girl, her face white as a sheet and her voice trembling. 'But it's not our parents. We're on a tour. The guide is giving them lunch.'

As she spoke the professor saw, far away on the horizon behind her, the sun glinting on the fuselage of a plane as it banked and tilted in its endless search. He thought for a long moment then, after a meaningful glance at Sid, turned back to the children.

'There's a bit of a problem. As you see this road leads away from the rocks and we can't drive across the ridge – it's too steep. We can't *walk* across because of the lions, so you'd best stay with us until we can get in touch with your group. What are your names?'

'I'm Ben Sharp and she's my cousin, Sarah Bonaventure,' said Ben.

'OK,' said the professor. 'We'll get on the radio and call up the park rangers.' He turned and winked at Sid – who looked at him blankly.

'We'll call the rangers *won't* we?' repeated the Professor giving a little cough and an even more exaggerated wink.

'Oh yeah, the rangers – of course!' said Sid as comprehension dawned. He picked up a radio transmitter and reported that the children were safe and that they would take them to the nearest settlement – but neither of the children saw that the equipment was switched off.

'Now there's just one more thing,' said the Professor. 'A trick I've learned after years of grappling with wild animals in the bush'.

The children stared wide-eyed at him – they'd never met a real hunter before.

'If you each give me a bit of clothing – something quite large like a top is best. Oh, and your hats; I'll leave them here. The lions already have your scent so if we leave something behind they'll think you're still nearby and it'll stop them following us to the next camp.' The children had no idea that this was the Professor's first ever trip to the African bush and that he had never seen a wild lion before in his life, and they were impressed with his fake bush-lore; the last thing they wanted was lions chasing them. They hurriedly slipped off their tops and gave them to the Professor.

'Great,' he said. Then, anxious to reassure Sarah who had turned her back to him, he added: 'Don't worry about your clothes. We've got plenty of stuff on board; we'll patch you up with a couple of our smallest bush-shirts and some makeshift hats until we reach civilization.' He turned and asked the men in the back to pass some clothes through, then jumped down and went to the back of the truck, out of sight of the children. He tore Sarah's top into pieces and scattered the fragments among the rocks. He made holes in Ben's shirt and rubbed it with dirt and sand. He then threw it as far as he could in the direction of the pride of lions and returned to the truck.

Nobody from the tour group had yet appeared over the rocks and, as Sid started up and drove away from the rocky ridge as fast as the road would allow, the professor set about winning the confidence of the children. He told them tales of his heroic adventures prospecting for diamonds in South America and about being kidnapped by villains who had eventually been eaten by wild animals. Ben was fascinated by the scars on his balding head.

'Were *you* attacked by wild animals too?' he asked. 'Is that what happened to your head?'

'Sort of,' Luke replied. 'As I was walking towards a plane I was attacked by a hawk who stole my pistol and then a tiger started to stalk me. As I backed away from it I walked into a rotating propeller and that's how I got my scars.'

'Wow!' said Ben. Sarah looked sceptical.

'I thought they didn't have tigers in South America,' she said.

'Well,' said the professor smoothly, 'I didn't realise you knew so much about animals; I was just using the term to indicate a big cat. The accident affected my memory,' he added hurriedly, 'and it may have been a leopard or jaguar or something.'

'What an interesting man,' said Ben later when they stopped briefly for a comfort break.

'Ye ..es,' said Sarah slowly. 'It's a bit funny though, for someone who's spent his life hunting animals and prospecting in the wilderness to make a mistake about a tiger.'

'But he lost his memory,' said Ben. 'He said he was unconscious for days.'

'Yeah, I suppose so,' Sarah replied but she still looked doubtful.

Sid's poaching experiences meant that he knew every track and road in the locality and they managed to leave the Serengeti by a remote route which avoided any encounters with rangers or official check points. Once out in the remote bushland to the south of Lake Victoria they stopped and set up camp. The Professor suggested that Fred set off to find fresh meat for their meal and that the children might want to accompany him. Ben was very excited at the prospect of going on a hunt, even though his request for a gun was politely refused. Sarah wasn't so sure about it but didn't want to be separated from Ben, so off they went with a somewhat bewildered Fred who wasn't heavily into child care.

When they had gone Sid turned to the Professor.

'What the hell's goin' on?' he snarled truculently. ' We can't get saddled wiv a couple of snotty kids!'

'Wait a moment and think,' said the Professor calmly. He pointed to the distant glint of another search plane on the horizon. 'They're looking for something and it's probably us. I don't know how much game you've killed recently but I *do* know from the records I saw in Nairobi that the authorities are on to you'.

'What records?' exclaimed Sid.

'You don't seriously think I would risk my life coming out here to join you without checking up on you first, do you?' Luke replied. 'I know a great deal about you – including the fact that you know how to survive out here and don't let anyone mess with you; you're just the guys I need.' Sid, placated by the compliment, returned to the discussion about the children.

'Yeah, whatever. But even if they are lookin' for us, so what? The kids can't help us in a shoot-out'.

'They certainly can,' said Luke. 'If we get caught in a police trap we can use them as hostages. Nobody will dare to attack us while we've got two kids with us. It would kill the tourist trade stone dead. They'll negotiate to get the kids back and our deal will be a free passage to Burundi. They'll be glad to get rid of us'.

'Yeah... but ...,' Sid's contorted face reflected the mental effort he was going through, '... but won't they chase us even more if they think we've kidnapped the kids?'

'Of course they would if they *knew*,' said Luke, 'but remember nobody has seen us yet. When the kids' tour group look for them they'll find some torn clothes, a couple of hats and a pride of lions and it'll just be another tragic case of children devoured by wild animals.'

Sid fell silent for a moment. The Professor's logic was undeniable.

'But what'll we tell the kids – and what'll we do with 'em when we're safe in the Congo?'

'Leave the first of those problems to me,' said Luke. 'In fact,' he added grimly after a moment's reflection, 'leave the second to me as well.'

Sarah and Ben were now enjoying themselves. The rangers would soon appear and return them to the others and, though they expected to get told off for having wandered away, no harm would be done. In the meantime they were having real excitement, not just sitting in a tour truck with a bunch of old fogeys with cameras, but crawling along the ground downwind of a herd of Thomson's gazelles. Fred had spotted the antelopes soon after they left the camp and had motioned the children to the ground with his finger to his lips.

'Don't worry,' he whispered hoarsely in Ben's ear. 'If they're grazing calmly there can't be any big cats around.' Ben wondered how, in that case, the predators ever caught anything but didn't like to say so to Fred. Soon Fred slowly raised his rifle and motioned to the children to cover their ears. Even though they did so, the crash of the rifle at close quarters was terrifying and both children were ashen-faced as they hurried after Fred to retrieve the carcass of a young buck. They watched in fascinated horror as he pulled an enormous knife from his belt and eviscerated the animal.

'Now back to camp. We gotta move quickly,' he said, nodding at the pile of steaming guts on the ground. 'The hyenas'll smell this stuff in no time.' He tied the feet of the animal together and slung it on his rifle, holding the barrel himself and giving Ben the butt to carry.

Sarah was very upset by the whole scene.

'Isn't it wrong to kill animals?' she asked tentatively, worried about Fred's possible response. He just laughed.

'It may be wrong or it may be right but it's how we eat out here. Anyway, there's plenty of 'em around and they don't belong to nobody

'Now back to camp...'

so what's the harm. An' ...,' he added, as if by way of justification, '... an' anyway, I dun plenty of wrong things; that's why I been in the slammer innit?'

'What's a slammer?' asked Ben. Fred gave a slightly shamefaced grin.

'The slammer? You know, the clink – jail – prison.'

Ben was enthralled.

'You've been to jail? Really? You're not kidding?' Fred laughed again.

'I bin lots of times. Brixton, Reading, Brixton again, Wandsworth, Singapore, Brazil – there's not much I don't know about jails.'

'Wow!' said Ben. He said "wow" several times again as they trudged along.

'Were there like... robbers and murderers and pirates and stuff?'

'Yeah, lots of 'em,' chuckled Fred, not adding that he had served time for all three of these offences in his action-filled criminal career. It was years since he had spoken to ten-year old children and he was beginning to enjoy the experience. It was the first time in countless years that anyone (with exception of law enforcement officers) had taken the slightest interest in his activities, much less looked up to him. The boy was now regarding him with something akin to hero worship and it was a novel experience for him.

'Yeah,' he added expansively, 'I seen all types in prison. A terrible thing for an innocent man to go through.' He suddenly felt the need to seem better in the children's eyes.

'You mean, you were wrongly imprisoned?' asked Sarah, who had been listening intently to this little exchange.

'Well, I obviously done *some* things not quite right,' said Fred, feeling as though he was getting a little out of his depth. 'But the cops and the beaks always 'ad it in for me – an' I only ever did wot Sid told me.'

By now they had reached the camp. Fred laid a fire, then skinned the gazelle and started to fix up a spit to roast it. At Ben's request he told Ben how to make the spit and let him do it unaided. Soon the little antelope was beginning to roast.

'Don't ever think I'm going to eat any of that,' said Sarah.

'Look, little Missie,' said Fred, not unkindly. 'This is wot we got. It's dead anyway, so whether you eat any or not makes no odds. If you want sumthin' else there's tins in the truck.'

Later, when they had all eaten the gazelle, including Sarah, and the men were smoking and drinking beer and arguing, the Professor came and sat next to the children.

'Listen, kids,' he said, 'I've been in touch with your tour operator and there's a bit of a problem. You know these bush fires that are sweeping across this area?' The children looked blank and shook their heads. 'No? Well, anyway, there are serious fires and one of them has cut off the only two roads between here and the place your parents are staying. I forget the name'.

'Arusha,' said Ben innocently.

'We never told you!' cut in Sarah with a frown. 'And it's not our parents – they're in the Congo. We're with my sisters and their friend, and I'm sure they must be getting very worried about us.'

The professor gave her a reassuring smile. He started to put a comforting arm round her shoulders but, seeing the expression on her face, thought better of it.

'Don't fret, my dear, I've had a long chat with the tour guide and he's keeping in constant touch with them. We've all agreed that the safest thing is for us to take you with us to the next big town with an airport and they'll fly down and pick you up. They know you're OK.' He paused, then continued: 'I suppose I should have told you this before but I'm a professor of zoology and we're on an urgent scientific mission for the United Nations Organization to save an endangered species in the Congo. We can't stop or divert from our planned route because of our visas.' He gave them a genial smile.

'Don't worry. I'll look after you. Just think of it as a special adventure and soon you'll be back safe and sound with your family and have an amazing tale to tell.' He patted them both comfortingly on the head, then made his way back to Sid.

'I think they're sorted for the time being. Just make sure those thugs of yours leave them alone. They're only useful hostages to us as long as they are OK.'

Sid was beginning to feel that the professor had taken control of events.

'Sure,' he said, 'but just remember, you're not in charge round here.'

'Of course not,' said the Professor with a disarming smile. 'But remember the old saying: "He who pays the piper calls the tune". I am going to make you a millionaire and you'd do well to remember that it's in your own best interests to listen to my suggestions.'

Meanwhile the children were discussing the latest developments. Both felt tearful but were determined not to appear weak in front of their rescuers.

'I think we've been kidnapped,' said Sarah.

'But they saved us from the lions,' said Ben.

'I know that but I think they then decided to kidnap us. I think they're crooks.'

'Will they kill us?' said Ben, his voice quavering a little.

'No, they'll want a ransom,' said Sarah confidently. 'I've read about things like this. If they were going to kill us they'd have done it already. We just have to stay calm and pretend to be their friends. Then one day we'll be ransomed – or we can escape when we get somewhere we can escape to.'

'But what about the Professor,' asked Ben. 'Professors aren't villains are they? Maybe what he said is all true – though,' he added, scanning the crystal clear horizon, 'I don't see any smoke from those fires. And...,' he stopped for a moment, gathering his thoughts, '... and one minute he thought we were here with our parents and the next minute he was saying that the tour operator was in constant touch with our family. If that were true, and he has been speaking to the tour people, surely he would have *known* we weren't here with our parents.' Sarah nodded in agreement; everything Ben had said made good sense.

'Anyway,' he continued, 'whether they're telling the truth or not, you're quite right. We just have to keep going until we can escape or get rescued. And don't worry, I'll look after you whatever happens.' And with that they hugged each other and went back to spend the night in the corner that had been allocated to them in one of the trucks.

11

African Pursuit

In the hotel at Arusha Lucy was feeling a little better, but although her upset stomach was settling she was very weak and still couldn't eat anything. Just as she was discussing how she felt with Clare, Clive burst into their hotel bedroom with his dreadful news. After hearing his story Lucy, tears streaming down her face, went out on to the little verandah belonging to their room and looked up into the sky. Before long a bird fluttered down and perched on the railings in front of her. Soon Clare saw the look in her face that meant she was communing with animals.

'*Greetings, O Promised One,*' said the bird. '*I heard thy call and am here to do thy bidding*'.

'*Greetings,*' said Lucy. '*I seek urgent tidings about my kin, two young Tailless Ones. Go thou to the great plains where the clovenkin roam and seek out the carrionquills who soar above. Ask if any of the manefangs or fleetfangs,*' she paused and thought, '*or cacklekin or wolfkin, have killed any Tailless Ones this day. If the young Tailless Ones are found, none is to harm them. Now go, and return in haste with any tidings.*'

The bird sped off with a clatter of wings and Lucy returned to where Clare and Clive sat hugging one another in their grief.

'All we can do now is wait,' she said. 'There's no point in ringing Mum and Dad or...,' she gave a sob at the thought of telling Ben's mother, '... or Auntie Jane until we know exactly what's happened.' The others agreed. 'If only I hadn't been ill,' sobbed Lucy. 'If I'd been there I could've told all the animals to keep an eye on them straight away.'

'There are always lots of "if onlys" whenever anything bad happens,' said Clive putting a comforting arm round her shoulders. ' "If only" that man on the tour hadn't been taken ill. "If only" that women hadn't fallen asleep. "If only" there hadn't been any lions around. We could go on and on, but all we can really do is hope and pray that by some miracle they're still alive.'

They switched on the TV to a local station in case there was any news, but there was no mention of the incident. They then sat in misery for the next hour trying to console one another and looking every few seconds towards the balcony. Eventually Clare pointed.

'Look!' she said. There in the blue sky was a tiny dark spot which rapidly grew larger and larger. A few minutes later a vulture settled clumsily on the verandah. They had all seen the vultures high in the sky ever since they had arrived, but they were astonished to see just how large one was at close quarters. It raised its ugly naked neck and spoke to Lucy.

'Greetings, O Great One.' Its voice was harsh and raucous and reminded her vividly of the condors she had spoken to when she had first discovered the valley of the Great Ones in the Amazon. *'I bear good tidings.'* Lucy's heart fluttered and she gave a thumbs-up sign to the others who were waiting breathlessly for some news. *'The manefang saw your kin but, before she could harm them, they were taken by some bearded Tailless Ones. Many of them. They put the young ones*

in two great houses that move, and they now travel to where the Brilliant One goes to his rest near the edge of the great water.'

'You have earned the everlasting gratitude of me and my kin,' said Lucy wholeheartedly, her voice trembling with relief, *'and now I have another boon to ask of thee. 'Go back and tell thine own kin to watch the houses that move at all times. If the young Tailless Ones seem in any danger they must be protected by any creature who can assist. A Malevolent One should always be near them at all times. Send word to me when the Brilliant One rises once again.'*

'It shall be so,' replied the vulture. *'Naught shall harm them.'* It tried clumsily to take off from the narrow balcony and Clive eventually had to assist it. Once in the air it was transformed from a clumsy, stumbling, caricature of a bird into a graceful flying machine. It flapped its way into a rising thermal air current and then started to circle upwards until eventually it headed off into the brilliant sunset.

'Well,' said Clare. 'I take it that was good news but now tell us the whole story – every detail, mind!'

'As you gathered, they're safe,' said Lucy. 'They've been picked up by some men in a couple of trucks. The funny thing is, though, they are heading west towards the edge of what sounds like a great lake. If they were tourists or rangers surely they would have brought them back to one of the rangers' lodges or a police station. Oh, yes,' she added. 'There were several men and they all had beards.'

Clive pulled out a map and they clustered round.

'Wow!' Clare exclaimed.' If the vulture's right, the great lake must be Lake Victoria.' *

This certainly is a 'great lake.' It is the largest lake in Africa and the largest tropical lake in the world with an area of 26,800 square miles (68,800 km2.)

'Where are they going? What the hell's going on?' said Clive, suddenly sounding concerned and angry.

'Well,' said Clare, 'to start with, the vulture may simply have been describing the general direction they were taking. They may already have changed direction and be heading for a ranger's hut.' She paused. 'Or...,'

'Or what?' said Clive impatiently.

'...or,' and I hate to say this, 'they've been kidnapped.' said Clare slowly. 'I really didn't like that bit about them all having beards. What group of tourists or rangers *all* have beards?' The others thought for a moment in horrified silence. She was right, of course. Clare continued: 'Remember all those stories we hear about terrorists targeting tourists? Maybe they are going to try and ransom them.'

'Huh!' said Lucy, scornfully. 'We'll soon put a stop to that. When my animals have finished with them they'll wish they'd never been born!'

Clare and Clive suddenly looked relieved again. Despite all their experiences with Lucy, it was difficult always to remember the enormous extent of her power over the animal kingdom and the ability it gave her to manipulate events, even over great distances, in circumstances such as these.

'If they *have* been kidnapped,' asked Clive, 'Shouldn't we tell the authorities before they get too far?'

'Absolutely not,' said Clare firmly. The others looked at her in surprise. 'First of all they'll be suspicious about how we know what's happened. There's no possible *normal* way we could know unless we were in on a scam with the villains. Secondly, we might put the children in danger. If some gung-ho cops go rushing in with guns blazing who knows what might happen! We're much better off using

Lucy's power to follow them, then to disable the villains and help the kids to escape when they're near a village or a town where we can go and rescue them as soon as Lucy's better.'

There was silence while the others digested what Clare had said. Then Clive nodded.

'You're right – as usual. That's by far the best strategy. What do you think Lu?' He looked questioningly at Lucy, who nodded in agreement.

'There's only one problem,' she said after a moment's thought. 'What should we tell the others?'

'It sounds awful,' replied her sister after a moment's thought, 'but we don't tell them anything until we've rescued the children. With any luck we can do it in a couple of days but if we tell them now they'll be worried sick. Mum and Dad will rush back from the Congo, Auntie Jane will fly out from England and there's nothing anyone can do anyway – except Lucy. And,' she added, 'in their panic they'll probably tell the authorities, which we've all just agreed, could be disastrous.'

Once again they thought over Clare's words and eventually, again, they all agreed.

'What if they hear through the media?' asked Clive.

'It looks very much as if the authorities are keeping a lid on this for the moment,' replied Clare, glancing at the TV which had been on throughout their discussion. 'It's now been several hours since the actual incident and there's been nothing on the telly. I can't say I'm surprised: if it gets out that two children have been eaten by lions it'll kill the tourist trade stone dead.'

'Never mind the authorities,' said Lucy, 'what about the other tourists who were on the truck with Ben and Sarah, won't they be telling everyone?'

'Actually, I don't think so,' Clive cut in before Clare could reply. 'They, after all, should have been keeping an eye on the children. They'll be the last ones to advertise the fact that because of their neglect and stupidity two children got eaten!'

'Good point,' said Clare, 'No, I think that there'll probably be a low-key article about children "lost on safari" in a few weeks time after they've had time to "tighten up" the guidelines for tourist companies. Anyway, if it does hit the headlines we can still ring the others immediately and explain we've got things under control.' The others nodded. 'And now,' she continued, 'I think it's time we got some sleep. Lucy's got to get fit as soon as possible so we can get into action.'

They went to bed, relieved beyond measure that the children were alive and apparently unhurt, but desperately worried about what the coming days would bring and whether they had made the right decisions so far.

The next morning Lucy felt well enough to try a little food. As she nibbled at some toast, they sat in her room awaiting further information. About mid-morning a pure white egret flew gracefully on to the verandah and gave an update.

'The young Tailless Ones are well and have eaten. The houses that move are once again running in the direction the Brilliant One goes to rest. Two fellfangs travel with thy kin lest any should wish them harm and two more travel with the others, but none knows of their presence. There are also scurripods in the house that moves who can tell the fledgiquills all that passes within.' Lucy thanked the bird who flew off towards the Serengeti, then turned to the others.

'They're fine and some kind of poisonous snakes will attack anyone who harms them. The mice in the truck are keeping the birds informed about any developments. They're on the move again though, still heading west.' Clive consulted his map again.

'Definitely looks as if they're leaving the country. They must be heading for Burundi or Rwanda. Our best chance would probably be to go into action at the border. We should try and get as near to them as possible. The trouble is, we're running out of time. The country is absolutely massive and they're already a day ahead of us.' He paused and gazed at the map, drumming his fingers on the table. 'Do you think you'll be OK by tomorrow, Lucy?' he asked.

'I think so,' she said. 'I already feel stronger now I've had breakfast and there's no sign of it coming back!'

'Well, by tomorrow they'll have nearly two days' start on us. It's going to be a long, hard drive and the roads are abysmal.'

'Let's fly,' said Clare.

'Good thinking,' said Clive.

'Cool,' said Lucy.

Clive got the map out again and they all pored over it.

'Looks like a choice between Shinyanga and Kigoma,' said Clive. 'It all really depends on where they're really heading.'

'I think they're heading out into the rainforest,' said Clare. 'Once there, they can't easily be seen from the air if a hunt starts up, and they'll be beyond the reach of the Tanzanian authorities where the crime took place.' The others nodded.

'In that case it's Kigoma,' said Clive. 'It's close to Burundi and we might yet beat them to the border.'

The next morning they were up at dawn. Lucy, thankfully, was feeling much better. They hurriedly packed some basic requirements and before leaving their hotel Clare asked a helpful receptionist to tell her parents if they rang from the Congo that they had gone on tour.

'Greetings, O king of the rocks...'

They then headed out to Arusha airport. Luckily they got a flight and by mid-afternoon they had reached Kigoma. Clive rented a Land Rover pick-up truck and headed north to Burundi. He stopped on the journey while Lucy received another update, this time from a large stork.

'The young Tailless Ones remain unharmed,' the bird reported, *'but the moving houses travel always towards the realm of the junglekin.'*

'What of that?' asked Lucy with a slight frown.

'They like not to speak the common tongue,' said the stork. *'But to learn more of this thou must speak to one greater than I.'*

For the first time since an accident in the Amazon, when she had temporarily lost her power, Lucy felt a chill of concern about her ability to communicate with the animals.

'With whom can I speak about this?' she asked urgently. The stork obviously wanted her to talk to a more intelligent species.

'*The arborimane dwell nearby,*' said the stork. '*One shall come hither at my call.*' The bird flew off. Clive and Clare looked at Lucy with concern.

'Something's up, isn't it?' said Clare. 'Are the children OK?'

'Yes, they're fine,' Lucy replied reassuringly, 'but there's something I'm not quite sure about. Apparently a baboon is coming to explain.'

A few seconds later a large male baboon with a mane as rich as a lion's appeared from some nearby rocks and sauntered majestically towards them. Some smaller males and females with young clustered behind, anxious to catch a glimpse of the Promised One.

'*Greetings, O king of the rocks,*' said Lucy, '*I wish to learn about the junglekin.*'

'*I can tell thee only what I know, O Great One,*' said the baboon. '*The junglekin are all those creatures who live in the great forest. They call*' the forest the Greater World and despise us who live on the plains in the Lesser World. They speak not the common tongue – or choose not to – and we of the Lesser World cannot pass through their lands.'

'How can I learn about my kin when they pass into the land of the junglekin?'

'You cannot,' said the baboon simply. 'Only the spotfang durst enter their realm and they speak both the common tongue and the tongue of the junglekin. The bravest and fastest of the fledgiquills, the fledgibanes, will also enter into that kingdom, but many who do so never return.'

'Know they not of the Promised One?' asked Lucy in horror. The baboon put on an expression as near to one of embarrassment as Lucy had ever seen in an animal.

'No... ,' he paused, uncomfortably, '...we speak not much to the spotfang whom we greatly fear, but I have heard tell ...'

'Heard what?' asked Lucy impatiently.

'The spotfangs have told the shieldkin, with whom we do talk, that for many moons the junglekin have spoken of ...,' he paused again, '... of a different Special One. One who fulfills their legend of a Tailless One for the junglekin.' The baboon saw Lucy's face and hurriedly sought to reassure her.

'But fear not for thy kin,' he added. 'The fellfangs stay near them, as do the scurripods and there are many fledgibanes that will risk their lives in your service.'

'I thank thee,' said Lucy, whose brain was now in turmoil. 'Stay close by for I may need thy help.' The baboon agreed and rejoined his troop who disappeared among the rocks and boulders.

'What's all that about?' asked Clare. 'Have you sorted out your problem?'

'Not really.' said Lucy. 'Although Sarah and Ben are OK it seems that it may be more difficult to track them and we can't rely on the help of the animals to rescue them.'

'Why on earth not?' asked Clive.

'Well, they've now entered the rainforest and apparently the creatures of the forest consider themselves a cut above the rest of the planet and don't talk to creatures outside the jungle. They call the forest the "Greater World" and everywhere else the "Lesser World" and they don't let the Lesser World animals in – except for the leopards which they can't stop. The only good thing is that our "own" snakes and mice are still with the kids. The snakes will protect them with their lives and the mice will talk to any birds who dare to fly into the forest – some Lesser World hawks do apparently, though the forest hawks and owls try to kill them.'

'The best-laid plans of mice and men...,'* said Clive bitterly, 'and for the first time in history it's literally true.'

'What else is there?' asked Clare. She knew her sister too well.

'Well,' said Lucy slowly, 'the next thing is *really* spooky. The leopards can go in and out a bit as I said. Apparently they're very independent and don't really go with this Greater and Lesser World gig. The trouble is, their favourite food is baboons, so they don't sit around with them swapping gossip.'

'But ...,' said Clare impatiently.

'But the baboons *do* talk to the tortoises, and the tortoises tell them that the leopards have been saying for some time that a Promised

---

* *Clive is quoting from a poem entitled* "To A Mouse, On Turning Her Up In Her Nest With The Plough", *written by the famous Scottish poet Robert Burns in 1785. The actual line he wrote is:* "The best laid schemes o' mice an' men, Gang aft a-gley", *often paraphrased as:* "The best laid plans of mice and men go oft awry".

One – except they call her the Special One – has appeared in the rainforest.' She ignored the gasps from Clive and Clare. 'Someone the junglekin have always been expecting and they are cock-a-hoop about it. They say it proves they are superior to all other animals – and, by the way, they've never heard of me.'

'Wow,' said Clive. 'The plot certainly thickens. What on earth do we make of all that?'

'Well, there's nothing we can do tonight,' said Lucy, 'except hope that with the help of some brave hawks we can carrying on keeping track of the villains. At least we know Sarah and Ben are safe. The snakes will bite anyone who touches them. I'll have another chat with the baboons tomorrow. They're really switched on and seem very helpful.'

They drove to the next town, Katara, and booked into a hotel where they all spent a restless night. In the morning they drove back to the crop of boulders where the baboons lived. On the way they were astonished to see herds of elephants, buffalos and giraffes, and several groups of wild dogs, cheetahs, hyenas and lions. All seemed to be moving west. When they reached the baboons the big male came out immediately to greet them.

'During sunsleep the animals of the plains have heard of thy plight. They assemble even now to seek thy kin. As well as those you see around you there are countless others surrounding the junglekin on all sides. The fledgiquills have flown many, many leagues to the lands that surround the forest and warned the animals of the desert and river and mountain and plain to come and serve thee. The hipposnorts and the Dreadful Ones have already entered the jungle, such is their eagerness to assist, but the others wait for thy command.'

Lucy couldn't believe her ears. Whatever had she started? She forced her mind back to their main concern.

'And what news of the young ones?'

'*The houses that move have travelled throughout all sunsleep and have passed many leagues into the great forest. Even now they cross the mighty river where the waters and the rocks have their eternal struggle and point towards the land of the bonobokin.*'

Lucy finally turned to the others.

'Gosh!' she said. 'Where to start? First, Sarah and Ben. They've been driving all night apparently and have reached something that sounds like a giant waterfall or cataract in the middle of the jungle.' Clive, as usual, had his map at the ready. He ran his finger across the page.

'That'll be the Stanley Falls!' he exclaimed, 'Oops, sorry, now called the *Boyoma* Falls.' He pointed to the middle of the forest as the others peered over his shoulder.

'And now they're heading for the land of the bonobokin, wherever that is,' said Lucy.

'That'll be the famous reserve at Salonga,' said Clare, looking intently at the map. 'I once did a project on bonobos – there it is,' she pointed at a spot about 250 miles to the southwest of the falls.

'Right, that's the news of the children and the villains,' said Lucy. 'And now for the animals. You're just not going to believe this. Those animals we saw on the way' – they nodded – 'they're just a fraction of all the animals surrounding the entire rainforest. Apparently when I give the word they are ready to invade the forest and rescue the children. I suspect they also intend to settle a few old scores at the same time. They can't wait to take the junglekin down a peg or two. The hippos and crocs have already gone into action. It sounds as though we are going to be responsible for a massive animal war.'

The other two just gaped at her. For once they were both lost for words. Then Clive reached for the radio. He fiddled through various Swahili programmes and then found an English broadcast:

'...*experts in Nairobi and at the Royal Zoological Society in London say there has never been such a massive migration since records began and it involves all the wrong species. Many of the grazers who usually move have stayed behind on the plains, and the predators who normally stay put are all on the move, together with some large herbivores such as elephants and giraffes. There are also reports of crocodiles fighting other crocodiles and hippos fighting other hippos. The experts think these unusual behaviour patterns are almost certainly some new manifestation of global warming. Several countries are already mobilizing soldiers to protect the migrating animals from poachers who are looking forward to a field day. Ex-colonial powers such as Britain and France who have long associations with some of the affected countries have already promised military and scientific aid.'*

'My God,' Clive said excitedly, 'What on earth have we started?' Lucy was appalled.

'We've got to stop this,' she exclaimed, 'otherwise hundreds of innocent animals will lose their lives.'

'What can we do?' asked Clive. They all thought for a moment as the baboon waited patiently beside them.

'Now things aren't going quite as planned hadn't we better tell the others? We'll have to go back to the hotel in Katara to do that though – my mobile can't pick up anything out here.' They all agreed. It was Clare who spoke first.

'We must get a note to the children while we still can and let them know we're coming to rescue them. As the villains seem as far as possible to be avoiding towns and villages we're probably going to have to rescue them in the wild. Perhaps we should ask the baboons what the chances are of a "hit squad" of leopards getting through to protect the children till we can get there. Next, we've got to try to find out about this other "Promised One" – if she or he exists. I still think the junglekin may be referring to Lucy but that somehow their legend has got distorted and they think she is only meant to relate to them. Don't ask me how we find out though – I haven't got the faintest idea!'

'You're right though,' agreed Clive. 'As thousands of animals seem to be getting mobilized, cracking the riddle of the two 'Promised Ones' may be the only way of stopping a horrendous animal war!'

'Right,' said Lucy. 'Let's swing into action.' She pulled out a notebook and started to scribble a note.

'Just a minute,' said Clare. 'We've never told Sarah and Ben that you can speak to animals. What are they going to make of a letter appearing out of nowhere?'

Lucy paused and thought for a moment.

'You're right of course. I'll have to word it carefully and when we meet up they're obviously going to have to know – it had to happen sometime soon anyway!' She tore up the note she had started and wrote a new one.

Don't let the men see you reading this

"Dear Sarah and Ben,

We are following you and are coming to rescue you. Some snakes and/ or leopards may come and frighten the men but they won't hurt you (I'll explain why later). Stay near the trucks and the leopards till we come.

Lots of love,

Lucy, Clare and Clive XXXXX

P.S. When you've read this note tear a corner off, put it back in the case and then just drop it on the ground or chuck it out of the truck. The animals will return it to us and we'll know you've read it. X

111

She then took her spare glasses case, made of soft leather and slipped the note inside. She turned and spoke to the baboon who loped off into the trees. Soon he returned and a few seconds later a hawk flew over and sat on the car bonnet.

He glanced around the group with a proud and haughty look. His speech was straight to the point as he addressed Lucy:

'How can I serve thee? I fear not the junglekin.' Just what we need, thought Lucy gratefully, reassured by the baboon's choice of messenger for the hazardous mission. They all admired the raptor's brilliant plumage, awesome beak and claws, and piercing eyes. None of them was to know that within a few hours one of those golden orbs would be gone, shattered by the beak of a jungle owl defending the junglekin from an intruder risking all in service of the Promised One. Lucy gave the spectacle case to the hawk.

'Take this to the young Tailless Ones. The bearded ones must not see thee or all is lost. Stay near until the young ones cast this to the ground, then return it hither.'

The hawk grasped the case and flew like an arrow to the west and the great forest, looking for all the world as if he held a small brown rodent in his talons.

'Right, now for the leopards and snakes.' Lucy turned to the baboon. *'I seek the aid of the spotfangs who live in the great forest. Can we send word to them?'*

'We are here to do thy will,' said the baboon simply. *'There are other fledgiquills such as the one you have seen who will brave the junglekin.'* The baboon went once more to the trees and almost immediately a second hawk flew across to the waiting trio. After greeting the bird Lucy gave it some instructions:

'Go thou to the spotfangs in the great forest. Assist them in seeking out

the young Tailless Ones. When you reach the houses that move, speak to the fellfangs who hide therein. They already have their instructions. Tell them their time has come.' She paused until she was satisfied the bird had understood, then continued: *'The spotfangs must protect the young Tailless Ones from the bearded ones and, once they are alone, from any of the junglekin that might wish them harm. The spotfangs must remain there until I come with my kin. Now, go like the wind and fare ye well.'* The hawk sped off towards the rainforest.

Lucy paused. What was the other thing? Of course. She turned back the baboon who had now returned:

'Finally, tell all the animals of the Lesser World to wait before attacking the junglekin. That includes the hipposnorts and the Dreadful Ones. I will meet with their Special One and then decide what must be done.'

The baboon agreed and trotted off to join his troop. A few seconds later a flock of egrets rose from the baboons' rocky outcrop and flew north, south, east and west with the words of the Promised One to the creatures of the Lesser World.

12

Into the Heart of Darkness

Joanna looked out from the plane across the seemingly interminable green canopy of the jungle, the second largest in the world after the Amazon and comprising almost twenty per cent of the world's remaining tropical rainforest. As she thought of the vast, dark impenetrable and forbidding landscape that lay beneath the sunlit canopy she recalled the description of the Congo penned by Joseph Conrad – "the heart of darkness". The term conjured up the magical and mysterious tales of the early explorers: tales of great cataracts and waterfalls, gorillas, pygmies, cannibals and mysterious animals ranging from giant serpents to dinosaurs. She thought of the words of the Latin author Pliny: "Ex Africa semper aliquid novi"* and reflected that for over two thousand years the great continent had continued to surprise scientists and naturalists as ever more bizarre and wonderful creatures and secrets were revealed by intrepid explorers.

Her own previous sojourn in the Congo had been one of mixed emotions: wonder at the marvels of nature and the fascinating studies she and Richard had undertaken; joy at the birth of Lucy, and intense sorrow at the loss of her other child amidst the horrors and brutality

There is always something new out of Africa

of civil war. And now, on her way back towards Kinshasa, the capital, she was again experiencing mixed emotions: hope that the feral girl they had read about might be indeed her missing child; fear that she might not be, or might not be found or, perhaps even worse, found and prove to be irreparably harmed by her bizarre and unnatural upbringing among wild animals. As Richard, tired out by his Kilimanjaro expedition the previous day, snored beside her, she went over once again, for the hundredth time, their plans to track down the mystery girl. They had started in London with enquiries at the Foreign and Commonwealth Office and she recalled with a mixture of amusement and annoyance the unhelpful phone conversation she had had with the official responsible for equatorial Africa.

'Hello, Tawkin-Tosh here. How may I be of assistance?' Tawkin-Tosh didn't usually answer the phone, but his secretary was away on a team-building course and he was on his own.

'Hello,' said Joanna, 'I wonder if you can assist me with some information. It concerns a newspaper article about a girl in the Congo.'

'The Congo, eh,' there was a brief silence. Joanna could practically hear the buffoon thinking. 'I think the Belgians are the ones you're after. I've got the number of their embassy somewhere.' There was the sound of shuffling papers.

'The Belgians left the Congo in 1960,' said Joanna. 'Perhaps that's something you ought to have known yourself.'

'Well, you learn something every day in this job! I've just moved from our South American section, so I'm still a bit shaky on the fine details. Always a new wrinkle, what?'

Joanna put the phone down. There was obviously nothing more to be learnt about the feral child until they got to Africa.

Now, on the plane, she felt eager to start on the quest. She felt comfortable about the other children who had waved them off cheerily at Arusha airport that morning and who were greatly enjoying their trip to Africa. She thought Lucy had looked a little pale, but put that down to the late night they had all enjoyed. Now she and Richard could devote all their energies to the task in hand.

There were two potential sources of information and help that they planned to use. The first was the UNESCO site at Salonga where they had worked on their previous visit and where the staff would undoubtedly have a great deal of local knowledge. The second was the British Embassy which, they felt had a duty to assist them in searching for what might be a lost British citizen. While the local enquiries were the ones they were principally pinning their hopes on, the British Embassy for the Congo was in the capital, Kinshasa, where their plane was about to land so it made sense to go there first before making the journey out to Salonga.

Joanna and Richard went straight to the Embassy from the airport. They introduced themselves at reception and explained that they had come for information about the feral child who had been reported in the news. They were asked to wait for a while and after a few moments an assistant appeared and took them to sit in a large office in front of a large desk. A distinguished-looking man came through another door, greeted them warmly, and introduced himself as the Ambassador.

Joanna and Richard exchanged astonished glances. They had expected some vague offer of assistance from a junior official.

'Can I start by just checking I've got this right?' said the ambassador. 'You are Dr. and Mrs. Bonaventure and you worked at the Salonga reserve thirteen years ago?' Richard tried to speak but his mouth was dry – so he just nodded.

'Yes, we are,' said Joanna.

'This is most curious,' the ambassador continued. 'In fact, I think it is the most curious thing that has happened to me in all my years in the service.' Joanna and Richard stared at him expectantly. For some reason Joanna found herself trembling as he continued. 'This very morning I received a package from the UNESCO office at Salonga. It had been taken there by a maid who said she had found it in the house of a Salonga park conservateur. He and his family had been arrested on suspicion of espionage a few weeks ago and, I understand from enquiries I have just made, exiled to Rwanda. On receiving this package the UNESCO officials, reluctant to get involved in something that might have political repercussions, sent it to me as I had been cited as an alternative recipient. Now we come to the interesting part and I think I should warn you to be prepared for some astonishing news. He opened the file and removed a letter and suddenly Richard leaned forward and peered more closely.

'Good heavens!' he exclaimed. 'Those – those are our old passports... and my papers and journals!'

'Precisely,' smiled the ambassador. 'And now I think you should read this letter.' He stood up and came round the desk and put Neema's guardian's letter gently into Joanna's shaking hands. She and Richard read it together. They sat in stunned silence for a while then, both weeping, turned and hugged each other as the ambassador rang a bell and asked an attendant to bring some tea.

'So it's true,' Richard eventually whispered. 'She survived that ghastly day.'

'But where is she?' asked Joanna, 'and what has she to do with the feral child?'

'Ah, that I don't know,' answered the ambassador. 'We are, of course, making urgent enquiries but you'll appreciate that I only learnt about any of this a few hours ago. We've established that the girl was not present when her foster family were arrested and the people at Salonga have not seen her since. I've sent someone in the area to have a quiet word with the maid. She may well know something but is obviously terrified of being arrested herself. There have been no reports of recent accidents or deaths in the area, so I think there's every possibility that the child running wild in the reserve really is your daughter.'

'But isn't she in great danger alone in the forest?' burst out Joanna.

'I don't know,' said the ambassador gently, 'and I don't wish to raise any false hopes. I have, however, just reviewed all the local reports that gave rise to the press article you saw and it is clear that the poachers who saw the mystery child– sorry, *alleged* poachers – were emphatic that the child was playing with the chimps. These bonobos have a reputation for being friendly and gentle and, incredible as it seems, it's just possible they're looking after her.'

'What do you think we should do next?' asked Richard.

'Well, we'll continue our own enquiries of course and let you know immediately of any developments.' He took a card from a carved wooden container on his desk and handed it to Joanna. 'Here's our contact details. Get in touch when you know where you're staying and we can then keep you posted. In fact –' he took back the card and scribbled on it with his pen, '–here's my home number. You can ring me any time of day or night if you need help.'

Joanna and Richard thanked him for all his help and kindness and turned to go.

'Just one more thing,' said the ambassador. 'We'll do our best but, to be honest, you're doing the right thing by going to the reserve yourselves. It's by far your best chance of finding the girl. I have to pick my way through a tricky political situation whereas you know the locality and the UNESCO people and you don't have to handle any sensitive diplomatic issues.' He looked at Joanna's distraught face and patted her on the shoulder as he ushered them out. 'When you find your daughter we'll have to fix her up with a passport. It's a unique situation so I may have to bend the rules a bit. I hope to see you again soon,' he said with a reassuring smile.

It was getting on in the day and they were both exhausted from the flight and the extraordinary meeting that had just had at the embassy. They decided to postpone the long and difficult journey to Salonga until the morning, and booked into a hotel in Kinshasa for the night.

When they eventually arrived at the reserve they found some suitable accommodation, rang the embassy with a contact number, and then visited their old haunts – those at least that had managed to survive two civil wars and endless civil unrest. The UNESCO officials gave them a warm welcome and told them about Neema and the long hours she used to spend with the animals. One of the rangers took them in a dugout canoe to the cabin where she had spent most of her time and as they looked out into the vast forest they realised the true enormity of their task.

'There's only one way to do this,' said Richard that evening. Joanna smiled.

'I know exactly what you're thinking,' she said. 'We need Lucy.' He nodded.

'She's got to know now anyway,' Joanna continued, 'so we may as well tell her and get her involved straight away.'

In the morning they rang the hotel in Arusha but, to their surprise the receptionist said that the party had all checked out.

'Though they did leave a message,' she added. 'Just a moment please'. There was a rustling of papers. 'Yes, here it is. "We've gone on tour. Mobiles not working but we'll keep trying. Leave a contact number with this hotel if you're now on a land line. Love from all".'

'That's odd,' said Richard, 'they never mentioned a tour but maybe they've heard of an exciting safari or something.' He left their number with the Arusha hotel who kindly agreed to act as a "post office" and they decided that there was nothing more they could do until the others got back in touch.

They tried to speak to the maid who had taken the package to UNESCO but she had fled back to her own village before she could get blamed for anything. All they could do now was to visit Neema's cabin in the reserve every day in the hope of catching sight of her.

13

Captive Cousins in the Congo

Sarah and Ben had settled into an uneasy existence with their captors. After the first couple of days during which they had not gone near any proper town they had both decided that they had been kidnapped and that the stories about returning them to their relatives were all a pack of lies. The stifling heat, the flies and the smell in the trucks were at times almost intolerable, but they comforted themselves with the thought that there had been no attempt to hurt them in any way and, as Sarah pointed out, they were worth much more to the villains alive than dead. They had both seen news stories and TV programmes about hostages and ransoms and just hoped that they would soon be rescued.

The only villain they had any liking for was Fred who was interested in them and was always taking them to see and do fascinating things related to animals and bushcraft. He regaled the children with stories about the jungle in Brazil. About how their camp had been infested with snakes and spiders; how one day an ant army had marched through the camp; how swarms of bees had attacked a plane coming to rescue them; how one of his mates had been blown to pieces by an accident with mining explosives; and how his brother had been eaten by caymans. The children were enthralled by his stories which all had the ring of truth and Fred revelled in being the centre of attention for the first time in his life.

The professor pretended to be kind and concerned for their welfare but they both instinctively disliked and distrusted him. Sid and the other men virtually ignored them. They had a corner of one of the covered trucks to themselves and shared the truck with Fred and two of the others. After leaving the savannah they passed through a mountainous region. Their vehicles roared straight through any town or village that couldn't be avoided, and the truck containing the children never stopped anywhere where there were signs of habitation. Fuel was always collected by the other truck and only transferred to the children's truck out in the bush. On many occasions on their long journey the trucks were stopped by soldiers or men in paramilitary uniforms at checkpoints. Ben began to notice that when they were stopped in this way the professor always disappeared into his truck and was not seen again until the obstruction or road block had been safely negotiated. He was accused of cowardice by some of the men but he explained that he was a scientist, not a thug, and if they did their job he would do his. Ben and Sarah, however, noticed a very curious thing which was that whenever these occasions arose the officer in charge of the militia, or any person threatening Sid with a gun or knife, would suddenly collapse as if struck from behind, or his weapon would suddenly point up in the air as he fired. Sometimes an officer even shot some of his own men as his gun inexplicably pointed in a different direction as he fired at Sid or the trucks. The upshot of this was that they never had any difficulty in passing through such blocks, however ugly the confrontation at first seemed. Sid himself seemed somewhat surprised at his own skill in overcoming armed men and soon became proud of his reputation as a block buster. Later, when Ben and Sarah were told about the professor's invisibility robe, they would recall with great amusement some of these mystifying scenes and realise what had really been going on.

They drove through more and more heavily wooded country until eventually they were in the depths of the rainforest. Sarah had noticed that there were mice living under some old blankets in the truck and she gave them morsels and scraps from her supper every night. Now and then birds came and perched on the tailgate of the lorry. Ben thought they were trying to catch the mice, but one day he was puzzled to see a mouse coming out and approaching a large hawk which had arrived and perched on the tailgate of the lorry.

'They look as if they're *talking* to each other,' he said to Sarah, and they both laughed at the thought.

One morning the children woke bruised and shaken after the trucks had driven all through the night over particularly dreadful roads. They could hear a continuous roaring and splashing and looked out to see an amazing sight. The river was thundering down cataracts and as they drove along they saw that the falls extended over many, many kilometres. The professor explained that these were the Boyoma falls, originally called the Stanley falls after a journalist who had journeyed through the Congo in search of the famous British explorer, David Livingstone. After leaving the falls the trucks headed south and west towards the Lomela river and the diamond lode that was the professor's goal. Their route took them into the densest jungle the children had so far seen. There was a great deal of carnage, most of it fortuitously hidden from the children who were in the rear truck of the convoy. Sid had by now developed a zero tolerance policy for road blocks and whenever they approached any group threatening to stop them he simply opened fire with an automatic and carried on driving. The children had by now got so used to the sound of gunfire that they hardly noticed the occasional bursts of automatic fire and the sound of splintering road barriers that punctuated their long journey. They travelled by day and by night along the terrible roads; in some places the track was so narrow that the lorries could barely force a passage through the overhanging trees and the undergrowth encroaching from the roadsides, and occasionally the men had to cut down a roadside tree to let them through.

On the morning of their third day after leaving the falls, they were continuing through similar terrain when Sid suddenly swore as the leading truck he was driving lurched to one side and ran into the bush at the side of the road. He got out and saw that they had a jagged puncture in one of the front tyres. The rubber was torn down to the wheel rim and was obviously beyond repair. Inspection of both trucks revealed that their spare tyres were missing, presumably stolen before the professor had acquired the vehicles. After cursing everything and everybody in sight Sid eventually calmed down and thought carefully for a moment.

'I'll take the other truck and go with Fred to find a new tyre somewhere – several tyres in fact; on these roads we're gonna get plenty more flats.' He paused and looked at the disabled truck by the side of the road. 'Get that one into the bush,' he added. 'If a bunch of rebels comes along you'll be sittin' ducks – 'specially as you'll be two men down without me and Fred.' One of the men got in and started up. The lorry bumped and jerked on the flat tyre but he revved up the powerful engine and crashed through a thicket of wild pineapples growing by the side of the road. He drove deeper into the trees until Sid was satisfied that the vehicle was completely invisible to any passing traffic. Then he and Fred set off in the remaining truck.

While the gang were waiting for Sid and Fred to return with the tyres, they pitched camp and ate a meal of roast cassava and monkey. After they had eaten the children sat together on a fallen trunk away from the men's cigarette and cigar smoke. As they sat Sarah noticed that a bird had settled close behind them and she nudged Ben who turned to look. It was some kind of a hawk they realised from its hooked beak, and it seemed completely fearless.

'Oh look,' said Sarah. 'It's hurt its eye, poor thing,' and sure enough one of the bird's eyes was closed and glistening as if recently injured. The bird hopped nearer and then Sarah gave a gasp. At its feet was Lucy's leather glasses case. She bent down and picked it up. How on earth had a bird found it and brought it to her? She felt inside for Lucy's glasses and instead pulled out the note. The first words jumped out at her and she hurriedly glanced across at the men. They were talking, drinking and smoking and paying no attention to her. She smoothed the note casually on to her lap and nudged Ben with her knee to read it with her. When they had finished she made sure she was unobserved as she tore a corner off the sheet, refolded the letter and replaced it in the case. She then slipped it behind her near the log. A few moments later the hawk emerged from a nearby tree and in a graceful swoop picked up the case and soared up into the sky. The children watched, spellbound, as it turned to the east and then was lost to sight as it disappeared above the forest canopy.

'How on earth did all that happen?' said Ben. 'And all that stuff in the note: how can leopards come and not hurt us?'

'It's something to do with Lucy,' said Sarah. 'She's always doing things with animals and they all seem to think she's marvellous. She's going to be a vet one day. Anyway, at last something is going to happen and she's got Clare and Clive to help her. I just hope they know these horrid men have all got guns and knives and things.'

'I'm sure they'll guess,' said Ben putting a protective arm around her. 'Don't worry. Everything's going to be OK.'

Meanwhile, Sid and Fred were still searching for a town where they could obtain some new tyres. They were in a remote area and it took the entire morning to find a settlement of reasonable size. There was a run-down garage but there were no tyres suitable for their army truck. They eventually found another town and Fred spotted a similar lorry to their own outside a cafe. In the cafe a group of rebel soldiers in para-military garb were sprawled across chairs and tables. They had obviously been drinking all morning and Sid's quick glance through the door went unnoticed.

At a nod from Sid, Fred climbed into the soldiers' lorry. He had intended to hotwire it but there was no need. The rebels, confident because of their brutal reputation that no-one would even contemplate meddling with them, had left the keys in the ignition. Sid hurriedly got back into their own truck and a moment later the two lorries moved off in convoy; the soldiers not discovering their loss until Sid and Fred had long disappeared into the vast depths of the jungle.

It was a long journey back on the terrible roads and it was late afternoon before Sid and Fred returned. They then transferred all the equipment from the hidden, punctured vehicle to their newly acquired lorry. During the transfer an acute observer might have heard a low hissing noise emanating from the ventilation holes in the ammunition boxes as they were carried from one lorry to the other. It was as well that nobody did, for they would have had a very nasty shock if they had opened the boxes. By the time everything had been transferred it was evening, and they decided to pitch camp for the night. Though the delay was annoying for the villains, losing a day was not critical now that they felt safe from pursuit deep in the rainforest, but the extra day was invaluable to Lucy, Clare and Clive who were now driving day and night to catch up with the kidnappers.

Now that they were nearing their destination Sid had become progressively more impatient with the presence of the children, and after supper that night Ben, who had gone behind some bushes to relieve himself, suddenly heard Sid talking to Fred and the professor nearby. The three had obviously moved away from the others at the campfire so their conversation couldn't be overheard.

'They're just a complete drag,' Sid was saying. 'We're not goin' to need 'em any more – it's like the wild west out here with all these soldiers an' rebels, an' the cops ain't takin' the slightest notice of us. I think it's time we wasted 'em.' Ben suddenly realised with horror that Sid was talking about him and Sarah.

'I think I agree,' murmured the professor. 'Leave it to me.'

'If anyone touches them kids I'll tear 'em apart!' Fred snarled suddenly. 'They ain't done no 'arm. We'll just drop 'em in the next town and scarper.'

'We can't do that.' said the professor. 'At the moment the heat's off because everyone obviously thinks they've been eaten by lions. If they suddenly reappear and start blabbing we'll all spend the rest of our lives in the slammer – and I wouldn't count on living to a ripe old age in jail in these parts.' Sid nodded.

'He's right, Fred. We gotta waste the kids.'

'Just you try, that's all,' said Fred. 'I'll be watchin',' he added as he stormed off to join the rest of the group.

'You can't let him put us all at risk,' said the professor when he had gone. 'He hardly ever argues with you, so he must feel very strongly about it.'

'He'll be OK when he settles down,' said Sid. 'You just do the business and I'll talk him round afterwards. We can bump up his percentage on the diamonds if necessary – if that's OK with you of course,' he added hurriedly. The professor nodded gravely.

'In the circumstances I think that would be entirely reasonable,' he replied. The "circumstances", he thought with amusement, being that the twins' only "percentage" was going to be a bullet through the brain.

Ben had heard enough but he stood stock still, hardly daring to breathe until the men had finished their conversation and moved off back to the campfire. He then slipped back to rejoin Sarah and told her what he had heard. That night they took it in turns to stay awake and keep watch, terrified every time something moved or rustled near the truck where they slept. Somehow they got through their night of fear and shortly after dawn the group had breakfast before setting off on the final leg of their journey. After breakfast the professor came over to the children and said in his most jovial voice.

'Come on you two, while the others are packing up let's pick some fruit to eat on the journey'. Sarah glanced at Ben and they both knew that the time had come to do something.

'OK,' said Sarah to the professor. 'We'll just go and get a couple of bags from the truck,' and before Luke could say anything she and Ben returned to their truck.

'As soon as we're hidden from him by the truck we'll run into the jungle,' Ben murmured as they went. 'It's our only hope.' Sarah nodded. The jungle was incredibly dense and with a few moment's start their slender figures might be able to get far enough away from the fat thugs to escape or hide. It was a pretty hopeless situation but there was nothing else they could do. As they approached the truck Ben saw a bird hop onto the back.

'Look,' he said. 'Another bird! Maybe it's got another message for us.' They looked around. The professor was scrutinizing his GPS and his compass, planning the next stage of the journey as he waited patiently for them. He had no reason to be suspicious for he had no idea that they knew of his plans. Sarah and Ben quickly scrambled in the truck to see the bird.

'We've got to see what it wants,' Sarah said breathlessly. 'Then we'll grab some water and run.' To their surprise and disappointment, however, the bird flew straight out again leaving no sign of a message.

'Must have just been after some crumbs or something,' said Ben. 'Let's go!' Sarah peeped round the corner of the truck before jumping out to check on the professor. She saw him walk behind a tree and then he seemed simply to disappear.

'Well, gives us more time to escape,' she thought, and started to climb out over the tailgate. Just then there was a hiss and there immediately below her was a long black snake. Its head was already on the ground and its body continued to emerge from the chassis and suspension under the truck's floorboards. She grabbed Ben and they shrank back into the truck. Then, to her horror she saw a second snake which came out of a tool compartment inside the back of the truck and slithered alongside herself and Ben, now huddled against the side. The mamba passed within inches of them but completely ignored them and reared up so that its head was looking out over the tailgate as if on guard. Then a strange thing happened. Suddenly the snake on the ground reared up and its forked tongue flickered. Its head arched back and it was clearly preparing to strike – but as Sarah and Ben watched in fearful fascination, they could see nothing for the reptile to attack. They then heard a curse and Sarah suddenly saw a footprint in the sand in front of the snake that she was sure had not been there before.

The stand-off between the professor and the mamba was an interesting one. The mamba relied on its eyesight to follow movements of its prey and was disconcerted by the apparent absence of the professor; on the other hand it had felt the vibrations of his approach and its constantly flickering tongue was testing the air and informing it that the professor was certainly present. It waited, alert and head erect for the slightest movement. For his part, the professor had approached the truck to finish off the children, confident that he was completely invisible. The appearance of the snake had taken him completely by surprise and as he stood in front of the deadly, swaying reptile he suddenly remembered reading that some snakes had thermal imaging detectors – presumably unaffected by invisibility. As it happened, the species of snake he now confronted did not possess this imaging facility, but the professor's herpetological knowledge did not extend far enough for him to be sure of this. He slowly inched his way backwards from the snake until he was far enough away to turn and run for the trees. Even then the snake could probably have caught him if it had seen him, for this was the fastest-moving snake on earth, capable of moving at twelve miles an hour, and one of the few snakes known deliberately to attack humans without provocation. Sarah, of course, was unaware of most of this drama but she heard the sound of running and saw the snake beginning to relax. Looking back at the group, she saw that the men had almost finished breaking camp and

Fred and the other two who shared the children's truck were coming towards her carrying pots and camp stools. At that moment she saw the professor reappear from behind the tree. He looked white and shaken and Sarah wondered what he had seen in the bush that had terrified him. As Fred and the men came nearer to the truck Luke saw them and shouted to them to stop. There were loud hisses and the men stopped and looked at the mambas in horror. The snakes swayed threateningly and the men slowly retreated backwards towards the other truck – which the professor had already hurriedly climbed into. About halfway Fred stopped, reluctant to leave the children, but his two companions joined the professor and the rest of the men in the other vehicle.

'What's going on?' asked Sid, who was already in the driving seat waiting impatiently for the loading to be completed.

'It's our truck,' called Fred, 'it's swarming with snakes!' Sid went white with fear. He and Fred both had a lifelong aversion to snakes. He thought briefly of getting out and trying to shoot them but the thought of shooting one and missing, or having another one streak towards his leg... he shuddered and made a quick decision.

'Leave the other truck. We can cope with one. We're nearly at the mines anyway.'

'But the kids,' said Fred, 'they're still in there with the snakes!' He was torn between his phobia of snakes and his genuine concern for the children as he stood between the two trucks, full of indecision. He didn't dare shoot at the snakes; for all he knew there were more than just two, and he might hit the children or hit the fuel tank of the lorry and incinerate them.

'Stay completely still, kids, and they won't hurt you,' he called to comfort them, his voice hoarse with fear, 'I'll soon think of something.'

But he didn't have time to think of anything for at that moment there was a coughing growl from the bushes and a leopard stalked towards Fred, its tail lashing angrily. Fred hurriedly scrambled into the back of the other truck and Sid threw it into gear and drove off.

'That solves one of our problems,' murmured Luke, who was sitting in front next to Sid. Sid grinned.

'Yeah. And we needed the extra room now we're down to one truck.'

After they had driven for about an hour the professor nudged Sid in the front seat, and leaned over so those in the back couldn't hear.

'I've been thinking,' he said in a low voice. 'We can't leave the kids in that lorry. Even after the snakes have killed them, they'll be found and everyone will know they were kidnapped. There'll be such a hue and cry that our chances of quietly setting up an illegal mining outfit down the road will be zero.' Sid frowned, then nodded.

'You're right. What do you suggest?'

'We'll have to go back and burn the lorry. As you know, there are burnt-out trucks all over the place. It won't be looked at for months – if ever. Even if it is, a few bits of charred bone will never be linked with a fake lion kill in the Serengeti.' Sid nodded slowly in agreement. It all made good sense.

'What about Fred? He'll never agree.'

The professor drew even nearer and they murmured for a while, then Sid drew into a clearing.

'Let's stop for a break,' he said cheerfully. 'The prof thinks he's left his briefcase by a log at our last stop. It's got stuff in it to do with the diamonds, so we gotta get it. I'll take 'im back while you guys 'ave a coffee and a bite.'

The men jumped down to stretch their legs. Fred sullenly started to make coffee on a camp stove. He was still upset about what had happened to the children and hadn't spoken to Sid or Luke since. Sid went over to him.

'Look, Fred, you're probably right about the kids. I'll see what I can do, but I'm not risking myself with any snakes.'

'Yeah!' Fred replied tersely. He didn't turn round. He knew his brother was lying and he was beginning to feel sickened by the whole expedition. Sid rejoined the professor in the truck, turned it round, and drove back up the track with the professor. Soon they arrived at the spot. The abandoned lorry stood by the side of the road. There was complete silence and no sign of any children, leopards or snakes. Sid briefly contemplated looking into the back for the children's bodies but the thought of having a snake or snakes striking into his face from the dark interior was unthinkable. If the kids had got out of the lorry, he told himself, the leopard would have attacked them and that was fine, for they'd never be found. If their bodies were still in the lorry he needed to destroy the evidence. He pulled a safe distance away and fired his machine pistol at the fuel tanks. Within a few seconds there was an almighty "whoosh" and the lorry burst into flames. The heat, even at a distance, was quite incredible and when the ammunition boxes started to explode Sid had to pull further away. Within a few moments the vehicle had been reduced to a charred shell in which nothing could have survived or remained recognizable. Sid looked questioningly at the professor who surveyed the scene with satisfaction and smiled.

'I think that wraps it all up rather neatly, don't you?' he murmured. Sid slid the lorry into gear and they drove off, leaving the wreck flickering with flames that would continue for several more hours.

Two hours earlier, after the villains had left, the children sat rigid with fear, eyes fixed in horror at the black mamba beside them. Once the rumble and vibrations of the departing lorry had faded the snake turned, casually slithered over Sarah's legs and slid under the tarpaulin covering stores opposite where the children sat. Even as it disappeared the head of the other snake appeared over the tailgate and it too slithered down, passed within inches of the children and rejoined its companion. The leopard, which had disappeared into the trees following the departure of the other lorry, suddenly re-appeared and sauntered over to the children. He stood on his hindlegs and put his forepaws on the tailgate and dropped a freshly killed squirrel into the truck at the children's feet. Then he dropped back to the ground and rolled on his back, legs in the air and purring deeply, for all the world like a domestic cat. Sarah looked at Ben. They had both relaxed a little with the disappearance of the snakes.

'This must be Lucy's leopard,' Sarah said. 'And he's brought us the squirrel for food. Even though,' she added wrinkling her nose, ' I wouldn't eat it in a trillion years. He's obviously here to protect us but what do you think about the snakes?'

'Well they could've bitten us ten times over,' said Ben thoughtfully, 'but they didn't, and Lucy did say in her note that leopards *and* snakes might help us. All the same, I don't feel very comfortable with them hidden just over there.' He gestured across the truck.

'I've got an idea,' said Sarah after they had sat chatting for a while, both immensely relieved by the departure of the gang. 'It doesn't feel very safe in this lorry with the snakes and if some of those dreadful soldiers we keep seeing come past they'll see the truck and find us. The leopard can protect us from other animals, but not from guns.

Why don't we move into the truck that's hidden over there behind the trees. No-one can see it from the road.'

'But that one's got a burst tyre,' said Ben.

'So what!' laughed Sarah, 'We can't drive it, anyway.'

'Good point,' said Ben immediately, with a smile. He started to clamber over the tailgate then suddenly paused and looked at the leopard; even though it could easily have leapt into the lorry and devoured them if it had wanted to do so, it somehow seemed foolhardy to step right down beside it.

'Come on, wimp!' said Sarah, teasing him with a grin as she jumped down first.

'Lucy said there'd be a leopard and here it is.' As if to prove her words, as soon as she was on the ground the leopard came over and nuzzled her reassuringly.

'It's fine,' she said. She unhooked the latches on the tailgate and let it swing down. 'Now pass me the stuff down and we can take it to the other lorry.'

Ben handed down their sleeping things and a large carton of water bottles that was next to them. They looked back at the other stores of water and canned food covered with tarpaulins. The snakes had disappeared somewhere into the interior.

'I daren't touch that stuff,' said Ben, 'even though we need it.'

'No,' agreed Sarah. 'We'll have to think some more about how to get it – but bring the squirrel; we don't want to offend the leopard!'

They trekked across the bushes with their bundles and the dead squirrel. The leopard prowled along after them looking from side to side. As they walked under the trees Ben looked up and saw two more leopards lying nonchalantly along branches, their tails hanging vertically down, so near that he could almost touch them. They let

'Look!'

down the tailgate of the concealed lorry and pushed their belongings in, putting the squirrel carefully to one side and climbed up. Just as they were about to close the tailgate Ben exclaimed and pointed.

'Look!' Sarah followed his finger and there she saw two mambas slithering along the ground. They stopped briefly in front of the leopard on the ground, then moved to the lorry the children had just put their things in. Sarah and Ben watched in fearful fascination as they wound their way up the back wheels, over the mudguards, and twisted themselves up into the lorry.

'They've followed us,' said Sarah.

'They *must* be on our side,' said Ben, 'didn't you see them talking to the leopard?' She nodded. 'That means we can go back and get the rest of the supplies,' he said confidently. 'Come on.'

They hurried back to the vehicle at the side of the road and Ben dragged the boxes to the back of the truck and handed them down to Sarah. When they had taken everything useful Ben jumped down and put up the tailgate, then the two of them started moving the provisions from the pile on the ground to the other truck. It was laborious work in the jungle heat and the entire job took the best part of an hour. As they carried the last box away Ben suddenly stopped and listened.

'Shush!' he said. 'What's that?'

They listened intently as, above the normal bird and animal sounds of the forest and the incessant dripping of water from the trees, a faint rumble became apparent.

'It's a lorry,' said Sarah. 'Quick!' They pulled the last box into the lorry that was their new home, secured the tailgate, and crouched down behind it. They both jumped as there was a thud on the tarpaulin. Stretched over the poles above them a shape bulged down.

'It's only the leopard,' whispered Ben. 'He's jumped up to hide from the lorry – and protect us.'

The noise of the lorry got louder, the engine note changing as it wound around the bends and tried to avoid potholes and dips in the dirt road. Eventually it came round a final bend and then, to the children's horror, stopped beside the vehicle they had just vacated.

'Good job you made us move,' Ben whispered to Sarah. She nodded but she was sick with fear and put her finger to her lips.

Suddenly there was the clatter of automatic fire and the canvas above them trembled as the great cat lying there tensed for action. Then there was a massive "crump" as the fuel tank on the other lorry exploded. The birds and animals of the forest fell into a stunned silence for a moment, then burst into a cacophony of alarm calls. The burning vehicle hissed and crackled as it burnt and the ammunition boxes the children had left behind started to explode. They lay still, hardly daring to breathe for fear of what might happen next but eventually, to their intense relief, they heard the newly arrived lorry start up, do a series of noisy manoeuvres to turn on the narrow road, then disappear the way it had come.

'How do we know they've really gone?' Sarah whispered to Ben after a few moments. He shrugged his shoulders in reply but gestured that they should remain hidden, a decision with which Sarah heartily concurred. Suddenly the truck vibrated as the leopard sprang off the roof to the ground. It stood with its paws up on the tailgate and looked in to the truck.

'I think it's giving us the all clear,' said Sarah. 'They must've gone.' They clambered down with some drinks and sat together on a log.

'I've been thinking,' said Ben after a few moments. 'I'm sure that lorry went back the same way that it came, didn't it?'

'Wow,' said Sarah, 'you're right. And that means ...'

'Yeah,' continued Ben. 'It means that whoever they were they weren't just passing – they knew the lorry was there and came deliberately to destroy it.'

'Which means... it must have been our lot coming back to finish us off,' finished Sarah.

'Exactly,' said Ben. 'And don't you see,' he added with a grin, 'that means they think they've finished with us, so we're safe.'

'Especially,' Sarah added thoughtfully, 'as other people are going to be less interested in a burnt-out truck than one just parked in the road.' It was true; they had passed many pillaged and burnt-out vehicles on their long journey west and such a commonplace sight was unlikely to excite much interest in any passing vehicles. 'So all we have to do now,' she continued happily, 'is sit here with the leopards and snakes guarding us and wait for the others to find us.'

Ben thought for a moment. Their situation had certainly improved dramatically, but there were still some seemingly impossible practical difficulties to surmount.

'How will they know where we are?' he asked.

'I don't know exactly,' said Sarah, 'but I'm sure it'll be OK. They found us to give us the message, didn't they? Maybe a leopard will go and find them or something.' She was remembering some of the tales the family had told about Lucy's adventures in the Amazon, and felt certain Lucy would somehow find them.

'What if one of those birds comes again?' said Ben. 'Shouldn't we get a message ready for it to take back?'

'Good idea,' said Sarah. She went back to the truck and got a pencil and paper. They discussed the note and then she wrote:

"We're safe and the bad men have gone. They think we're dead. We're hiding in the forest near a burnt lorry on the road. It took us two days to

get here from the Stanley waterfalls. The leopards and snakes are guarding us and we have enough food and drink to last ages.

Love, S and B.

PS I mean two days and nights!"

She folded the letter up small and twisted one of her elastic hairbands round it.

'There. Now we just wait for a Hogwarts' post bird to arrive!'

14

Jungle Jeopardy

Clare, Clive and Lucy drove steadily through more mountainous terrain towards the rainforests. They had purchased visas at official border points but, as they had been warned, were subjected to frequent requests for "extra" visas and bribes at various key junctions and roadblocks. The further west they progressed the more aggressive and intimidating these requests became. Sid and his gang had coped with this problem by unseen help from the professor and by brute force, but these options weren't open to the unarmed trio and soon Lucy started to resort to assistance from the animals. Gun-toting para-militias at unofficial roadblocks would suddenly lose all interest in the Land Rover when large snakes appeared on the scene or venomous insects landed on their jackets. The roads got worse and worse and they soon realised that the current spell of dry weather was a true blessing; many of the roads they were using would have simply been impassable in the wet. Soon the animals warned Lucy that they were about to enter the realm of the junglekin and Clare and Clive saw that she had become very thoughtful. She was recalling an episode in the Amazon when a blow on the head had deprived her of the ability to speak to the animals. She had recovered within a couple of days but those two days had reminded her just how lonely and helpless she could be without the support of her animals.

Now as they lurched along the dreadful roads towards the forests she suddenly wondered whether she could really track down and save the children from a bunch of desperadoes with only minimal help from the animals. Their interactions with officials, soldiers and paramilitary groups at roadblocks and river crossings had reminded her just how much she needed the animals' support in this hostile and lawless environment. The more she thought about the problem, the more urgent it seemed to find a solution. Clare was driving and after some further pondering Lucy suddenly leaned forward and tapped her on the shoulder.

'Stop! I need to make some preparations.'

'I wondered what you were hatching up sitting there in silence,' said Clare with a grin as she pulled onto the side of the road. Unfortunately the long grass on the verge was concealing a storm drain alongside the road. The Land Rover gave a sickening lurch to the side and ground to a stop at a drunken angle.

'Oh ****!' said Clare. 'I'm so sorry.' They jumped out and Clive fetched the spade that all bush vehicles carried for such emergencies. He tried to build up some earth in front of the front wheel but the drain was so deep that the body of the vehicle was embedded into the earth and his attempts to free it were hopeless.

'Looks as if it's over to you Luce,' he said. 'Shades of a stuck aeroplane?' They all had to smile despite the seriousness of the situation as they remembered Lucy enlisting the aid of various animals to free a plane from a bog in the Valley of the Great Ones.

'Let's just hope and pray,' he said, looking serious again, 'that nothing's damaged. I should think any kind of help will be a long time coming in these parts.' Clare agreed and then pointed to Lucy. She was already standing with the look on her face that they both knew meant she was calling to the animals. Soon a small flock of birds appeared and after consulting with Lucy flew off in different directions. Clare and Clive exchanged amused glances: they had witnessed such little scenes many times before.

'While we're waiting,' said Clare, 'just before my piece of precision parking you were about to announce some plans. Tell us all.'

'Well,' Lucy replied, 'I've already told the birds what I need – as well as getting help for the car – and now we need to make some preparations. First we need a box; then we need some space in the back of the truck where we can put a blanket or groundsheet.' With a puzzled look, Clive fished out a cardboard box from their provisions in the back and emptied it.

'Perfect,' said Lucy and cut a hole in the side with her nail scissors. Then she took the spade lying by the front wheel and propped it up at an angle against the back of the truck. Clare and Clive were by now both completely mystified.

'OK,' Clive said, 'We give up. What on earth are you doing?' Lucy laughed.

'I was thinking about how we were going to cope in the forest without the help of the local animals – except possibly the leopards. I decided the best thing to do was to take those we need *with* us.' At that moment a bird flew back and perched on a twig near Lucy.

'The nearest cornukin is but a league away. He cometh hither at thy bidding and will be here anon.'

Lucy thanked the bird, then turned to the others.

'The RAC is on the way but won't get here for a bit. That gives us time to settle the others in'.

'What's the RAC?' asked Clive. He was a member of the RAC in England – the Royal Automobile Club which gave roadside assistance – but wasn't sure what was going on here.

'... and who are "the others"?,' asked Clare. But Lucy just smiled and pointed. In the distance, across the scrub and bush, a small black cloud had appeared and was approaching rapidly. Soon they could hear a buzzing sound that got louder and louder until the bees came up to the Land Rover and landed in Lucy's box, the lid of which she had left open. When the swarm was inside she shut the lid and after a few moments one or two bees came out of the hole she had made and started to explore nearby.

'Look!' said Clive suddenly, and pointed to the side of the road in front of them. A puff adder had appeared and was slithering towards the car. Soon, from other points on the verge, a rock python and two black mambas emerged.

'Ah, the others,' said Lucy happily as the snakes slithered up the spade into the back of the truck and curled up in the space Clare had prepared with a blanket. 'The snakes don't care about coming into the jungle and I told them we'd bring them out again later,' she explained. 'From previous experience I think they could come in very useful. The bees were more of a problem because I didn't want to move an existing hive. I asked the birds to see if they could find a swarm looking for a new location and they did just that. This is their new home,' she pointed at the box. 'I expect they'll find moving about a bit confusing but I'm sure they'll be OK. We'll bring them back again later if they want, but maybe they'll just settle for somewhere in the jungle when we've finished with them.'

After about half an hour the bushes parted and an enormous shape loomed into sight. For such a large creature it made remarkably little sound and as it approached Clive and Clare instinctively moved behind the Land Rover.

'Here we are,' said Lucy to Clive. 'The Rhino Automobile Club awaits your instructions!'

Clive explained what was necessary to Lucy and she passed his instructions on to the rhino. Clive was desperately worried that the metre-long horn on the animal might damage some vital part of the underneath of the car. In the event, one might have been forgiven for imagining that the creature had been brought up on a garage forecourt. With exquisite precision it inserted its massive horn into a perfect position on the underside of the chassis and lifted the vehicle into the air as though it were a twig. Twisting its neck it gently flicked the front of the car sideways onto the road and then withdrew to survey the result as if it were an artist stepping back from an easel.

'Good God!' was all Clive could bring himself to say. He crawled under the front of the car to check things out but neither the original calamity nor the rhino's intervention seemed to have caused any significant damage. 'Phew,' he said as he got up and dusted his knees. 'I think we're OK'. He got in the car, started it up and tested the steering and the brakes. 'I think you can thank the RAC and send him back to the office,' he said to Lucy with a relieved smile. 'Everything's just fine. Just one question: how on earth did you find him – I thought rhinos had been practically wiped out in this area?' Lucy turned and spoke to the rhino before replying.

'I think you're right. He says that he and two others were brought from far away and they're the only ones round here. People keep checking on them. It sounds as if they're on some kind of private reserve to re-establish the population.' She spoke again to the rhino and he lumbered away into the bush.

'Right,' said Clare, getting back behind the steering wheel. 'Are we ready to go?'

'Hang on,' said Lucy, 'I think the remainder of "the others" are

Lifted as though it were a twig...

just arriving.' As she spoke two eagles plummeted towards the vehicle and perched on the roof. 'OK,' she continued. 'We're now all present and correct – I'm not sure we'll be able to find any messengers in the forest, so we're taking a couple with us.' Clive, a keen birdwatcher, was impressed.

'Those are Bateleur eagles,' he said, admiring their haughty orange faces and striking black and white plumage. 'Why did you ask for them?'

'I didn't,' said Lucy with a smile. 'I just asked for something a bit heftier than a hawk. If the owls in the forest are going to be unfriendly it seemed sensible to take along something that could look after itself!'

They had now lost a lot of time and had no idea how far behind the villains they were. Clive and Clare shared the driving and they

tried to keep going without stopping except for fuel. On the advice of the car hire company they had taken a substantial amount of fuel with them but Clive was anxious to preserve this for later in the trip and they filled up wherever the opportunity presented itself. The almost inevitable attempts at extortion by the fuel vendors were usually brought to an abrupt halt by the black mambas who reared up and swayed threateningly in front of anyone who Lucy felt was trying to exploit them. One glance at the most dangerous snakes in existence always brought a surprisingly rapid and satisfactory end to any negotiations.

As they passed into the rainforest there was a distinct feeling, even to Clive and Clare, that they had passed into hostile territory. They had become accustomed to animals and birds going out of their way to assist, or merely catch a glimpse of, the Promised One but now there was a dark and forbidding atmosphere in the depths of the jungle. Any road block they came across they now dealt with immediately using the animals they had on board. The bees proved invaluable. As soon as somebody stepped into the road with a gun he was surrounded by a swarm and disappeared under cover in an instant while Clive and Clare drove through the block. Lucy would later be proud to announce at the end of their adventure that she didn't think a single bee had lost its life in her service: the experience of simply being enveloped in a swarm of the insects seemed to be more than enough deterrent for the most aggressive of soldiers or rebels. At road blocks they increasingly noticed that the wooden posts that could swing up and down like barriers at a railway crossing were broken or even torn out of the ground. They would have been greatly amused had they realised that their journey had been made easier by the previous handiwork of those that they were chasing, for Sid had simply driven through such minor obstacles.

Clive was depressed by their slow progress. The roads were frightful and, as they could not call on assistance from the forest elephants or hippos they had to be extremely careful not to get stuck. Often they could not progress at more than five or ten miles an hour. The only consolation was that they realised that the villains ahead of them must have encountered the same problems, perhaps even worse, for the birds' descriptions suggested that the lorries they were pursuing were much larger and heavier than their own vehicle. After a day deep in the forest when they had seemingly made little progress, Lucy sent one of the eagles on an exploratory mission. It did not return that night, and Lucy began to fear that it had fallen victim to the predators of the forest, but the next day it returned clutching the children's note.

'Great,' said Clare in relief after they had all read the note. 'At least they're out of the clutches of the thugs – and seem to have some supplies though quite how that's come about is a mystery. No doubt we'll find out soon.'

'Now all we've got to do is find them somewhere in the middle of the greatest jungle in Africa,' said Clive.

'I'm going to try and use the eagles to guide us,' said Lucy. 'One of them now knows where the children are and it may be able to sort out the best route for us if I can get it to understand we need to stay on the roads.' Sure enough, after a consultation with the birds, Lucy was happy that they were on a road that would eventually lead to the children. Clive got out the map while Clare was driving and tried to work out where they were heading.

'It looks as if we're going towards a river called Lomela,' he said. He paused and his brow furrowed. 'How extraordinary,' he murmured.

'What? What is it?' asked Clare.

'Where did you say your Mum and Dad were going, Salonga or something?'

'Yes, the Salonga National Park is a massive reserve – the largest in the Congo. Full of unusual trees for them to get excited about.'

'Well look,' Clive pointed and both the girls leaned over. 'It's further on than the Lomela river but we're heading straight for it.'

'What an amazing coincidence,' said Clare. 'Talking of which, I wonder how they're getting on. I hope they got the message we left at the hotel.' As they were speaking a small hawk glided down. It looked exhausted after its long and dangerous flight. Lucy spoke to it.

'I come with tidings from the arborimane,' it said. *'The tuskikin, cornukin and greatkine are gathered in great numbers and are ready to trample the junglekin at thy command. The manefang, fleetfang,*

*cacklekin and wolfkin will go where the giant greypods cannot pass and
the hipposnorts and the Dreadful Ones will make the jungle waters safe for
thee.'* Lucy turned and spoke to one of her eagles which immediately
flew off, then addressed the messenger bird.

'I thank thee,' said Lucy. *'When thou hast rested and eaten thou
must return and tell the arborimane that he has done well, but that no
creatures must attack the junglekin until I have spoken to their Special
One.'* As she finished the eagle returned with a plump rodent and laid
it in front of the messenger hawk which flew with it to a stump and
started to devour it ravenously. Lucy then turned to the others.

'The plains animals are dead keen to start beating up the junglekin.
So far it looks as if they've obeyed my previous instructions to wait,
but I've told them again to be on the safe side.' Clive switched on
the radio and flicked through the stations. They were all in French,
which Clare spoke fluently, and when she heard one broadcasting
some news she gestured to the others to keep quiet.

*'...and the largest congregations of elephants ever reported in recent times
have assembled in Western Tanzania, Northern Zambia and Northern
Angola. Large herds of buffalo are also moving north towards the rainforests.
An even more astonishing phenomenon is the apparent migration of large
groups of predators such as lions and cheetahs towards the fringes of the
Central African rainforest. Unprecedented numbers of hyenas and wild dogs
have also been reported in these areas. The rivers close to forested areas are
packed with crocodiles and hippos, the general trend of movement in these
animals being always in the direction of the forests. Wildlife experts are
completely perplexed by these events. There are no reports of any previous
such behaviour and in many cases the observed movements are completely
inappropriate for the animals concerned in terms of the season and the present
and future availability of suitable food supplies. An emergency meeting at*

the United Nations to discuss the problem is planned for ...' Clare switched off and told the others. They sat in silence for a moment.

'We've got to sort out this "Special One" as soon as possible,' said Clive. 'We're causing havoc!' The others nodded.

Lucy got out of the Land Rover and stood looking into the impenetrable forest. Clive and Clare watched as she obviously called in vain. It was the first time they had ever seen animals fail to respond to her call and it brought home to them just how alien this world of the junglekin was in terms of what they now knew about animal behaviour and legend. Lucy knew from her conversations with the baboon that the only animals that regarded themselves as belonging to both the Greater World and Lesser World were the leopards and she surmised that they would be her best chance of establishing the truth about the "Special One". She asked an eagle to locate the nearest leopard and they waited impatiently for it to return.

In less than ten minutes it swooped down to the Land Rover and informed Lucy that a leopard was on its way. Soon a lithe dark shape appeared in the trees. The black panther* sprang to the ground beside them and they all gasped at its beauty. Lucy was reminded vividly of Melanie the black jaguar which had assisted her in the Amazon.

'Greetings, O darkfang,' said Lucy.

'Greetings,' replied the panther in the common tongue. *'Thou art The Promised One of the Lesser World.'* It was a simple statement of fact but it told Lucy that she was on the right track.

'That is so,' she said, *'and it is told that there is a "Special One" of the Greater World. Know thou of such a one?'*

*Leopards, cougars and jaguars may have black fur, a melanistic variation, and are known as black panthers.

'The junglekin speak of a Tailless One – with eyes of magic light such as thine – but she is guarded by the bonobokin and ventures not from their realm.' Lucy gasped in astonishment.

'And whither is their land?' she asked, to see if the answer matched up with what Clare had thought earlier.

'They live where the Brilliant One sinks beneath the trees. I have never hunted there but my kin speak of wondrous beasts that also live in those hidden places.' Lucy's mind was in turmoil. She thanked the panther and asked him to stay within calling distance. Then she shared her news with the others, including the astonishing fact that the Special One seemed to wear glasses.

'She,' exclaimed Clive. 'Huh, women seem to have bagged all the top jobs in the animal world. It's obviously not just human beings they like bossing about!' Clare and Lucy ignored him.

'It sounds as if there really *is* another one,' said Clare. 'I wonder who on earth she is – and how old she is.'

'And can she speak to animals?' Lucy wondered aloud. She called back the black leopard. 'Canst thou speak to a fledgiquill of the forest? One who can seek out the Special One of the junglekin?'

'I can,' replied the panther. He paused and glanced scornfully at Lucy's eagles, perched on the back of the truck, before continuing, 'But fledgiquills cannot understand the matters of which we speak. Their minds are not like mine and thine.'

'That is true,' said Lucy suppressing a smile, 'but they can at least tell us if another Special One approaches.'

'It shall be done.' The panther padded off to the nearest tree and leapt effortlessly into the branches. Soon a bird flew up through the canopy and headed off into the western sky. Lucy explained what was happening to Clare and Clive. They all agreed that if the Special One existed *she* would easily be able to locate *them* using the junglekin and that their own next priority was to find Sarah and Ben as soon as possible. Clive started up and they drove off as quickly as the appalling road permitted. Three hours later, their eagles, who had been shuttling backwards and forwards, informed them that they were now very close to their objective. Clive slowed down and as they rounded a bend in the road they saw the burnt-out truck by the roadside ahead of them.

'Let's stop here,' said Lucy. 'If Sarah and Ben hear the car they may get frightened and run away and hide.' Clare agreed so she pulled in close to the bush and stopped. They all got out and walked towards the blackened hulk of the lorry.

'I can hear voices,' said Clare excitedly, 'It's them!' She and Clive broke into a run. As they did so Lucy had an amazing feeling. It was as though an animal were calling her but it was different and stronger than an animal, and it wasn't calling her, it was just ...just there like a brilliant beacon in her mind. She shook her head and hurried to catch up with the others.

15

Chatting with Chimps

Neema sat in the fork of a tree eating a banana and listening to the excited bonobos chattering around her. Something was going on. First a bird had flown into their group from the east, then several bonobos from different family groups had joined them from various directions, finally a crocodile (a species the bonobos normally stayed well clear of) had emerged from a nearby river and clambered up the bank to speak to the chimps sitting in the trees above. Soon Jambo swung over to speak to Neema.

'*There are mysterious tidings from near and far,*' she started. '*First, my kin who remained near the place we usually dwell say that two Tailless Ones come every day to thy little house and call for thee. They carry no thundersticks. Then others of my kin come whence the Brilliant One rises. They tell of two small Tailless Ones who sit alone in a house that moves. They are guarded by spotfangs who threaten any of the junglekin who approach.*'

'*Are those of whom you speak not the Little Tailless Ones?*' asked Neema, wondering if Jambo was referring to the forest pygmies.

'*Nay, O Special One. They are young ones – younger than thee. Their skin is pale –paler indeed than thine own, and the head of one is as corn when the Brilliant One shines.*'

'How far are they from here?' asked Neema in astonishment.

'They are many leagues hence,' was the reply, *'close to the great river of those parts. But there are other matters of great import that I must impart to thee. A Dreadful One comes from where the river leaves the forest and flows to the Great Salt. He tells of a mighty gathering of the creatures of the Lesser World. They threaten to enter our kingdom. We are cleverer than they but many of them are mighty creatures and we shall suffer grievously should they enter here.'* Jambo paused. She looked distinctly uncomfortable and Neema immediately sensed she was withholding something.

'Is there aught else to tell?' asked Neema?

'It is said ...,' the chimp hesitated again.

'It is said ...?' prompted Neema.

'It is said that the creatures of the Lesser World also have a Special One – with eyes such as thine from which the Brilliant One can shine. The fledgiquill who came hither,' she pointed to the messenger bird sitting nearby, *'tells that even now she travels hither from afar.'*

Neema was utterly bewildered. What on earth was going on? Animals invading the rainforest. Strangers at her cabin in Salonga – did that mean the police now knew about her? Children lost in the jungle and, most mysterious of all, another "Special One" who wore glasses. Who on earth was she and why was she coming? Suddenly Neema realised that this other Special One might be in pursuit of the young children she had just heard about, in which case she should be helped or stopped, depending on her motives. Finding them should be her own first priority. She thought for a while then spoke to Jambo.

'I would like thee to take me to the young Tailless Ones. Is it a journey suitable for me?' Jambo consulted with her cousins.

'The jungle snortikin will carry thee...'

'We can take thee there in safety. Most of the rivers have places we can cross in the trees; where we cannot, others will assist us.'

'What of the spotfang?' asked Neema nervously. 'Whom do they serve?'

'The spotfang believe they belong to both the Greater and the Lesser Worlds. They fear none, but if we tell them thou art special to us they will not harm thee.' Relieved by this, Neema then spoke to the crocodile.

'Return to the edge of the Greater World, O Mighty One, and ask none to attack the creatures of the Lesser World until I give word.'

The great reptile grunted in assent and slid soundlessly into the black depths of the river. Neema saw the water swirling in his wake as he began his long journey to the edge of the great forest. The bonobos set off with Neema through the jungle. Until now she had seen them merely foraging or cavorting in the trees and bushes but now they had a mission she was astonished at the speed and agility with which they could move through the densest forest, helping her to follow by smoothing out branches and assisting her across gaps. When she began to fall behind they enlisted the help of others. She rode on an okapi for several miles and was amazed at its ability to slip through the thickest undergrowth. On another part of the journey she clutched on to a bongo as it gave giant leaps across water-filled

pools and clumps of tangled undergrowth. They crossed innumerable rivers and ponds and swamps by climbing across the overhanging and interlacing branches of trees but eventually they came to a wide river which the trees did not overreach. Jambo stopped and sniffed the air in different directions, then spoke to a youngster who swung off effortlessly upstream while the group waited patiently. Within ten minutes the bushes parted and a forest elephant pushed her way through.

'*Sit thou on the tuskikin, O Special One,*' said Jambo. Neema swung down onto the elephant's back and clutched on nervously as the creature waded into the river. Soon Neema realised that the river was wide at this point because it was relatively shallow, and though the brown waters swirled up to her knees they came no higher as her massive steed took her safely to the other side. She thanked the elephant.

'*Farewell,*' said the gentle giant, '*From this day on I shall be honoured among all my kin for, alone among them, I have borne the Special One upon my back.*' Later in the journey they came to some swampy ground and Jambo once again gave instructions to a youngster.

'*The jungle snortikin will come,*' she assured Neema, '*and carry thee over this perilous place.*' Soon the giant forest hog appeared and knelt for Neema to mount. She clutched its coarse black hair as it plunged through the swampy terrain, the bonobos leaping nimbly from one reedy tussock to the next. The giant hog continued to carry her through the undergrowth after leaving the swamp, until Jambo indicated that she should return to the trees.

'We draw nigh to the young ones,' she said. *'Even now my kin speak to the spotfangs who guard them.'*

16

Reunions, Revelations and Reconciliations

After thanking the hog Neema clambered silently to a spot next to Jambo and saw that they were above a road. By the side of the road was a burnt-out lorry and for one sickening moment she thought the children had been burnt. Then she followed Jambo along a broad branch stretching right across the road and linking with the trees on the other side. There, a few yards into the forest on the far side, was a small clearing in which a second lorry was parked. Around the clearing she could see leopards in the trees. They looked at her, but made no move either to threaten her or to pay homage to her. Then she heard voices and there in the clearing, sitting on a log and eating bananas, she saw a boy and a girl. As she inched nearer she realised they were speaking in English. She had no idea that she was gazing at her own sister and cousin. She called down:

'Hello there!'

The children, startled, looked up and Sarah squealed in delight.

'It's Lucy!' she shouted. 'How did her hair get so long!' And she and Ben jumped up and ran under the tree in which Neema was sitting. As they did so she felt something emanating from beyond them that she had never experienced before. It was similar to communication with the animals but much stronger and somehow pleasant and joyous and lovely. She shook her head and focused back on the children, smiling down at their upturned, joyful faces.

'Who's Lucy?' she asked. The children laughed, and then their mirth turned to puzzlement as they realised from the girl's expression that the question was genuine.

'What do you mean?' asked Sarah.

'I'm Neema,' said the girl in the tree. 'Who are you? And who's Lucy?'

'*I'm* Lucy!' The voice came from the other side of the clearing behind the children who spun round and then ran squealing with shrieks of delight into Lucy's arms. Even as she hugged them she looked up into the tree and her mouth fell open. The girl in the tree was a mirror image of herself. As Ben and Sarah detached themselves and rushed to greet Clare and Clive, Lucy realised that the intense sensation she was experiencing had its source in the other girl who was now clambering down to the ground. Soon they stood looking at each other and an awed silence fell upon the scene as the bonobos stopped chattering and the birds paused in their song. Clive and Clare, their arms around the younger children, stood and gazed at the two girls, identical in height and shape, as they faced one another. Both turned down the "beacons" in their brains as the prodigious energy they felt radiating from the other threatened to overwhelm them. 'Hi, I'm Lucy,' repeated the Promised One. 'Lucy Bonaventure.'

'Bonaventure!' gasped the Special One. The contents of her grandfather's desk came flooding back to her. 'You were born here – near here – in Salonga?' she stammered. Lucy nodded, utterly bewildered. How on earth did this girl know where she had been born? 'I am Neema – Neema... Bonaventure,' said the other. 'And I think... I think I'm your twin sister!'

'I think I'm your twin sister...'

Lucy felt faint. She sat down on the log where Sarah and Ben had been sitting and patted the space next to her.

'You'd better tell us everything,' she said, her voice barely louder than a whisper. The others, speechless, came over and sat round the pair in a circle. Neema told them about her childhood and the discovery one day of her "grandpa's" file. She could remember the letter almost word for word. She then told them of her discovery that she could speak to animals.

'I've never told anyone about it before,' she said, 'but I can see that you've all been through this already.' Lucy, Clare and Clive all nodded. Sarah and Ben looked puzzled and Clare leant over and whispered that she would tell them everything later. Neema then told them about the arrest of her family, her escape into the jungle with the bonobos and the story of how she had come to find the children. When she had finished Clare got up, gave her a long hug and kissed her.

'You really must be our sister.' she said. 'This is a wonderful day for us all.' There was much hugging and weeping and kissing as they explained to Neema who they all were, then Lucy said she would tell Neema her story.

'First,' she said turning to Ben and Sarah with a kindly and somewhat regretful smile, 'I must tell you that some of this story will be a surprise for you. We were going to tell you the family secret when you were a bit older, but you now know so much already it would be unfair not to tell you the whole story.' So then, as Lucy told Neema her tale, Sarah and Ben heard everything about Lucy and the animals and all kinds of things that had puzzled them over the last two years suddenly became clear. When Lucy had finished Clare then told Neema and the children all that had happened in the last few days. Suddenly Neema gasped.

'Your parents! ...my parents...*our* parents.! They must be the people the bonobos told me about. I didn't tell you that bit as I didn't realise it was important.' She then told them of the couple who went to her cabin every day in Salonga and called her name.

'But why would they be looking for you?' asked Clive, with puzzled frown. 'They don't know about you.'

'Of *course* they know about her!' interrupted Clare with a laugh. 'She's their daughter! *We're* the ones who didn't know about her. For some reason they must have decided to come here to look for her. Our African holiday was obviously just an excuse for the trip, but they didn't tell us the whole story in case they couldn't find her.' They all fell silent as they thought about what she had said, then nodded in turn. It made perfect sense. Neema was the first to break the silence:

'I must send them a note and tell them I'm OK.' She paused. 'Oh, sorry,' she said, 'I'd better explain. I've found I can send notes using the animals.'

Clare, Clive and Lucy looked at each other and smiled.

'Been there, done that,' said Clare with a grin, and then explained to Neema how their lives had been saved by Lucy's animal notes on more than one occasion.

'Now,' said Neema, 'about this note to...,' she hesitated, '...Mum and Dad.' She smiled. 'Funny – that's the first time I've ever been able to say that. Or...,' she frowned and looked at the others, '...or should it be " Mummy and Daddy" – or "Mother and Father"?' They all laughed and Clare said,

'Whatever. They'll be so pleased to hear from you, you could call them anything.' Neema pulled a pencil and paper from the belt round her waist.

"Dear Mum and Dad,

I've met up with Lucy and the others. Everyone is OK. Stay in Salonga.
Keep visiting the cabin every day and we'll all come and join you.

Lots of Love

*Neema (*Grace *in English).*

X X X X"

She showed the note to the others. 'Do you want to add anything? Oh, and by the way I've decided to call myself Grace from now on. It means the same as Neema, and if I'm going to rejoin my family I think I should have an English name.'

They all scrawled their initials with a kiss and then Grace folded the note, tucked it into a palm husk and gave it to a bonobo. She adopted the expression Clive and Clare had seen so often on Lucy's face when talking to animals and they exchanged a smile. For Lucy the experience was even more fascinating for she could actually hear Grace giving her instructions to the ape. She told Grace after the ape had swung off and they both giggled.

'We'll have to have a pact to filter each other out when we're together,' said Grace, 'so we don't know what the other's thinking.'

'It's a deal,' said Lucy, grinning, but they both knew that they shared a power that would be extraordinarily useful in the future.

'Look,' said Clive. 'We've got lots and lots to talk about. Why don't we set up camp, make a proper meal and sort out what happens next?'

They all readily agreed to this and set about preparing for a reunion barbeque. Clive drove the Land Rover off the road into the bush so as not to attract any unwelcome visitors and after a wonderful dinner they sat round the fire on logs and camp chairs from the lorry and started to swap stories.

'Let's hear from you and Ben first,' said Clare to Sarah. 'I'm dying to know what really happened.'

The children told them everything from first seeing the lion cub until finally seeing Grace in the tree. They interrupted and corrected each other constantly as they babbled excitedly about their adventure, and the others were fascinated by their tale.

'So you really did nearly get eaten by lions,' said Clive, 'and the men really did save you. I wonder what made them decide so quickly to kidnap you rather than hand you in to the park rangers?'

'Well they were obviously poachers,' said Clare. 'We know that from what Sarah and Ben have told us about all their guns and stuff.'

'True,' said Clive, 'but they could still have dumped the children in a town or somewhere safe without identifying themselves. And why have they crossed three countries and come into the depths of the jungle? It's almost as though they've another mission and took the children along as an insurance policy – to use them as hostages to get out of a police trap, for instance.'

'I think that they *are* doing something special,' said Ben excitedly. 'The professor kept talking to Sid about exact locations and stuff and they were always looking at the map. Sometimes with a big magnifying glass.'

'The professor?' Clive interrupted. During their story the children had been referring to him as Luke. 'So Luke is a professor?' The children looked at each other in amusement and nodded. Clive looked at Clare and Lucy. 'Tell us a bit more about him.'

'He's had all kinds of exciting adventures in the Amazon,' said Ben, '– and he's got a massive scar on his head where he got hit by a plane as he escaped from a tiger.'

'– or leopard or whatever,' corrected Sarah. 'Oh,' she continued, 'and he and Sid and Fred were always talking about someone called Chopper.'

'...and Sam,' added Ben.

'Oh my God,' whispered Clive. He clutched his head between his hands. 'It's got to be him, hasn't it?' Clare and Lucy nodded.

'I take it this is someone you know and don't much care for,' said Grace, hesitant to seem to be interrupting.

'It's a long, long, story,' said Clare. 'Clive and I never met Sid and Fred but we know the professor and Lucy can fill you in on the others.' She looked at Sarah and Ben. 'You've learned a lot of new things today and, I'm afraid, you're about to learn some more. She was about to tell Grace and the children about their adventures in South America when Clive lifted up his head and interrupted.

'Sorry, Clare, I've just *got* to ask Ben and Sarah something *before* they hear what you're going to say.' The children looked curious.

'In all the time you spent with the professor,' he asked, 'did you notice anything... funny about him. Did he do anything like ...magic tricks?'

The children thought.

'Well, he kept suddenly disappearing,' said Ben '–but we thought it was because he was a coward, not a conjuror.'

' – and there was that weird footprint in front of the snake,' said Sarah, 'that was more like a conjuring trick.' Clive groaned. They had said enough.

'I can't believe it,' he said despairingly. 'The ******* has somehow got hold of another robe. We've got to stop him or heaven knows what will happen!'

'Sorry to seem stupid,' said Grace, 'but what on earth are you talking about?'

'Let me start right from the beginning,' said Lucy who had been silent so far, 'and unbelievable though it may sound, all will become clear.' They sat until almost dawn over the dying embers of the fire, listening to each other's tales and discussing their future plans, then collapsed in the lorry to sleep, exhausted after one of the most extraordinary days in their extraordinary lives.

They rose late the next day and the bonobos brought them a "brunch" of delicious and exotic fruits. After they had eaten they put their new plans straight into action. First Lucy and Grace stood in the middle of the clearing and called the animals. Lucy had lent Grace some clean clothes from her bag in the Land Rover and Clare had cut her hair and given her some shampoo. They now stood alongside each other looking like peas out of a pod. Clare nudged Clive and whispered:

'If anyone had any doubts about Grace's letter, they wouldn't have them any longer looking at those two, would they?' Clive grinned and agreed. The two "special ones" had decided the previous night that rather than "share the throne" and risk confusion, Grace would remain affiliated to the "Greater World" and Lucy to the "Lesser World", but they would make it clear that they acted in unison in all things.

As they called out together a vast procession of animals appeared from the dense and seemingly impenetrable undergrowth. Forest elephants, hippos and pygmy cape buffaloes jostled for space among giant forest hogs, red river hogs, bongos, okapi and crocodiles. In and around their hooves and feet clustered countless smaller animals: duikers, pangolins, otters, jackals, cervals, golden cats, mongooses, civets and porcupines. Leopards appeared in the trees, surrounded by pottos, tree pangolins and monkeys of every size and shape. Snakes and various reptiles slithered and crawled to every spare spot and birds of every description appeared, from bustards and buzzards to peafowl and parrots. At the centre, closely surrounding the girls, was a cluster of bonobos. Clare, Clive and the younger children stood in amazement at the sight. They had no concept that such a bewildering number and variety of species could possibly exist in the immediate locality and Sarah and Ben, seeing Lucy's power in action for the first time, were completely overawed. Grace was the first to speak to the assembled throng:

'Welcome all ye creatures of the forest. I have great tidings for thee. The Promised One of the Lesser World is here and she is my sister, born in the same brood.' She put her arm round Lucy. *'You have all waited countless moons for us to come and now we start to restore the ancient ways. First there is to be harmony between the creatures of the Greater World and the Lesser World which will, henceforth, be called the Inner World and the Outer World. Animals will, of course, chase and kill and eat each other as they have done since the beginning of time. The clawkin devours the clovenkin and the great eat the small. This is right and has always been so. But there must be no distinction henceforth between the junglekin and those outside. The junglekin will speak once again the common tongue when they meet with those who know not the forest tongue and there is to be no strife between the two worlds.'* Then Lucy spoke.

' Hearken all ye denizens of the Inner World. I too desire that the ancient enmity between the Inner and Outer Worlds should end.' She held her arms outstretched in front of her and the two eagles she had brought with her fluttered down on to her wrists. *'See, I now send the raptoquills yonder to the Outer World to proclaim peace. The*

'Welcome all ye creatures of the forest.'

tuskikin, the greatkine, the manefang and the Dreadful Ones who even now gather in great multitudes to slaughter the junglekin will now return to the plains and mountains and swamps whence they came.' She lifted her arms and the eagles flew up above the canopy, then separated, one to bear the message to the north and west, the other to the south and east. A wave of sound rippled through the assembled junglekin as the animals growled and grunted and chattered in approbation. Then Grace spoke to them again.

'Now go quickly and tell all thy kin these tidings. And you –,' she looked up at the canopy, ' *– you jungle fledgiquills must fly with haste to the edges of our kingdom, as do the raptoquills, and tell the junglekin to leave in peace those who now turn away to return to the plains and swamps.'* There was a clatter of wings as dozens of birds of every description took off and flew in every direction. Then Jambo spoke.

'The legends that our mothers spoke of have come true, and we are fortunate indeed to see this day. Now go all of thee, and do the will of the Special Ones.' The animals dispersed with surprising rapidity and Clare grinned.

'It's going to be fun for the next few weeks listening to all the animal and climate experts telling us exactly why all the animals suddenly decided to turn round and go back this morning.' They all laughed.

Lucy then took Sarah and Ben to the Land Rover to see the bees and snakes that had protected them on their forest journey.

'I bet our snakes are bigger than yours,' said Ben as they went, and they all laughed.

As soon as the younger ones were out of earshot Clare turned to Clive, who had been looking pensive ever since his conversation with Sarah and Ben about the professor.

'OK, come on,' she said, 'what's on your mind?' He gave a rueful smile.

'That obvious, is it? Well we had to discuss it soon and it may as well be now.' He was about to continue when Clare interrupted.

'It's all right, I can guess. You want to go and find him don't you?' Clive gave a resigned shrug.

'I don't think we have any option. He's obviously got an invisibility robe and as long as he's got it he's a danger, not just to us but to anyone in the world. The power it confers on him is simply unimaginable – and we're probably the only people who can succeed in getting it off him. We're the only ones who know he's got it, for a start, and only somebody with Lucy's power could hope to go up against him, with any chance of winning. This has got to be the best – probably *only* – chance of anyone stopping him.' Clare nodded slowly.

'You're right of course,' she said, 'and we'll need Lucy, but I don't want the younger ones involved in this in any way.'

'I agree absolutely,' said Clive. 'I was thinking about this during the night and I think we should split up. If you're happy for Grace to look after Sarah and Ben, she could take them back to your mum and dad at Salonga, while we go with Lucy to sort out the professor.' Clare thought this was a good plan and over coffee she and Clive discussed it with Lucy and Grace, while Sarah and Ben played with the bonobos. Soon Grace called the pair over.

'Now I know you two have had a pretty dull time recently,' she said mischievously. 'How do fancy coming with me for a *really* exciting adventure?' A few moments later a delighted Sarah and Ben, each with a rucksack, were sitting astride okapis. Grace, revelling in the company of her new-found family, called the bonobos together and the expedition set off on the jungle journey to Salonga – a magical experience that Sarah and Ben would both remember in vivid detail for the rest of their lives.

17

Desperate for Diamonds

The professor was now consulting his GPS with ever-increasing frequency and getting progressively more excited as they neared their goal. Although the roads they actually drove along seemed to bear little relation to those shown on Sid's maps, eventually they reached a spot that corresponded precisely with Peter Flint's map reference. The location seemed unremarkable. They had driven up a long hill with dense forest on either side and then came out into a more scrub-like, rocky area.

'See if you can pull out onto that rocky stuff,' Luke said to Sid. 'I think we've actually got here.' Sid pulled off the road and followed a stony gully up a further small rise in the ground and then stopped. Luke jumped out and walked to the top of the ridge. An astonishing view lay in front of him. He was standing at the edge of a small narrow gorge. A river coursed one hundred feet below, parallel to the road they had just turned off. To the left, the west, the river ran down a series of cataracts along the gorge before disappearing into the depths of the rainforest which, from his elevated vantage point, he could see stretching to the horizon in all directions. On the opposite side of the ravine, easily accessible from this side by large boulders straddling the river, was a cliff similar to the one he was standing on. The side of the cliff had been eroded over the centuries and various rock strata were easily visible. To the right, the east, the ridge he was standing on gradually diminished in height and disappeared into the forest. On the opposite side, however, the stratified cliff ended abruptly in an escarpment that plunged down almost vertically to a giant swamp that stretched for several miles to the north-east. The river itself arose from the swamp, its greenish-brown waters starting their immense journey to the sea by gushing through the boulders immediately below him. The professor felt a surge of excitement as he gazed at the striking geological feature of the cliff opposite. This was obviously it. Even the colour of the principal visible rock stratum reminded him of the rocks he had collected in the Amazon crater. He looked down. There was a flat grassy area adjacent to the river that was free of trees, probably a meander left where the river had changed its course. It was adjacent to the boulders that led across the river and was an ideal site for a camp. Getting the stuff down from the truck to the riverbank would require some labour and he decided a psychological boost was necessary. He knew from long experience that there was nothing like greed to get things moving along. He turned back to the men who had all alighted and were now coming to see what lay beyond the ridge.

'This is it, boys,' Luke said cheerfully. 'We've arrived – at last! And there ...,' he waved expansively at the cliff opposite, '... is the best diamond ore on the planet – enough for me to make millions of gems. In a month we'll be the richest men on earth.' The excitement in the group was almost palpable. The thugs did high fives, cheering and congratulating Luke on his navigation. 'But now,' Luke continued, 'there's work to do. We've got to build a camp and a cabin where I can process the minerals we're going to extract.' He didn't add that the only minerals any of them were going to receive at the end of their labours would be cupronickel and lead in the shape of a bullet. His psychology was perfect and soon the men were eagerly unloading boxes from the lorry and manhandling them down the steep rocky slope to the river bank below.

The professor took a geologist's hammer and a pair of binoculars and went with Sid across the river to reconnoitre, picking his way carefully from boulder to boulder. He inspected the entire cliff face with the binoculars, then grunted with satisfaction. Viewed in close-up, the rocks comprising the principal stratum looked identical to the samples he had left in the South American crater. He scrambled up to the nearest seam and hacked at it with his hammer. As he did so Sid looked over to see how the men were coping with the hill and his eye caught a glint on the hilltop. He counted the men; they were all visible. He saw the glint again.

'What's that, Luke?' The professor turned. 'That glinting over there, above the men.' The professor looked through his binoculars. The sun had glinted off somebody's spectacles; somebody who, with two companions, was looking down at the men below. As they began to look up again Luke recognized them instantly and groaned. He immediately turned back to the cliff – he was pretty certain they hadn't seen him.

'What is it?' said Sid.

'It's strangers,' said the professor. Don't look!' he added sharply as Sid started to turn to stare. 'I don't want them to know we've seen them.'

'Who in Gawd's name is out 'ere in the middle of nowhere?' asked Sid in astonishment. Luke thought rapidly: he needed Sid on side for the moment.

'It's prospectors,' he said. 'I recognize them from another dig. They're after our diamonds.' He paused; he might as well use the opportunity to gain a little extra credibility with Sid. 'And the reason they're here is the same reason we're here. They are among the world's leading mineralogists and, like me, they've obviously worked out that this is likely to be the richest lode of diamonds in the world – even without the benefit of my enhanced extraction technique.' he added hurriedly. Sid was clearly impressed.

'What are we goin' to do?' asked Sid, 'should we follow 'em?'

'No,' said the professor. 'They're smart. They'll be away before we reach the top of the hill. But they'll be back. They were just spying out the land. And when they come, we'll be waiting for them.'

As they made their way back across the river Luke was feverishly working out what had happened. He remembered telling them all about the ore needed for invisibility robes in the crater so they must be after the photogyraspar, just as he was. But how on earth ...? In a flash it came to him. Peter Flint of course – he was in contact with both the Bonaventures and the Fossfinders and he had copied them in on the e-mail about the Congo deposits. Well, if they thought they could start making invisibility robes they had another think coming. But what to do about it? He was more than prepared to kill the three of them without compunction but he knew there were others in the family and that the three he had just seen were almost certainly part of a larger expedition. No, he had to deal with this problem at its source and that meant using Hans. But how? His mobile was useless out here. His problem was solved by a shout from Fred who was leading the working party of men they were now approaching.

'Half the stuff we need for buildin' the camp – saws an' axes an' spades an' stuff was in the other truck – the one with the snakes.' Sid swore but the professor saw his chance.

'Let them carry on as best they can with what they've got,' he said to Sid, 'and I'll come with you in the truck. We'll find the nearest town and nick all the stuff we need.' Annoying though the situation was, Sid could see there was no alternative course of action and soon he was driving the truck out on to the road with the professor next to him. It was over four hours before they reached a settlement, fortunately a small town which even had a general store. As Sid was choosing the equipment he needed Luke slipped on his invisibility robe and walked into the police station. He picked up a phone and dialled a number in Kinshasa.

'Hans,' he whispered, facing the wall in case his disembodied voice attracted attention. The phone he held against the wall as though it were still on its hook.

'Hans, I can't go into detail but our little plan is threatened by some characters I know of old. They're called Bonaventure and Fossfinder. I want them out of the country. See if you can get their visas cancelled or something, and chuck them out. If you don't, we can kiss our fortune goodbye.'

'Bonaventure,' said Hans thoughtfully. It was an unusual name. He didn't tell Luke that he knew exactly where the Bonaventures were. His inferiority complex made him want to impress Luke by appearing to manage to track them down. 'I'll get straight on to it. Ring me when you next can for news. Good luck.'

'Auf weidersehen' said Luke and put the phone down.

'Bonaventure,' Hans repeated slowly to himself. He was determined that nothing should stop Luke creating the wealth that would be his own salvation. 'I think I can do better than just getting them kicked out,' he murmured with quiet satisfaction as he picked up the phone again.

Luke slipped out of the police station and, still invisible, returned to the store where Sid was deep in conversation with the shopkeeper about the relative merits of two spades. A pile of items he had already selected was lying at the base of the counter, hidden from the shopkeeper's view. Luke picked up several items from the pile and took them out to the truck, taking three trips in all to transfer everything. He then removed his robe and rejoined Sid who was now looking about for his other goods. Luke murmured in his ear, upon which Sid hurriedly paid for both the spades he was holding and they made a rapid exit.

'I can't believe you did that right under his nose,' he said to Luke as they got in the truck. 'You must be a bloody magician.' As they drove off Sid saw the shopkeeper come out and look about, scratching his head. As they hadn't quite got everything they needed they stopped at a couple of farms as they left town and each time the professor told Sid to keep his head down and keep the engine running. Then he got out, slipped his robe on, and helped himself to various tools.

'You must 'ave 'ad a very interestin' life,' said Sid as the professor climbed back into the cab after his second successful sortie. 'I thought I knew 'ow to nick stuff, but I ain't never seen anyone op'rate like you before.' The Professor gave a modest smile.

'I expect it's because I don't really look the part,' he explained. 'If people don't expect to see a thief, or see someone who doesn't look like a thief, they just don't see one even if he's there.'

Sid still looked perplexed as they began the long and arduous drive back to the camp with their booty.

18

Eagles, Snakes and Crocodiles

Clive loaded as many of the supplies from the children's lorry as he could fit into the Land Rover. He drained the fuel from the lorry's tanks and filled the Land Rover and his spare fuel cans. Then the trio set off in search of the villains. Since the rapprochement between the inner and outer worlds Lucy was now able to use the animals of the forest as well as those she had brought with her and a constant stream of birds guided them to where the villains had stopped and set up camp. Occasionally they were stopped by paramilitary groups, but the bees continued to prove incredibly effective in bringing any such encounters to a speedy conclusion. As they drew nearer to the villains the road became worse and worse and eventually the birds took them off the road altogether up along a narrow gully – fortunately dry and stony. Suddenly Clare told Clive to stop and pointed. Through the bushes ahead they could just make out the shape of the lorry. Lucy sent a convenient squirrel along to check if the vehicle was empty, which it was. They got out of the Land Rover and crept up to it. An amazing view met their eyes. The lorry was parked at the top of a cliff and below them a river splashed and tumbled along a narrow gorge. In the brilliant sunshine a rainbow was visible in the clouds of spray rising from the water. On the other side of the gorge was another cliff which disappeared into the jungle on their left but to their right ended in a steep escarpment overlooking a giant swamp from which the river emerged. The villains were in the process of building a camp just below them, beside the river and two men had crossed the giant boulders through which the river raced and were now examining the cliff on the other side. Different rock strata were clearly visible where the cliff had been eroded and one of the men appeared to be hacking at the rocks in the cliff while the other erected a tent.

'What next?' whispered Lucy.

'Well we know where they are now, and the layout of their camp,' replied Clive. 'Let's keep out of sight while we think how we can best use the animals to find out what they're up to.' They crept back to the Land Rover and Clive drove it right into the bush so that it was completely invisible from either the main road or the gully. They sat beside the car and drank coffee from their Thermos flask while they chatted about what they had seen.

'I think he's after some rocks to make invisibility robes,' said Clare. 'You must remember how he told us all about that special ore back in the Amazon crater – and he's using a gang of thugs to help him just like he did last time.'

'I'm sure you're right,' said Clive. 'What I can't figure out is why he didn't go back to the original crater which is full of the stuff and why, of all other places he might pick he's chosen here in just about the remotest, most dangerous and most inaccessible place on the planet.'

'I'm sure all will become clear if we're patient and stick around,' said Lucy. At that moment they all jumped as they heard the lorry start up.

'Quick,' said Clare, 'they're moving on. Keep out of sight.' They all crouched in the bushes and saw the lorry lurch past on the uneven stones. Sid was driving with the professor next to him but as the lorry disappeared they could see clearly that the back was empty.

'It's OK, they've left the men behind,' said Clive. 'They've just gone for some supplies – and did you see? It's definitely the professor!'

It was well after dark by the time the lorry returned and when all was quiet the trio eventually relaxed and went to sleep, secure in the knowledge that Lucy's animal lookouts would warn them of anyone approaching. The next day dawned bright and clear and after breakfast the three once again crept up to the edge of the cliff to spy on the villains. The men were already back at work building the camp and the professor had obviously decided that this was a suitable spot for his base. A herd of wild pigs rooted at the edge of the swamp, seemingly unconcerned by the activities of the men nearby. Vultures soared on their endless patterns high in the blue sky, and a fish eagle circled lazily over the swamp on its massive wings. As they gazed down they heard the click of a rifle being cocked behind them.

'Don't even think of movin',' said a coarse voice. Sid then raised his voice and shouted to the men below at the base of he cliff. 'They've arrived and I've got 'em'. The men below looked up and started climbing up towards them. 'Shall I do 'em now?' he called.

'No, wait!' the unmistakable voice of the professor floated up. He was slightly breathless as he began to clamber up the rocks. 'I need to talk to them.' Sid prodded Lucy with his boot.

'So it's you again, yer bleedin' little toerag. Well when the prof's done we'll fix yer proper this time!' The three lay motionless as the professor climbed. Clive could feel the muzzle of the rifle pushed hard into the back of his neck and knew that the slightest movement would be the last he ever made. Suddenly there was the sound of rushing wind and as Sid looked up he saw a dark shape hurtling down from the sky. He screamed as the talons of the fish eagle sank deep into his face and the force of three kilos of solid muscle hitting him at speed knocked him backwards to the ground, his gun clattering to the rocks. Clive leapt up immediately and grabbed the gun. Sid was grappling with the great raptor with both hands, desperately trying to protect his eyes.

'Quick!' Clive shouted, 'start the Land Rover. I'll be right there.'

'Don't tackle him,' shouted Clare. 'Just run. The eagle will stop him.'

But now Clive wasn't anywhere near Sid. He ran to the thugs' truck and fired at the tyres. He knew nothing about guns and prayed that Sid had released the safety catch if there was one. There was a deafening crash as he pulled the trigger and as he aimed at each wheel in turn the lorry settled to the ground among pieces of fragmented rubber. He ran to where Clare had pulled the Land Rover out into the gully and jumped in. As they lurched and bumped their way out on to the road Lucy looked back and saw the first man's head just appearing over the edge of the cliff. Clare drove as fast as she dared until they were safely clear and then pulled off the road and steered through the bush until once again they were near the top of the cliff and invisible from the road. Lucy spoke to a nearby bird.

'Fly in haste to the Tailless Ones near the house that moves. Tell the gilliquill his work is now done. Return with thy tidings.' The bird flew off and returned in a few moments to speak to Lucy who then turned to the others.

'It's OK. they're not following,' she reported. 'They're just standing round the truck shouting and arguing,' she added, slightly gleefully.

'That was really quick thinking, Clive,' said Clare. 'When I heard the shots I nearly had a heart attack but I was busy reversing out

'The eagle will stop him.'

and couldn't see what was happening. Then Lucy told me what you'd done.'

'If the gun hadn't worked,' Clive replied, 'I'd have had to open the bonnet and smash the carburettor or the engine electrics with the butt, but it would have taken much longer – we only just made it as it was. Anyway,' he said modestly, 'the really quick thinking was by you, Lucy.' He smiled at her. 'You had that fish eagle over in no time flat.'

'We were really lucky he was cruising nearby,' she said. 'Getting the vultures down would have taken ages. Anyway, all's well that ends well. What next?'

'Well they're now immobile which gives us a massive advantage,' said Clive. 'We can spy on them at will. I'd love to get their guns off them, though. They're obviously trigger happy and wouldn't think twice about potting us if they catch us again – especially that bloke who's just got a new face.'

'That's Sid,' said Lucy. 'He's a really nasty piece of work – though I'm still not sure I don't prefer him to the professor, given the choice.'

'Which reminds me,' said Clive. 'I meant to ask you how on earth you think the professor got to know Sid and Fred and bring them here.'

'I've got no idea,' said Lucy. 'Maybe Chopper and Sam mentioned them to him before they got killed but how he tracked them down is a mystery.'

'Talking of mysteries,' said Clare, 'I've just remembered something else. We were *ambushed* today, they were expecting us and Sid was lying in wait. How did they know we were coming?'

'They must have seen us yesterday when we peeped over the edge,' said Lucy. 'We'll have to be much more careful in future.'

'Which brings us to the next point,' said Clare. 'What *is* the future. How are we going to get the robe off the professor?'

'It's not just a question of getting the robe,' said Clive. 'Now we know why he's here it's vital that we stop him getting any of these rocks that he thinks are so important. Otherwise, presumably, he can just make himself another robe. But, to answer your question, how we go about tackling him? Well, as usual, I leave *that* up to you clever sisters!'

They decided to have lunch while they made some plans and in the afternoon they crept to the edge of the cliff once again. They had driven about a mile from their original parking spot near the villains' lorry and were now simply further along the cliff, away from from the swamp. The men had resumed work on the camp and were still clearly visible, upstream in the gorge. Lucy sent some rodents ahead of them to establish there were no guards at the cliff top above the camp and then the three of them made their way quietly through the bush along the cliff until they were almost back at the truck with the shattered tyres. They peeped cautiously over the cliff, taking extra care this time not to be seen. The men had now stopped for a break and were drinking coffee immediately below them. Sid and the professor had crossed to the other side and were hacking specimens from the rock face and loading them into canvas bags. Sid's head was bandaged and even from across the narrow gorge they could see that his face was swollen and bruised almost beyond recognition. Suddenly there was a screech and two fish eagles started swooping and buzzing at the men. Clare and Clive looked enquiringly at Lucy but she shook her head.

'Nothing to do with me,' she whispered. 'Maybe the men are threatening their nest site.' One of the men cursed as the female struck his hand with her talons and then started shooting. The others laughed at his vain attempts to hit the birds which dived and spiralled at an astonishing speed.

The professor and Sid spun round at the noise of gunfire but turned back to their task when they saw that it wasn't an attack but a bird shoot. Soon all the men were firing and when they ran out of ammunition the birds were still unharmed and persisting in their angry protest. Two of the men clambered up to the truck to replenish their ammunition supplies and Clare, Clive and Lucy shrank down behind a boulder. They heard the men rummaging in the truck. Suddenly there were cries of fear and the men leapt from the truck and started scrambling back down the cliff. Clare and Clive once again looked enquiringly at Lucy but she shrugged her shoulders.

'I didn't do anything,' she said with a puzzled expression, 'let's find out what's going on.' The trio didn't dare move so Lucy looked about for some animal help. She was about to talk to a squirrel but then caught sight of a colobus monkey in a nearby tree and decided that his superior intelligence might be useful. She called him over.

'Knowest thou of these Tailless Ones?' she asked.

'Aye, I dwell in this place and see all they do. When the Brilliant One last went to his rest they killed one of my kin with their thundersticks and devoured her.'

'Why do two of them now flee from the house that moves?'

'I go to the house every day to eat their food when they are gone, but have seen nothing amiss. I will go once more.' While he bounded off to the truck Lucy turned to the others.

'They had roast monkey for supper last night, so they're not flavour of the month with this guy. I'm sure he'll help us all he can.' The monkey returned with exciting news.

186

'*The Tailless Ones sought new food for their thundersticks. But when they removed the roof of the wooden nest the fellfangs arose. I spoke to them in the common tongue. They speak not much but say they are in thy service.*'

'*Thank thee. These are good tidings indeed,*' said Lucy. '*Soon these Tailless Ones will be gone and this place will once again belong to thee and thy kin.*' She turned to the other two. 'Great,' she said. 'Some of the snakes we asked to protect the children are still in that truck They were hidden in the ammunition boxes and when the men came up to re-load their guns they got a nasty shock!'

'So, if they've all run out of ammo'...,' said Clare.

'...and I've still got Sid's gun back at the car ...,' said Clive.

'... then we're armed and they're not!.' finished Lucy.

'Unless the professor's got a gun,' said Clare. 'We'd better just bear that in mind'. The others agreed, then they peeped over the edge again. The men were all now clambering back up the steep slope in consternation at the news from the terrified two.

'This has got to be our best chance,' said Clive. 'Anything you can do Luce?' Lucy called the monkey back.

'*If thou wouldst be rid of these Tailless Ones in haste, find us a spotfang.*' The monkey bounded off and the three hunched down again behind the boulder. Soon the men gathered round the truck nervously. One of the two who had come previously peeped cautiously into the back of the truck and then leapt backwards at the sound of a loud hiss.

'What can we do?' he said, his voice trembling. 'We can't get at the stores or any ammo!'

'One of us'll 'ave to go and tell Sid and the Prof,' said Fred, who had turned white as a sheet at the prospect of facing snakes once again. The man nearest the cliff turned to go back down and then stopped dead. There, standing silently on the edge, was an enormous leopard, its exquisite markings shining in the afternoon sun. Then a growl rumbled behind the group and another leopard appeared. The men stood stock still, trapped between the two great predators, clutching their useless weapons.

'Don't move and they won't hurt you,' said Lucy, jumping up and walking towards the truck.

'Come on,' she turned and beckoned to Clare and Clive, 'let's go and get what we came for.'

'I can never get over just how powerful this kid is,' Clive muttered to Clare as they rather hesitantly got up and walked past the astonished villains to the truck.

'Look out,' called Fred, 'there's snakes in there!' as Lucy clambered over the tailgate.

'Thanks, I know,' Lucy called back over her shoulder. 'They're my pets; they're called Sid and Fred and they do anything I say.' Clive and Clare grinned as they followed her, then they all rummaged through the contents of the truck looking for the invisibility robe. At a glance from Lucy the two mambas had settled down and curled up calmly on the floor.

'Any luck, you two?' called Clare, as she emptied out another box onto the floor.

'Nope,' said Lucy.

'I think,' said Clive, 'that he wouldn't leave it anywhere. He probably carries it with him at all times.'

'You must be right,' said Lucy. 'Let's go and get it.'

'What, now?' said Clive.

'When else do you suggest,' said Lucy with a grin. 'Are you going to try and fix an appointment with him?' Clive had to laugh.

'You're right' he said. 'No time like the present!'

'*Carpe diem*!' added Clare.

They jumped to the ground and the snakes renewed their guard over the truck. The men still stood transfixed in a tight group. They gazed in stupefaction as the trio walked past snakes and leopards with equal impunity.

'You can sit down if you like,' said Lucy, as Clive lifted down a box of bottled water from the truck. The men sat down obediently and opened some bottles of water. 'There you are. Good boys!' she turned to Clare and Clive and gave an impish grin. 'I should be running a primary school.' The thugs glowered at her. If looks could kill she would have been vaporized on the spot. 'We'll be back soon,' she announced gaily. 'Oh, and the leopards will kill anyone who tries to leave.'

19

The Demise of a Dastardly Duo

Clive, Clare and Lucy left the men under the watchful eyes of the leopards and started off down the cliffside. Meanwhile, across the gorge Sid, who had turned to put some rock samples in a basket, glanced across to check that the men had restarted their work after coffee. He did a classic doubletake at the sight of the three climbing down to the camp. He grabbed the professor and pointed.

'What the hell's going on?' His speech was muffled by the swelling of his mouth and jaw. Deep, red, angry gashes were gouged out of his upper cheeks and nose. The professor looked over, his face flushing with anger.

'Those... bloody... kids! Whatever I do they come and mess with me. I'll kill everyone of them today, so help me!' He drew his automatic and ran with Sid towards the river as the youngsters started to jump from boulder to boulder across the stream towards them.

'Isn't it about time you pulled your next rabbit out of the hat?' Clive said to Lucy between jumps. 'They're getting very near and I think the prof's holding a gun – looks as if Clare was right. And Sid could have a knife or something.'

'All under control,' replied Lucy calmly, and even as she spoke a massive crocodile lunged out of the river on to the far bank and waddled at a surprising speed towards the oncoming pair, jaws agape.

'My God, look out!' shouted Sid who was leading the way. He turned round hurriedly, bumping into the professor as he did so, then started scrambling back up the hill. The professor paused and emptied his gun at the great reptile, to no apparent effect. He swore, then threw the useless weapon at the animal before turning and racing up the hill after Sid. They reached the top of the cliff and started running along the ridge at the top, away from the swamp and towards the jungle. The rock python was lazing in the afternoon sun when it heard Lucy's call. It had not eaten for several months and was just thinking about beginning to move and start looking for its next meal. It would need something large – a pig or a gazelle for it was a giant of its kind, over eight metres long and as thick as Lucy's waist in girth around its widest point.

At the sound of the Promised One it raised its head three feet off the ground and looked for her. Instead it saw two men hurrying towards it. Sid didn't see it until he was only a few feet away and stopped short with a gasp. He turned and ran back towards the escarpment overlooking the swamp. The professor was nowhere to be seen, though Sid felt as though he had brushed past something as he ran. As he reached the edge of the precipice he glanced back over his shoulder. The python was slithering towards him and now it was completely uncurled he was for the first time aware of its enormous size. With his lifelong phobia of snakes this reptile was a creature out of Sid's worst nightmares, immeasurably bigger than anything he had ever seen, its beautiful tan and black markings glistening in the sun as it sped towards him, its tongue flickering out of its blunt, diamond-shaped head. At Lucy's instruction the snake suddenly stopped.

'Don't move, either of you,' she called up, 'and you'll be quite safe. The snake and the crocodile will do as I say, and if you give yourselves up you'll both have a fair trial.'

Sid looked down the sheer cliff face. He was damned if some slip of a girl was going to trap him. The greenish-brown surface of the swamp was a hundred feet below. It was only a very short distance for him to swim back to the base of the cliff and he was sure he could beat the crocodile back over the river boulders to the safety of the camp on the other side. He saw the surface of the swamp ripple slightly as some fish or reptile moved in its murky depths. The sight reassured him: if the surface could ripple it was probably a soft landing. He took a deep breath and leapt out into the void. Clive, Clare and Lucy looked on in horror. As if in slow motion, Sid dropped towards the swamp and as he fell an extraordinary sight met their eyes. A giant head on a long neck emerged from the depths and its great jaws gaped. It rose to meet its prey and twenty feet from the surface Sid was caught as neatly as a fish thrown to a sea lion. Even as the serpentine neck disappeared beneath the surface a sickening crunch was clearly audible to the shocked onlookers. After a stunned silence Clive was the first to recall the professor.

'Hang on – where's the prof?' he shouted. The others looked in vain and then the truth dawned on Clare.

'He's put the robe on,' she shouted. 'Everyone keep their guard. Stay together.'

'Professor,' Lucy called. 'The snake will know where you are. Take off the robe, then come down and you'll be safe.'

On several previous occasions in his life the professor had underestimated the power of animals to detect his invisible form and this was to prove his last. He started to edge his way past the python and towards the youngsters. Lucy saw the snake stiffen.

'...an extraordinary sight met their eyes.'

'Don't move!' she screamed. But the professor ignored her. Unlike the mamba he had previously encountered, this species of snake *did* have thermal detectors to catch prey in the dark and it knew precisely where Luke was. Despite Lucy's request for the snake to remain still, the professor's sudden movement triggered an unstoppable reflex in the reptile and it struck with lightning speed. The trio watched in horrified fascination as the snake spiralled its great coils around its victim. The professor was still invisible, so the snake looked for a moment as if it were creating a vertical corkscrew shape with nothing inside it. Then it started to squeeze, its primitive instincts continuing to make it deaf to Lucy's entreaties.

Then the shocked onlookers then witnessed a quite extraordinary sight. The professor's head suddenly appeared above the coils of the snake, then his whole body as he managed to clamber out of the robe and leave it in the ever-tightening grip of the reptile. He started running along the ridge towards the rainforest and was soon lost to sight. Lucy called to the python and as they walked up it slithered away in disappointment, back to its sunny rocks. Clive bent down and felt about on the ground. It was an eerie feeling suddenly making contact with the invisible robe. He felt all over it and located an energy pack with a button. He pressed the button and they all watched in wonderment as the robe de-energized and gradually became visible.

'What about his head?' said Clare holding up the robe as it she were in a dress shop.

'Good thinking!' said Clive, and he felt about again until he located a soft helmet with its own tiny energizing unit. 'Well,' he said gathering the robe and helmet up to carry them back. 'This is what we came to find and which has cost so many lives and had so many hopes depending on it. I feel as if I'm carrying the Holy Grail. I'm tempted to burn it on the spot but I think we'd better get it back to Lucinda. It's probably her original prototype.'

'We should definitely keep it,' said Clare. 'And you never know, it could just come in useful before we're done!'

'What about the professor?' asked Clive.

'He can't get far without transport or weapons,' said Lucy. 'We'll keep an eye on him through the animals and round him up when we've decided what to do with him.' When they had crossed the gorge and returned to the lorry the men were still sitting huddled together in a group, the leopards prowling back and forth around them.

'What are we going to do with them?' said Clive.

'That depends,' said Clare. She asked Lucy which one was Fred and then turned to the assembled thugs.

'The professor and Sid won't be coming back – ever,' – she stated. She didn't elaborate, and the villains looked at her with new respect. Here was a woman to be reckoned with. She sensed their attitude and had no doubt they would tell her the truth. 'How long will the supplies in the truck last?' she asked Fred who had turned pale under his tan, wondering what had happened to Sid.

'Dunno, three weeks – four, mebbe,' he replied hoarsely. Seeing his face she felt a pang of sympathy for him.

'I'm sorry about your brother. We never intended that he should be harmed. We wanted to bring him to justice for kidnapping the children. We tried to stop him but he leapt off the cliff into the swamp.' Fred nodded in silence. He knew that what she had told him must be true.

Clare turned to Lucy and Clive. While clambering back up the cliff she had she had been making plans, but now suddenly remembered that she hadn't discussed her thoughts with the others.

'OK if I carry on?' They both nodded. They were still stunned by the suddenness of the gruesome and tragic events they had just witnessed, but Clare seemed to have recovered her composure and her wits and they both had complete trust in her judgement. She turned back to the men.

'All right, you lot, here's the plan. I don't know what other crimes you've committed, but as far as kidnapping the children is concerned I think that the professor and Sid were mostly to blame. The children, one of whom happens to be my little sister, said that the rest of you didn't bother them and that you,' she pointed to Fred, 'were especially kind to them and tried to protect them. So we're going to let you all go.' The leopards will go away shortly after we leave. One of them will follow us to protect us, so don't try and find us. We'll chuck most of your guns into the swamp but we'll leave you one to defend yourselves. The snakes will move out of the truck tomorrow when we'll be miles away and you'll then have access to food, and ammunition for the remaining gun.' She paused and spoke to Clive. 'I presume they can't ever use this truck again.'

'No,' he said, but I'll make sure anyway.' He opened the bonnet and smashed the carburettor with a rock. He then climbed into the back of the truck and lifted out a case of beer. 'I'll borrow this, boys, if that's OK. I've run out and you've got plenty left by the look of it. Oh, and I'm taking your spare fuel – I don't think you'll be needing it!' Clare turned back to the men.

"We're now going to Kinshasa,' she continued. 'We'll tell the authorities that you're stranded and where you are, and they'll come out to look for you. If you feel happy to face the DRC police then you can wait in safety here till they pick you up. If any of you have got a guilty conscience about something you've done previously and don't want to see the cops, you can make your own way through the rainforest and organize your own salvation. You've got several days to decide and your fate's in your own hands. Any questions?' There were none. Clare looked enquiringly at Clive and Lucy. 'OK with all that?' she asked. They both nodded.

'I'll just say one thing,' said Fred. 'You're a fair bird with lots of guts.'

'I second that,' Clive whispered to Lucy, 'what an amazing sister you've got!' She smiled and nodded. They collected up the guns, allowing Fred to select the one they should leave and Clive threw the others into the swamp. Lucy acquired a river hog to help them transport the spare fuel cans and the beer, and after she had spoken to the leopards, the three of them left to walk back to the Land Rover.

'You didn't speak to the snakes,' said Clare as they made their way along the cliff top.

'No, they aren't great intellects,' said Lucy, 'and I thought it best not to get too complicated with my instructions. They can stop the men getting at the ammo' tonight and I'll just send them a simple message tomorrow telling them to leave!' Clare glanced at Clive and they both grinned. As far as animals were concerned, Lucy had it all worked out, as usual.

When they got back they cooked a barbeque, opened a few cans of the villains' beer and, inevitably, discussed the day's events. As they chatted one of the leopards appeared silently from the bush and stood guard.

'I'm dying to talk about that Loch Ness monster that ate Sid,' said Clive 'but I suppose that first we ought to sort out our plan of action for the professor.' They all agreed and, thought for a few moments.

'He's so evil and dangerous,' said Clare eventually, 'that we've *got* to make sure he's brought to justice and locked up safe and sound for a very long time.' The others agreed that he would have to be caught and delivered to the authorities and they were just working out the best way of achieving this when the problem was resolved. A kingfisher flew up from the gorge and alighted in the nearby trees. A few seconds later it flew back to the river and the colobus monkey emerged. It loped up to them and spoke to Lucy who soon turned to the others.

'It looks as if the matter's been taken out of our hands. After we'd gone the professor returned and tried to cross back over the river. He slipped and the crocs got him. The monkey says that from what the kingfisher told him there can be no question that he's dead.'

There was a brief silence as they digested the news.

'Well I for one am not going to lose any sleep over him,' said Clive bluntly. 'He was a thief and a murderer and a kidnapper, and if he did go to jail he would be forever plotting and planning to escape and make another invisibility robe. The world is definitely better off without him – and so are we. It would have been a hell of a performance trying to get him captured by the police and convicted without telling anyone about Lucy's power or the invisibility robe. I'm sorry, but I'm relieved at what's happened.'

'I know all you say is true,' said Lucy, 'but I can't help feeling that, directly or indirectly, I'm responsible for both those men's deaths today.'

'Look,' said Clare, 'Those men kidnapped Sarah and Ben and had every intention of killing them – we have overwhelming evidence to that effect. Ben actually *heard* them plotting to kill them; the professor tried to entice them into the bushes and was only stopped by the snakes. They left the children, as they thought, to the mercy of the snakes and they then returned to incinerate them, live or dead. I rest my case your honour.'

'Hear, hear,' said Clive 'and remember, Lucy, that you did your utmost to bring them to justice. You warned them several times and they ignored you – despite their experiences in the Amazon. You couldn't have done anything more.'

'But if we hadn't gone this afternoon,' said Lucy, 'none of this would have happened.'

'True, but how could we have left that evil man to do untold harm throughout the world with his invisibility robe and the power to make new ones? And, as we said the other day, who else could have stopped him? Sometimes in life you have to make difficult choices. This was one we had to make, and I think we made the right one. I'll believe that until the day I die!'

Lucy was reassured by his logic and they eventually retired, safe under the watchful eyes of their big cat.

The next day they rose early. Now that they could call upon assistance from the junglekin, they were no longer dependent on the animals they had brought with them. The bees in the box had decided that they liked the flora near the river and the swamp and elected to stay in that spot; Lucy thanked them and the swarm disappeared to find a hollow tree to colonize. The snakes said that they too liked the forest and slithered out of their makeshift accommodation into the nearby bush. Lucy then sent a bird to call off the snakes guarding the villains' ammunition and thanked the leopard who had guarded them overnight. They refuelled the Land Rover using one of the drums Clive had taken from the villains and then set off on the long, dusty, and bumpy road to Kinshasa, where they planned to meet up with the rest of the family before flying back to London.

20

Diplomatic Duplicity

Richard and Joanna stood near Neema's observation hide as they had done every day and looked out at the ever-changing scene before them as animals darted to and fro; monkeys swung through the trees; insects, reptiles and other small creatures went about their business on the forest floor; and birds and butterflies winged their way across the glade. They were astonished when a bonobo suddenly emerged from the trees and made its way shyly towards them. Hardly daring to breathe for fear of frightening it they stood stock still as it came right up to them, deposited something at Richard's feet and scampered away.

'What on earth...,' Richard exclaimed in surprise as he bent down and picked up the husk with its embedded note.

'It's a letter!'

'From Lucy? Up to her old tricks again?' asked Joanna with a smile.

'No – o,' said Richard, his expression changing as he read. 'It's not from... Lucy.' He handed her the note, his eyes moist. Joanna read it and then turned and hugged him tight.

'I just can't believe it's all come good,' she whispered eventually, 'after all these years.'

They made their way happily back to their boat and returned to the villa they had been allocated near the park headquarters. They opened a bottle of champagne, toasted their new-found daughter in her absence and passed the evening discussing the various possible ways in which the children might have all managed to find each other and join up. The next day they returned to the hide and waited eagerly for the party to arrive. In the afternoon, just as they were about to leave, there was a shout and Sarah and Ben rushed through the clearing. Even as they hugged and kissed the youngsters Joanna saw another form move silently into view. She looked up.

'It's Lucy,' she said to Richard.

'No – it's Grace!' the girl said, and ran across to greet them. After a very emotional few minutes Richard cautiously asked where the

...they hugged and kissed the youngsters...

201

others were. 'They've gone to catch an invisible professor,' said Grace. 'They said you'd know exactly who they were talking about, but I'm sure Sarah and Ben are going to tell you the whole story. The others are going to send us a message through the animals when their mission is completed and they want us to meet them in Kinshasa.'

'But without Lucy how did you get back safely with Sarah and Ben?' asked Richard. He knew what the answer would be, but the question had to be asked. Before Grace could reply Sarah burst in:

'Grace can speak to *animals,* Daddy – can you believe it; she really can!' Richard looked at Joanna and they both smiled.

'Yes, love, I do believe you.'

'Well, if we're not expecting anyone else today,' said Joanna, 'let's get back and celebrate – after you two have had a bath,' she added with mock severity as she pretended to sniff Sarah and Ben, who were looking travel-stained to say the least, after their prolonged experiences in in lorries, camps and the jungle. They all returned to the house in Salonga and talked far into the night. Just before going to bed Grace spoke to Richard and Joanna.

'Mummy...Daddy,' she said hesitantly, shy about the unaccustomed form of address. Joanna and Richard smiled encouragingly.

'What is it, love?' said Joanna.

'There's something you should know. My family – my foster family,' she corrected herself, 'were arrested recently and the police are looking for me to arrest me as well. If I stay here with you I think I may put you all in danger, so tomorrow I think I should return to the animals until you've managed to sort things out.' Richard assured her that the ambassador was already working on it and that there was nothing to worry about. On that happy note they all retired.

The morning brought two developments, one pleasant, the other distinctly unpleasant. Just after breakfast a monkey appeared at the window. Grace talked to it for a few moments and then reported to the others.

'Great news! They say it's all sorted out and they've set off for Kinshasa.'

'I wonder what they've actually done,' pondered Richard who had been very worried about the prospect of them grappling with the wily professor again, notwithstanding Lucy's power.

'Well they've obviously achieved something and at least they're safe,' said Joanna. 'That's all I was really concerned about.'

'If they've already set out for Kinshasa, maybe we should do the same,' said Richard. 'It was a bit of a problem journey getting out here and I don't expect getting back will be any easier.' Joanna nodded.

'And we'll need to get some clothes and stuff for Sarah and Ben,' she added. Just then the phone rang. It was the ambassador's secretary at the British Embassy. 'It's good of the ambassador to ring back as he promised,' said Joanna to Richard as she held the phone waiting for the secretary to connect the ambassador. 'He really cares – and he'll be so pleased to hear what's happened!'

'Hello, sorry to keep you,' the secretary said, 'the ambassador is just coming on the line now.'

'Hello, is that Joanna Bonaventure?' She recognised the ambassador's voice instantly. 'Good. John Moriarty here.'

'Thank you so much for ringing, ambassador.'

'Not good news. I'm afraid.' His voice adopted a grave tone. 'First of all there's no further news about the lost girl.' Joanna smiled to herself – she had news for him there. 'Then there is a problem with your visas: it seems that in the confusion surrounding your emergency departure during the rebellion thirteen years ago, we have no record of your actually having left the country. It wouldn't normally have come to light, except your current visa has triggered an automatic check on your records. As your original visa thirteen years ago was only for one year, it means that technically you have been illegal immigrants for the entire intervening period. Worse than that, the authorities have got wind of the fact that you have come to look for the feral child, and consider that your search represents the potential abduction of a Congolese citizen.'

'How on earth did they know why we had come?' said Joanna, her voice trembling.

'I don't know. Maybe some busybody at Salonga saw you suddenly appear and start taking an interest in the lost child. They must have put two and two together.'

'What does all this mean,' asked Joanna, her face ashen.

'Well you can't leave the country and you can't try and get in contact with the child. You're not allowed to leave your present accommodation so you're effectively under house arrest. It's possible that the police will come and check on you, but I've tried to placate them and given them an assurance that you will not move about.' He paused briefly, then continued. 'There's just one other point. Are you expecting any other family members to join you?'

'Yes,' said Joanna. 'They're driving over from Tanzania.'

'Well when they get in touch please inform them that they too are forbidden to move about in case they try and assist in the abduction of the missing child. There'll be roadblocks to pick them up, but if they get in touch it might be helpful if you could forewarn them and explain what's going on.' His voice softened. 'I'm so sorry about this. We are working night and day here to try and sort it out for you. Just sit tight, and I'll get back with any further news. Don't even think of breaking the non-movement order. If you do I'll lose what modest influence I have with the civil authorities and you'll almost certainly end up in jail for an indefinite period – could be years. Good luck, and don't hesitate to ring me with any further questions.'

'Th-thank you, goodbye,' stuttered Joanna.

'What in heaven's name's going on?' said Richard. 'You look as if you've seen a ghost.'

Joanna explained what had happened and they set down in a state of shock to try and work out what to do.

'We obviously have to stay here until we get more news from the Embassy,' said Richard after some thought. 'Thank goodness we've got them on our side. But it sounds as if Grace's decision to return to the forest was a good one. A bunch of police might turn up at any minute.'

'What about Sarah and Ben?' asked Joanna. 'I forgot to tell him they were already here.'

'Probably just as well,' said Richard thoughtfully. 'It would have been pretty difficult to explain how they got here on their own without the others – but it doesn't solve the problem of what to do with them.'

'Can I make a suggestion?' asked Grace hesitantly. She was not used to family discussions and wasn't sure if she should participate.

'Of course,' said Richard and Joanna in unison.

'I've seen what the police and paramilitaries can do and I would be very worried about leaving Sarah and Ben here. I think they should come with me to the forest – as soon as possible before anyone arrives. I'll look after them with the bonobos until the Embassy has managed to sort things out.'

Although it seemed an extraordinary course of action to send two young children into the rainforest, the more Richard and Joanna thought about it the more they realised that it was the safest and most sensible thing to do. Sarah and Ben, who had been exploring around the house and garden, were called in and told the plan, with which they were, of course thrilled. Joanna hurriedly put some things a bag for them and, taking care to remain as inconspicuous as possible, Grace and the youngsters slipped away to start their boat journey to the bonobo reserve.

Back at the Embassy Moriarty put the phone down with a smug smile. It had been surprisingly easy. They seemed to have swallowed the entire pack of lies without question – but then, when he thought about it, why wouldn't they? The ambassador himself ringing them in person. Of course they would believe him; they had no earthly reason to doubt him. He thought he had handled it rather well: just the right mixture of grave concern and the promise to try and sort things out. He was particularly proud of the phrase "the police may come". They wouldn't of course: they knew nothing about the Bonaventures, but the thought that they might appear would certainly make the Bonaventures think twice about moving about. He couldn't wait for Luke's next call; even he would have to acknowledge that his cousin had done a great job.

21

Benign Blackmail

Several days later, after a painfully slow journey, along terrible roads made worse by heavy rain, Clive, Clare and Lucy eventually arrived in Kinshasa in the late morning. They had received a note from Grace *en route* informing them of the situation, so Clive didn't return his hire car at this stage and they checked into a hotel under false names. Now that they had a landline they rang Joanna and Richard who told them that no police had appeared to enforce the house-arrest order, but that they had complied with the ambassador's request not to break it and had not left the house. There had, as yet been no further news from the embassy.

On the long drive to the capital they had all been wondering why on earth the professor had suddenly decided that the middle of the African rainforest was a good place to look for photogyraspar and Clive had decided to contact Peter Flint to see if he had any ideas. He rang home to England to update his parents on the situation and obtain Peter Flint's contact details at the same time. That afternoon, when he calculated it would be about the right time in Rio, he rang Peter. He was pleasantly surprised to get through first time.

'Peter Flint here.'

'Peter,' said Clive, 'we've never met, but I'm Clive, Helen and Julian Fossfinder's son. I went to the Amazon crater with them.'

'Ah yes. I've heard all about that from Lucinda. Quite a party! Also, your parents gave me some samples that saved me a great deal of time and trouble so I owe you guys a favour. What can I do for you?'

'I've got a rather unusual request and I can't think of anybody other than you that might be able to help. I'm in the Democratic Republic of Congo with the Bonaventure family and the most extraordinary thing has happened.'

'Let me guess, though I hope I'm wrong,' interrupted Peter. 'You've come across Professor Strahlung.' Clive was astounded.

'How on earth did you know that?'

'Oh dear,' said Peter, 'I was hoping against hope that he wouldn't get there but he obviously has.'

'Before we go any further,' Clive replied, 'I should tell you that the professor is dead – eaten by crocodiles.'

'*Nihil nisi bonum de mortuis* as they say, but it couldn't have happened to a nicer chap.' Clive couldn't help grinning at Peter's sardonic humour. He was beginning to like this man.

'So what's the story?' he asked.

'Well the first point,' said Flint, 'is that before we knew your parents had rescued some rock samples from the crater Lucinda, my fiancée, was desperate to get hold of more photogyraspar. You probably weren't aware of the fact, but the crater is now a completely protected site – something your Dad and Mum got the UN to do. That's brilliant for the flora and fauna of course but it means that it's out of bounds for prospecting. I then undertook a geological analysis of the ore in which photogyraspar is found and, with the help of an expert in England who has a massive database of prospecting samples, discovered that an almost identical ore exists, guess where, in the middle of the Congo.'

'But how on earth did the professor find that out?' exclaimed Clive.

'I discovered that through a real stroke of luck. I knew of course that he'd escaped from hospital and, for anybody in the know, it was obvious from the bewildered police report that he'd somehow got hold of an invisibility robe. A few days after I'd read about his escape my head of department asked me to deal with a query from the university switchboard supervisor. She was interested in an international phone call made from my department in the middle of the night. I should tell you that we recently introduced a system to economize on the university's massive phone charges. Any long distance calls made between the hours of 8 p.m. and 8 a.m are logged in the switchboard, the call is recorded and a record kept of the number dialled. It's basically to stop unsupervised nightstaff spending hours on long-distance or international phonecalls to relatives in the middle of the night. Every week the switchboard supervisor contacts heads of departments with a list of calls so they can either be justified or docked from the departmental budget. Now, when she played back this call for me it was unmistakably the voice of Luke Strahlung – you'll remember I know him well because he used to work here. He must have got in here in his invisibility robe and gone through my stuff which is obviously how he found out about the Congo lode of ore.'

'Well, that's amazing,' said Clive. 'Thanks very much for solving the mystery.'

'Wait, you haven't heard the half of it yet!' said Peter. 'Don't you want to know where the professor was calling?'

'Gosh, I hadn't thought about that,' said Clive, 'Where was it?'

'It was to a number in Kinshasa – and before I say more, have you got a fax or e-mail in that place – I'd like to send you a transcript of the conversation. The professor's obviously in cahoots with someone over there.'

'Hold on a sec,' Clive checked with the hotel receptionist and then gave Peter a fax number. 'I'll ring you back when I've read it.'

A few minutes later an excited Clive rang Peter back.

'Wow, quite an incriminating phone call. I'm a bit puzzled, though, the professor's such a wily old ******* – how on earth did he make such a stupid mistake?'

'That's because the monitoring system is so new. It wasn't here in his time; in fact it only went in two weeks ago and this is the first time they've picked up a call from our department.'

'Well whoever this Hans Moriarty is, he's got a serious problem if anyone gets hold of this script,' said Clive.

'Ah yes, that's the final twist I was coming to,' said Peter gleefully. 'Out of pure curiosity I checked on the number in Kinshasa.'

'And ...,' said Clive. Peter was certainly spinning this out.

'... and it's the number of the British Embassy!'

'What! So there's somebody in the British embassy bribing the locals and helping the professor to extract minerals illegally?'

'Exactly. I'm not quite sure what you can do about it, but it sounds as though a quiet word in the ambassador's ear might be a useful next step.' Clive thanked him profusely for his time and help and then went through to Clare and Lucy and recounted the story.

'The funny thing is,' he mused as they read the transcript together, 'I've seen that name Moriarty somewhere else recently, but I can't for the life of me remember where.' Clare looked up from the fax.

'I remember,' she said.

'I do too!' Lucy interrupted. 'It was the password on Luke's computer in the crater. You thought it might be his mother's maiden name.'

'Of course,' Clive slapped his knee. 'That's where it was. Things are beginning to fall into place.'

'What's falling into place?' asked Lucy. But Clive was looking hurriedly at his watch.

'Sorry, Luce, tell you in a moment. It's nearly five o'clock and I want to catch the ambassador before the embassy closes down for the day. We've got to stop this Moriarty person in his tracks as soon as possible – if he hears nothing from the professor and can't contact him he may think his cover's blown and make a run for it.' He picked up the phone again and asked the hotel operator to put him through to the embassy.

'Hello,' said Clive when the embassy answered. 'Could you put me through to the ambassador please?' There was a pause and a click.

'Hello, this is the ambassador's office. His PA speaking. How can I help you?'

'Good afternoon,' said Clive. 'I would like to speak to the ambassador on a very confidential matter. If he's free, can you put me through please?'

'I'm afraid Mr Moriarty has just left the office for the day. If it's urgent you could leave me a contact number and I'll do my best to track him down.' Clive was too stunned to answer for a few seconds, then pulled himself together.

'Er, no...thanks. I'll call again tomorrow.'

The girls looked at him.

'Well?' asked Clare eventually.

'Sorry, I've just had a bit of a shock. You're not going to believe this, but Moriarty is the *ambassador*!'

After they had all discussed the implications of this interesting discovery, Lucy asked Clive about his previous comment about "things falling into place".

'Ah, yes,' said Clive, his brain now spinning. 'As soon as you reminded me where we'd seen the name Moriarty before, I began to suspect that he might be the professor's cousin. And now...,' he paused for thought and looked at his watch, '...yes, a perfect time to ring London; I know just what to do.' He picked up the phone again and rang London.

'Dad, it's me again. Yes, we're fine thanks. I've just had a most interesting conversation with Peter Flint – tell you all about it later. Meantime can you do me a favour. Are you still friendly with that political journalist, Ferret? Great. Now this is what I'd like you to do...'

The next day a fax arrived from Julian.

"Dear Clive,

Hope this helps.

Love, Dad.

John Moriarty, currently British Ambassador in Kinshasa, Democratic Republic of the Congo. Was born Johannes Klaus Moriarty in Wilhelmshaven, Germany in 1949. He was the son of a German Naval Officer, Lucius Moriarty and an English Army Nurse serving in BAOR. The family came to England in 1952. Hans (as he was known) was educated at Wimbledon College and studied law at King's College London. After working in a legal capacity for the civil service he became a career civil servant and with his fluency in several languages entered the foreign office, now calling himself John Moriarty. After a meteoric rise in the FCO and service in embassies in New York, Paris and Rio, he was appointed as ambassador to the DRC in

2004. He is married with two children but there are no other known living relatives. His mother was an only child. His father had one sister who is believed to have emigrated with her husband to Brazil at the end of World War II, but whose current whereabouts, if she is still alive, are unknown.'

'Wow, you're right Clive,' said Clare. 'He obviously is Luke's cousin. Luke must have been named after his uncle, Lucius.'

'And now he's up to no good,' said Clive, nodding in agreement. 'Either Luke had something over him or, in return for favours ...'

'... Such as fake mining concessions...,' Clare burst in.

'... exactly,' said Clive patiently. 'In return for those, the professor is cutting him in on the fortune he hopes – *hoped* – to make on the invisibility robes.'

'And more importantly for us,' Clare exclaimed, 'after the professor saw us at the crater he obviously tipped the ambassador off to make life as difficult as possible for us all.'

'Yes,' said Clive slowly, 'the question is, has he *actually* got the authorities involved – which would be pretty risky if the truth came out – or has he just lied to Mum and Dad to put the frighteners on us all and stop us moving about, a certain way of making sure none of us could visit a certain photogyraspar deposit.'

'There's only one way to find out,' said Clare, 'that's to ask him, and remember, we now hold all the trumps. We've got the incriminating fax, the invisibility robe and two sisters for whom any animals will do anything. Let's get started! But first I'll ring Mum and Dad so they can start to relax a bit.'

After Clare had rung Richard and Joanna, Clive rang the embassy and spoke to the ambassador's secretary. She told him that the ambassador was in meetings all day and couldn't take any calls. Clive smiled grimly to himself.

'Can you just pop in and say that it's Luke with a message for Hans. I'll hold the line.' A moment later Hans came on the line after he had gestured for his secretary to leave the room.

'Luke,' he said. 'Good news, I've tracked them down and slapped some fake restrictions on them. I can guarantee you'll be free from further interference.'

Clive had the phone on speaker mode and the three of them grinned at each other. All their hunches had been correct.

'This isn't Luke, I'm afraid,' said Clive, 'it's Mr 'X' from London who is *very* interested in your extra-curricular activities. I'll see you in half an hour in your office.' Before the stunned ambassador could answer Clive put the receiver down.

'That'll make him sweat a bit,' he said cheerfully. The girls laughed and Clare clapped her hands.

'Very subtle,' she said. 'I just loved that dramatic "Mr X". What a cliché!'

'Now where's that invisibility robe?' asked Clive. 'I've been dying to try it out.' They got it out and as Clive was taller than the professor they adjusted the velcro hem so that his feet were invisible. Though they had all "seen" the professor in the robe they had never actually seen anyone disappear in front of them at close quarters, and when Clive stood in front of the mirror and activated the robe and the helmet and then simply vanished they were all lost in wonder at the almost miraculous power of the invention.

'Bye girls,' said a disembodied voice and the door opened, apparently by itself, and then shut itself again. A few seconds later it opened again and a few seconds later the faxed transcript rose up from the desk, folded magically in space, then disappeared.

'Sorry,' said the voice again, 'forgot the main exhibit! Bye again.' The door finally shut.

Outside the ambassador's office Clive looked up and down the corridor, slipped his robe off and folded it into a bag he had held hidden under the robe. He then walked in without knocking. The secretary looked at him aghast. 'Who are you?' she asked, 'and how did you get past security?'

'I'm Mr X,' replied Clive. The ambassador is expecting me. Oh, and I think security were all fast asleep.'

'The ambassador has just made me cancel all appointments because of you,' she said coldly. 'It had better be good. I'll tell him you're here.' She went through to the next room where the ambassador was sitting with his elbows on his desk and his head in his hands, and announced the arrival of Mr X.

'Thank you,' said the ambassador wearily. 'Please show him in – and close the door. Nobody is to disturb us under any circumstances.'

Clive walked in and caught his breath. If there had been any doubt in his mind that this man was a relative of Luke it was now dispelled. The cousins could have been identical twins.

'My apologies for the somewhat unconventional approach,' Clive began, 'and as we have delicate matters to consider I can assure you that nobody in the building other than your secretary is aware of my visit. I'm sure you don't need me to explain why.' The ambassador's haunted look told Clive that no explanation was necessary. Here was a man who knew he was about to hear some unpleasant truths.

'First, in fairness to you and out of common courtesy, I must tell you that your cousin Luke is dead. He fell while attempting to ford a river and was attacked by crocodiles. I don't know how close he was to you but please accept my sympathies at your loss.' The ambassador nodded in acknowledgment, but said nothing. He wanted to know what was coming next. In truth he had never been close to Luke, and apart from being jealous at his academic success, had not had any interest in him. On the few occasions they had met, when the ambassador had worked in the Rio embassy, he had not particularly liked him. The ambassador was, however, desperate for the fortune that his association with Luke had promised to yield, to save him from professional ruin, and that now seemed very unlikely to materialise.

'The other thing I want to talk about,' Clive continued, 'is this.' He slid the faxed telephone transcript across the desk. 'I think I'm safe in saying that if this goes to the right desk in London you can say goodbye to the Foreign Office, your reputation and probably your pension.'

The ambassador paled under his tan but remained completely impassive as he read the document. Then he looked at Clive and said.

'This is blackmail, isn't it? Who are you and what do you want?' Clive thought carefully before replying.

'Yes, I'm afraid it is blackmail. I am not, however, seeking to destroy you, I simply want you to correct the injustice you have done to me and my friends the Bonaventure family – who incidentally have now discovered their missing child, Grace.' What happened next took Clive completely by surprise. He had expected denial, expostulation, aggression, threats, even violence, but the ambassador slowly leant over the desk and put his head in his hands.

'I've been such a fool,' he said, his voice trembling.

Clive instantly felt a twinge of sympathy for the man. He knew only too well how the professor could manipulate people. After a moment's thought he reached over and retrieved his transcript.

'Look,' he said, 'this document isn't in the public domain; I came across it by chance and the malpractice discussed in it will never actually take place now that Luke is dead.' The ambassador nodded. 'So if I destroy this, London will never know about it and in return you can lift the unjust restrictions placed upon us and set about legitimizing Grace's position with a British passport and a proper birth certificate.'

'I could certainly do that,' the ambassador replied. He had a hunted expression, 'and I appreciate your decency in offering not to expose me but I'm afraid there's another complication. I will almost certainly no longer be ambassador by the end of the month – that's next week – and embassy business will be thrown into turmoil. Grace's complicated passport application will then be merely routine business and may have to wait until a new ambassador is appointed. It could take weeks or even months.'

'Why might you not be ambassador?' asked Clive.

'It's a long story,' said the ambassador wearily, 'and there's nothing anyone can do about it.'

'I've got all the time in the world,' Clive retorted. 'Why don't you tell me about it anyway? You've got absolutely nothing to lose: at best this is probably going to cost you your job and your reputation; at worst, you're going to spend the rest of your life in a Congo jail.' He paused briefly before adding grimly, '– and that would be a very short life from what I've heard.'

The distraught man thought in silence for several moments. Then he looked up.

'OK,' he said, 'you're right – but first let's have a cup of tea. He pressed a buzzer and spoke to his secretary. 'May as well make use of these little privileges while I can,' he said giving Clive a twisted smile.

'Now let me bare all. As you say, I've nothing to lose. The reason I so desperately needed money from Luke was because I have a secret passion for gambling – *had* I should say, because now, although it's too late, I've given up the habit completely. I got into debt with a gambling syndicate based here in Kinshasa and my debt reached such a level that they demanded some kind of security until it was repaid; otherwise they would expose me. I stopped gambling and repaid the debt – fortunately I had a generous legacy from a distant aunt. Then, to my horror, they refused to return my security. I had thought there was some honour among thieves, but realise now that I was being totally naïve.'

'What was it – the thing you gave him?' asked Clive.

'You won't believe I did this,' said John, 'but remember I had no choice.' The secretary came in and gave them tea and biscuits on beautiful Victorian crockery. 'The embassy has certain assets,' the ambassador resumed after she had closed the door behind her. 'In addition to financial credits in banks we actually own a significant number of artefacts. These are mostly presents from visiting potentates, heads of government, other ambassadors, tribal chiefs and similar dignitaries. They are often indigenous products – traditional wooden carvings, tapestries and such like. Some are extremely valuable and are kept in a vault to which only I have access. By far the most valuable of these assets is a diamond that was owned by King Solomon, a truly fabulous stone called "The Wisdom of King Solomon". Legend has it that when Solomon was visited by the Queen of Sheba she saw the stone on a pendant round his neck and tried to seduce him into giving it to her. He was wise enough to refuse and that is how the stone got its name.' Clive nodded – he had read Rider Haggard and knew that King Solomon's legendary diamond mines were thought to be somewhere in Africa. 'I'm sure that I don't now need to tell you,' continued the ambassador, 'that it was this precious jewel that I used as security against my debt and when the syndicate refused to return the stone I was simply devastated. I couldn't tell the police or make a fuss because of course my gambling and my "borrowing" of a precious embassy possession would be exposed and I would be ruined.'

'How much do they want?' asked Clive bluntly.

'A great deal – as I suspect you've already guessed,' the ambassador replied. 'The actual stone is flawless but isn't much use to them; they can't sell it because it is too famous and its provenance is universally known. If they cut it up its value will only be a fraction of what it is worth as a single unblemished gem. So, of course, they'd rather have money and it's insured for one million pounds. That is the amount that Luke was going to give me.'

'Where is it?' asked Clive. The ambassador gave a hollow laugh.

'Don't even think about it. Retrieving the stone would be quite out of the question. It currently resides at the home of one of the gambling syndicate. He lives by extortion and is one of the richest men in Kinshasa. His enormous villa is in the western suburbs of the city and is impregnable.'

Clive suddenly remembered something that had been said earlier.

'You said you might not be ambassador in a week,' he asked. 'What's magic about a week?' The ambassador groaned.

'That's the final twist of the knife,' he said. 'Every year the embassy assets are checked and audited. The audit is usually in late September, but for some bureaucratic reason to do with tax or insurance or whatever, they've brought it forward. The auditors come in on Monday. Once I open the vault I'm destroyed.' He drank his cup of tea then put it down and walked to the wall cupboard. 'I think I need something stronger – will you join me?' Clive nodded and they sat together drinking the finest whisky the embassy possessed as they contemplated the bleak situation.

'It does seem to me,' said Clive slowly, 'and without in any way condoning what you have done, that it would be in everybody's best interests if the diamond could be in your vault before the auditors arrive on Monday. It would help me and my family, especially Grace, it would preserve the reputation of our embassy and indeed our country, and it would also help you. The only ones for whom it would be bad news are the extortionist syndicate who have cheated you.'

'That would all be fine, even though I wouldn't deserve it,' said the ambassador, 'but for one single fact, which is that the retrieval of the stone is simply not feasible.' Clive took a sip of whisky as he pondered on how to say what he wished to say.

'You have been very honest with me,' he eventually said after a long pause, 'and I will now be honest with you in return, but I must first ask you a question. Did Luke ever tell you how he proposed to make this fortune?'

'No. All I know is that he said he'd invented something incredible that couldn't fail.'

'Well first of all, just to set the record straight, it wasn't *his* invention, though it did come out of his department. I can't tell you exactly what it was because I'm honour bound to keep it secret. I can tell you, however, that his description was no exaggeration. It *is* incredible and it *does* work. It is also in my possession and I intend to return it to its rightful owner, a young scientist in Rio. In the meantime, however, I intend to use it to get us out of the situation we are in.'

'But how can you possibly make enough money in time for it to be any use?' said the Ambassador.

'It only makes money in an indirect way,' Clive explained, picking his words carefully. 'What it actually does is to make people unaware of what is actually going on.'

'You mean a kind of hypnotism?'

'I suppose that's as good a way of imagining it as any,' Clive replied, with a nod. 'It's certainly all I'm going to tell you about it. You'll have to trust me that I think we've got a chance of retrieving your precious stone. The great thing is, the villains won't know that you've got it back – they'll just think it has been pinched from them. If they should ever bring up the question of payment with you again you simply ask to see the stone first and there can only be an embarrassed silence. And they certainly can't ever check in the embassy vault to see if you've got it or not.' The ambassador's face lightened. He was beginning to believe that Clive's plan might be just feasible, and was already looking more animated than he had so far looked since Clive had first come in. Then he frowned.

'I believe everything you've told me about the invention,' he said, 'Luke was very convincing about it and you sound just the same. There is a problem, however – a very big problem.'

'What's that?' asked Clive.

'This hypnotism – or whatever – may work with people, but this character's villa is protected by animals – dangerous animals. He has rottweilers and cheetahs roaming the grounds, and his valuables are rumoured to be protected by crocodiles. Your invention will presumably be useless against them. I never heard of anyone hypnotizing a croc.' Clive just smiled.

'It'll be OK. Trust me!' He drained his glass and pulled a town map from his pocket and spread it on the desk between them.

'Now, where exactly does this interesting gentleman live?'

A minute after Clive had left the room the ambassador saw that he had left the fax transcript on the desk. He quickly rang security at the front gate.

'I've just had a visitor,' he said, 'and he's left something behind. Please let him know and then send someone up for it.'

'Yes, sir.' A few minutes later, the security guard rang back and the secretary put him through. 'We're just about to close the main gates for the night sir, but there's been no sign of your visitor. Shall I wait a few moments more?'

'No-oo,' said the ambassador thoughtfully. 'No, he must have left earlier. Thank you. Good night.'

'Goodnight, sir.'

So, whatever this invention is, it really does work, thought the ambassador as he put the phone down. He picked up the fax. Maybe Clive had left it as a sign of good faith. He locked it in his private wall safe and picked up the phone to his secretary.

'Put me through to the Bonaventures in Salonga please – oh, and while I'm on the phone to them, check and see if anyone's still working down in passports.'

22

Clare Copes with Crocs

That evening Clare rang her parents in Salonga to tell them that the situation was improving and was delighted to learn that the ambassador had already contacted them to tell them their travel restrictions had been lifted, that their visa problems would soon be sorted out and that he was working on Grace's passport.

'It looks as though he's keeping to his side of the bargain he made with you,' she told Clive, 'so we'd better get on with ours!' They all then had a long discussion about the best plan for retrieving the diamond. Clive had assumed that he would be the one to go, but Lucy said that if they could adjust the invisibility robe to fit her it would be better, as she could talk to any guard animals directly.

'In case you've both forgotten,' said Clare after listening to them arguing. ' We're in Kinshasa where they speak French. As you're both hopeless at French, you won't know if anything useful is being said. *I'm* the one who should go and Lucy can fix the animals from outside before I go in. Anyway,' she added with a smile. 'I'm dying to have a go with that robe at least once.'

Her logic was unassailable so it was agreed that she should go and they adjusted the robe to fit her. She then rang the ambassador on the home number he'd given Clive to get an exact description of the diamond.

'He's not getting you to go in there is he?' the ambassador said in genuine distress. 'These are vicious ruthless people who'll stop at nothing.'

'Don't worry,' Clare reassured him. 'It's going to be a combined operation.'

'Well, the very best of luck to you,' said the ambassador. 'I think you're very courageous. Oh, and please thank Clive for leaving the fax and tell him that after he left today I rang his parents in Salonga.'

The next morning Clive and Lucy took a taxi from their hotel and went to a large villa in an affluent suburb. The villa was invisible from the road because it was surrounded by a high wall surmounted with barbed wire. An imposing drive led from the main road up to a guard house adjacent to two massive iron gates. Beyond the gate a cheetah was just visible, sauntering across the drive.

The taxi door opened.

'Goodbye! Good luck!.' The door closed. The taxi driver glanced in the mirror before driving off and was astonished to see that there were still two people in the back. Tourists! he thought. Always changing their mind. He was just about to ask where they would like to go instead when the door opened again.

'What about the animals?' a voice said.

'Gosh, sorry, I forgot all about it!' Lucy and Clive got out and asked the driver to wait a few moments. They walked up and down as though admiring the gates while a security guard with a heavy automatic weapon eyed them suspiciously. They walked away from the gates to some nearby trees and soon a monkey swung down to sit on a low branch. He seemed very interested in Lucy. After a few moments Lucy spoke – apparently to nobody in particular, as far as the guard could make out.

'Everything's fine,' she said. 'He's intelligent. In fact he's going to go in and stick around all the time you're there. He says the crocs aren't too bright and may not get it quite right, so it's best if he's there.'

'Crocodiles! Nobody said anything about crocodiles!' said a disembodied voice.

'Well, you were the one who insisted on going.' replied Lucy. 'It was a straight choice between speaking French and speaking crocodile and you won the argument.' Clive smiled at this sisterly interchange. Lucy suddenly grinned.

'Everything's fine,' she said. 'I was only teasing. Good luck!' She and Clive went back to the taxi as the monkey swung effortlessly over the wall into the villa grounds.

'Were you really teasing?' said Clive as the taxi moved off. 'I thought the ambassador did mention crocs, but maybe I didn't tell you.'

'No, I wasn't teasing,' said Lucy with a grin. 'But she was being a bit of a wimp and I'm sure the monkey'll see she's OK.'

After the taxi had driven off Clare suddenly felt very alone and vulnerable. Her confidence of the night before suddenly seemed to have evaporated. She began to worry what would happen if the robe's energizer suddenly failed – it didn't bear thinking about. Even Lucy's reassurance that she and Clive would soon hear from the animals if anything went wrong didn't completely assuage her fears.

Just then a large car drove up to the gates and the guard jumped to attention. He spoke to two other heavily armed guards who came through a small door beside the main gates and asked the occupants of the car to get out. They then frisked them and examined the contents of their briefcases, the interior of the car and the boot, before nodding to the guard and standing back and saluting. He then pressed a button and the gates swung open and the car passed through followed closely by Clare. Once inside she felt a surge of adrenaline and confidence. The guard hadn't taken the slightest notice of her – so the robe was effective, and a cheetah sniffed at her, then nonchalantly strolled away – so Lucy's instructions to the monkey seemed to be working. She hurried up to the house where the door was open and a maid greeting the visitors who had just arrived. Clare slipped in and followed them into a meeting room. It was thick with acrid tobacco smoke and, she thought, possibly other kinds of smoke and she had to resist a sudden desire to cough. The newcomers sat at the only three remaining vacant spaces at a large ebony table. At the head of the table sat a large, fleshy man with a nose stud and a cruel face. He was dressed in expensive clothes, wore a large Rolex watch and had heavy rings of gold and precious stones on his stubby fingers. To Clare's horror he started speaking in Lingala, but after a brief statement in this tongue he switched to French and she relaxed.

'Thanks again for coming, and welcome to our syndicate,' he said. 'I think our little club is getting so large,' he continued, ' we may have to meet in a larger room next month – or even a larger house.' The group all laughed at this – they all knew there wasn't a larger property anywhere in Kinshasa. Clare couldn't believe her luck. She had obviously stumbled in on a meeting likely to provide a great deal of information.

'Anyway, it's a sign of our continuing success that we are growing in number and I'm pleased to announce that, for the first time since we formed our little business group, our returns this month from the – ahem – *personal* documents and photographs that have fallen into our possession, has actually exceeded the income from our legitimate gambling saloons and casinos.' He turned and addressed the three newcomers directly. 'And I understand that, as a little gesture of goodwill on being invited to join us, you have brought along some new paperwork to add to our little collection.'

The leading newcomer smiled, nodded, and passed a large folder to the main man. He flicked through the letters and photographs and beamed after looking at one or two in detail.

'Excellent, excellent,' he murmured and he started to pass examples round to his crew. There were approving noises and grunts as the group perused the documents and several members congratulated the newcomers on the quality of their material. They went on talking for another two hours and Clare was just beginning to wish she hadn't had that extra coffee after breakfast when, to her intense relief, the chairman called the meeting to a close. He gathered up the new material into a folder, and led the way into a large reception room lavishly decorated with polished hardwood furniture and imported cutlery, glassware and china. Exquisite African carvings filled numerous alcoves and the floor was covered in exotic animal skins. The tusks and horns of various protected and endangered species adorned the walls and the head of a magnificent leopard graced the panelling behind the top of a polished mahogany table which was covered in canapes and cocktails.

As the group helped themselves to the nibbles and drinks the boss man excused himself for a moment and left through a side door with the folder under his arm, followed closely by Clare. He went along a corridor and out of the house on to a large flagstoned patio which was open on all sides and was covered by a thatched roof supported on wooden beams. On the patio there was a long table covered with delicacies. These were protected from flies by embroidered muslin covers and cooks were preparing a further selection of meats on barbecues and spits. The smell was delicious and Clare began to feel hungry. The man she was following nodded to one of the cooks who immediately picked up a large hunk of raw meat and accompanied him. Still followed by Clare they walked through a small garden, where peacocks strutted, and soon they came to a small lake which was entirely surrounded by a high fence of steel netting. The top of the fence curved outwards and was strung with barbed wire bearing a voltage sign with a skull and crossbones on it, to indicate it was electrified. There was an entrance gate in the fence and from this a concrete causeway led across the water to an island on which stood a small wooden cabin. Along each side of the causeway ran steel grooves. Something moved as the three of them approached and Clare saw that the pool was teeming with crocodiles, three or four of which were basking on the causeway. She made a mental note to deal with Lucy later.

At the entrance to the gate was a security panel. The man lifted the flap on this and inserted a key from a gold chain around his neck. He then gave another nod to the cook who lifted the flap on a small aperture in the fence and threw the meat he had brought into the pool. There was a thrashing of tails as the crocodiles fought to reach the snack and the animals on the causeway immediately slid into the water to join the fray. As soon as they had all gone the man turned the key and two metal fences arose from the grooves alongside the causeway. He turned and made a dismissive gesture to the cook, who returned to his duties.

The man then tapped out a code on the security pad. Clare was now standing right beside him and memorized the six-digit code. As soon as he pressed the last button the gate slid open and he now had a clear path to the cabin door, the steel fences on either side of the causeway protecting him from the crocodiles. He moved quickly across the causeway, followed by Clare and went into the cabin using the same code. There were three rooms inside: a large office, a kitchenette and, much to Clare's relief, a toilet. The office contained a table with a phone, a filing cabinet with three drawers, and a computer. The top drawer of the filing cabinet was labelled (in French) "Syndicate accounts"; the second drawer, "Letters and photos"; and the bottom drawer, "Items". The man put his folder on the table and took out the material the newcomers had given him. He opened the second drawer, put the documents in a file marked "unsorted" and closed it. The cabinet was unlocked, somewhat to Clare's surprise, then she reminded herself that the entire crocodile enclosure was, in effect, one large walk-in safe.

The man went to the door, keyed in the same code as before, and returned across the causeway. Once the far gate had closed behind him he took the golden key from his neck and stuck it into the security console. Seconds later the causeway rails retracted into their seatings and within moments some crocodiles had hauled themselves out onto the causeway again for a sunbathe. The man hurried back to join the pre-lunch reception and, after a quick trip to the loo, Clare set to work. The top drawer of the filing cabinet contained accounts related to the restaurants, bars and casinos run by the syndicate and seemed straightforward and non-incriminating. They were obviously documents concerned with the legitimate front of the organization and would, no doubt, be the only ones submitted for perusal by auditors and tax officials. The second drawer was much more interesting. It contained, in addition to the 'unsorted' file, a meticulously labelled set of envelopes, each with a name and address on it. Clare opened one which contained a letter of a highly personal nature and a photograph, which Clare suspected, the owner would dearly love to have back in her possession. She flicked through some of the other envelopes; all contained similar documents. Some bore the titles and addresses of people who were prominent officials – either on the outside envelope or on the material within. All the letters and papers contained information about which the original owners were obviously being blackmailed. Clare knew that the names and addresses on the envelopes would be in the computer and every week or month an address label and letter would be generated with a request for a monetary payment. If the payment didn't appear, the secret material in the cabinet would be made public – a risk none of those being blackmailed could possibly afford to take.

Clare remembered what she had come for and opened the bottom drawer. It was the most fascinating section of all, containing a vast and motley range of items: cuff-links, scarves, wristwatches, brooches, knives, a handgun, theatre tickets, a nightclub cloakroom tag, and various articles of clothing including a pair of slippers and, bizarrely, a single shoe. Each item was tagged neatly with a name and address and a note as to where it had been obtained. As she gazed at the apparently innocuous pile of assorted objects she realised that every one of them, because of the circumstances in which it had been found or stolen, was so compromising to its original owner that he or she was prepared to pay a fortune to the blackmailers in order to protect themselves from exposure. She felt physically sick as she thought of the ongoing mental anguish and torment that the contents of the cabinet represented for the hundreds of victims of the extortionists. At the bottom was a box covered in maroon felt bearing the British royal coat of arms and Clare knew without examining the label that she had found what she sought. She opened the spring lid with a click and gasped in wonder as she saw the exquisite stone nestling in its bed of finest satin. Clare had brought under her robes a large bag. She had expressed surprise at its size when Clive had produced it, for she already knew from the ambassador the modest dimensions of the lost diamond box.

'I just think you may find it comes in useful,' Clive had said enigmatically and now, as she looked at the files in front of her, she knew what he had meant. First she took the jewel box, then she took all the contents of the document and photograph file. There wasn't much room left in her bag but she took some of the smaller items from the bottom drawer and squashed them in. Then she walked to the door and prayed that the security code didn't change according to a protocol every time it was used. She tapped in the code she had memorized and the cabin door slid back. She saw the crocodiles scattered across the causeway and faltered, but then, on the meshed roof of the enclosure, she saw Lucy's monkey calmly sitting grooming himself and felt reassured. She wedged the door open with a chair then returned to the filing cabinet and threw the remaining contents of the items drawer into the pool. The shoe and slippers and pieces of clothing were instantly swallowed or torn to bits by the crocodiles. The inedible items sank into the soft muddy bottom and disappeared.

She then went back and pushed the computer over so that its cooling grilles were uppermost. The cabin had several torches and oil lamps for use during the frequent powercuts and she poured oil from the lamps into the computer grille until it started seeping out at the bottom through joints in the casing. She then lit the wick from one of the lamps and placed it on the floor in the pool of oil leaking from the computer. As the oil began to burn she rapidly took the syndicate accounts from the top drawer of the filing cabinet and stuffed them

under her arm. They stuck out a bit through the invisibility robe but she didn't worry – she wasn't taking them far. The computer was now engulfed in flames and she hurried across the causeway, stepping carefully between the recumbent crocodiles, opened the gate in the fence with the code and wedged it open with a large stone. She glanced around to check all was clear, then slipped off her robe and looked at the monkey. She pointed at the crocodiles and then pointed through the garden to the outside dining area. The monkey didn't react, so she repeated the gesture and mimicked eating. Suddenly the monkey twigged and swung down the side of the enclosure to speak to the reptiles. Soon they were waddling across the garden towards the barbecue. The peacocks scattered, letting out harsh cries of fear. The cooks took one look and ran for cover as the crocodiles fell upon the roasted meats. Two or three of the reptiles clambered

'The cooks took one look and ran for cover...'

onto benches and then on to the table and commenced to clear the delicacy-laden boards of everything edible. At that very moment the syndicate and their guests emerged to have their lunch. Smoke from the burning cabin was now beginning to curl over the trees and drift slowly towards the house.

Clare, hidden once again in her robe and clutching her bag and the syndicate files, slipped past the guests, foregoing the pleasure of seeing their faces, and went back to the conference room where she stuffed the syndicate accounts file into the briefcases of the visitors. If the security was as strict on the way out as it was on the way in, she thought, the newcomers were going to have a great deal of explaining to do and would fall under instant suspicion for the whole operation. She walked down to the gate, past several cheetahs, and picked up a large stone with which she banged hard on the gate. The security guard looked up from his lunch and looked out. She banged the gate again and rattled it. The guard came out, peeped through from side to side and shook his head in puzzlement. As he turned back to the guard house he noticed that his lunch had disappeared. The gate rattled again and looking back he saw his lunch scattered on the driveway outside the bars of the gate. Some birds were already hopping towards it. Then he noticed that his hat and a large bunch of keys had also been pushed through the bars of the gate. He called to the back of the guard house and the two security men appeared. One of them unslung his gun and held it at the ready as the guard pushed a button and the small side door slid open. The security officer went out cautiously, weapon at the ready, looking nervously from side to side before retrieving the hat and keys and retreating hurriedly back inside. He was unaware of Clare sidling past him. The side door closed. The monkey appeared on top of the wall and was joined by another from a nearby tree. They came to the ground and sniffed until they located Clare. They then set off along the roadside path, turning back to look at where they knew Clare to be. Their intention was unmistakable and she followed them immediately. After a mile or so they came to a small deserted sideroad with a taxi parked in it. The driver was smoking and reading a comic while Lucy and Clive strolled about admiring the trees and tropical flowers. Suddenly they seemed to feel that they had seen enough of nature and got back into the taxi. The doors shut and Clive leaned forward to the driver.

'British Embassy, please.' A few hours later, after a long chat with a very relieved ambassador, they were about to leave his office when he stopped them.

'There's just one more thing,' he said. 'As you already know, I rang your family in Salonga after you had left me yesterday. One of the things they asked me about was Grace's foster parents. I can assure you that I had nothing to do with their exile – that was something to do with local jealousies and political dirty work. Today, however, I made some enquiries and it looks as if the matter was handled by the Ministry of the Interior. I'm afraid I have no influence there – they naturally resent any foreign interference in internal matters – but I did get the name of the key player in the affair.' He slid a scrap of paper with a scribbled name over the desk, then added. 'Having seen what you guys are capable of I thought this might come in useful.' They thanked him and emerged from the embassy a few moments later clutching exit visas for the entire family and, the greatest prize of all, a brand-new passport for Grace Neema Bonaventure.

'The embassy could only issue a temporary one,' Clare explained after collecting it from the passport section, 'but it'll get her back to England and that's all that matters.'

'Well it saves us from having to break the law and play our final trump card,' said Clive.

'What's that?' asked Lucy.

'Why, the invisibility robe of course. I presume it got the professor into Tanzania so I'm sure it could get Grace out of the Congo!' They all laughed and then Clive and Lucy congratulated Clare on her conversation with the Ambassador who had, of course, been fascinated by her retrieval of the jewel. Clare had given the ambassador a bowdlerized version of the retrieval of the stone, and had been able to reassure him that not only could nobody link its disappearance with him, but that any suspicion was likely to fall on a group of villains who were well deserving of the unexpected privilege. Back at their hotel Lucy and Clive listened to the account of what had really happened with delight and were astonished at the pile of incriminating blackmail documents that Clare had brought with her.

'What on earth are you going to do with these?' asked Clive.

'Well, I could just destroy them,' said Clare, 'as I did the other stuff I couldn't get out. Then the blackmail demands would suddenly stop, but the victims would never know why and always be wondering whether they might start up again sometime. That's why I've got a better idea.' She went to her laptop, composed a letter and showed it to the others.

'What d'you think? I'm going to fill in the right name and then send one of these marked "strictly confidential" to each of the addresses to which the blackmail demands are sent.' Lucy and Clive peered at the little screen.

"Dear X,

On a recent stroll through the suburb of Gombe I came across an envelope labelled with your address, lying by the roadside near a large walled villa. I took the liberty of looking inside the envelope to check that it was empty and had simply been discarded, but to my astonishment found the enclosed document/letter/photograph (to be deleted as appropriate).

It struck me that if this item should happen to come into the possession of any unsavoury characters who happen to reside in the neighbourhood, they might seek to exploit it for purposes of financial gain and I am therefore returning it to you with my compliments. It has not been copied.

With best wishes for a more relaxed and prosperous future.

From a well-wisher from whom you will never hear again."

'Brilliant!' cried Lucy, clapping her hands.

'Isn't it amazing how much good has come out of this,' said Clive, nodding in agreement. 'Because of the ambassador's confession, dozens of people are going to sleep happier in their beds after getting your surprise letter through the post.'

'Not just the ambassador's confession,' said Clare quickly. 'Don't forget your generosity to him.'

'And *your* courage going into that awful villa,' said Lucy to Clare. 'It looked really spooky from the outside.'

'Not forgetting your amazing power, Lucy,' added Clive, determined to have the last word in this compliment competition.

'And,' she replied, beating him, 'the invisibility robe which you insisted on tracking down and capturing.'

They all laughed, then went down to the hotel restaurant to have the most relaxing meal they had enjoyed for a long time.

The next morning Clive looked thoughtful over breakfast.

'What's up?' asked Clare. All we've got to do now is wait for the others to get here from Salonga. There's nothing else, is there?'

'There is something,' Clive replied. 'You remember what the ambassador told us yesterday about Grace's foster family?' The girls nodded as Clive opened his wallet and retrieved the scrap of paper that the ambassador had given them. 'I was just wondering if...,'

' Of course!' Clare interrupted. 'Fingers crossed everyone!' Lucy looked bewildered; then light dawned as her sister snatched the piece of paper from Clive and dashed over to the files she had retrieved from the villa. She started feverishly flicking through the pile of incriminating documents. Suddenly she pulled out a large photograph with a flourish and waved it in the air. 'Tara-tara,' she pretended to trumpet. 'We've got him!'

An hour later a mystified senior official at the interior ministry gazed once again at the contents of the package that had somehow materialized in his office. He reread the anonymous note and looked at the torn half of the photograph lying on his desk. He would do practically anything to get back the other half as well; lifting an exile order was the least he could do. Shaking his head in bewilderment he picked up the phone and started to make several phone calls, starting with a number in Rwanda.

A week later the family held a grand reunion in the hotel in Kinshasa. Grace's foster family had come up with the others from the reserve, still astonished by the apparent sudden shift in political forces that had seen them welcomed back to their house and to their jobs in Salonga. They were all agog to hear each others' tales and after they had exchanged countless stories Clive turned to Ulindaji and told him about the creature that had risen from the swamp and eaten Sid. Ulindaji was very excited to hear Clive's account and asked him to describe the creature in as much detail as was possible from a single fleeting glimpse.

'It sounds very much as this is the water monster known as Lukwata,' he said, 'but all previous sightings have been in Uganda. I've never heard of it being seen near here, but Neema – sorry – Grace, has become our expert on legendary animals,' he turned to her enquiringly. 'Have you ever seen anything like this?'

Grace told him about the creatures she had thought to be plesiosaurs which sounded to be the same species of animal. With his encouragement she then told the others about her sightings of other strange creatures and she and Lucy decided there and then that they would write a scientific paper with "grandpa" on Congo cryptids. They talked until late in the night, particularly about how Grace was going to keep in touch with her foster family, and it was agreed that the first visit would be one by Ulindaji, Shangazi and Mzuri to London to see Grace's new home, and meet Ben's family and Clive's parents. Eventually Joanna had to coax them all to go to bed.

'We've got a long flight to England tomorrow,' she said, 'and it's a plane I definitely don't want to miss; we've had enough complications here to last us a lifetime.'

23

Clare's Last Card

The plane roared northwards across the Sahara desert towards home and safety. Clare and Clive sat together and smiled at the sight of Lucy and Grace sitting across the aisle talking animatedly about all the things they planned to do together.

'There's one thing I meant to ask you,' said Clive. 'After you'd talked to the passport people at the embassy about Grace, where on earth did you manage to get her photograph?' Clare laughed.

'I see I fooled you as well as the embassy and the people at the airport. It *isn't* Grace of course. It's Lucy. She opened her bag and took out a little wallet. 'I keep them of all the family wherever I go.' Clive flicked through them. All the family's photos were there except the one of Lucy which Clare had given to the embassy. There was also one of Clive. 'Oh, I don't know how that got in there,' said Clare, blushing as she snatched the wallet back. As she replaced the wallet in her bag, Clive glimpsed two envelopes.

'What are those?' he asked. Clare smiled.

'Don't be so nosy!' Then she relented. 'If you must know, they're our "get out of jail free" card and our "travel insurance".' Her smile widened to a grin at the puzzled look on Clive's face. 'You remember all the blackmail documents I posted yesterday?' he nodded. 'Well

I kept two back. I thought I'd post them in London once we knew nothing else could go wrong.' Clive looked at the envelopes. One was addressed to the Chief of Police, Kinshasa; the other to the Under-Consul, British Embassy, Kinshasa. His eyes widened in amusement and admiration.

'As you can see,' Clare said, 'the ambassador wasn't the only embassy official up to naughty tricks! I'm glad I didn't have to use blackmail for us all to get home safely, but there's a first time for everything.' She smiled happily as she snuggled up to him. Their drinks arrived and they switched on the in-flight movie.

24

Guidance from Grandparents

Lucy and Grace sat on the seafront at Littleporkton with Grandma and Grandpa. They had come down for a few days before returning for the new term at school. Their grandparents had been thrilled to meet Grace and had been fascinated by the account of their African adventures. Lucy had taken Grace to the dolphinarium and introduced her to Jonathan, the dolphin with which she had first discussed her powers and which had told her what the animals expected of the Promised One. They had both had further long discussions with the dolphin and now that Lucy had experienced at first hand the devotion of countless animals in different situations and their expectations of help from her, she was in a much better position to appreciate the dolphin's views. When they finally left the dolphins they met Grandma and Grandpa on the seafront as arranged and sat eating a picnic in the brilliant late summer sunshine.

'I asked you once,' said Lucy, 'when I first learned I was the Promised One, what I should be doing to improve the world for the animals and you told me not to expect to be able to do much before I was grown-up. Now I have seen so much more of the world and spoken to so many animals – and to Grace – we can both see that there is so much to be done. The forests are being cut down, the seas are polluted, the ice caps are melting, the earth's atmosphere is changing and everywhere humans and animals are competing for space and resources. We can see now that we do have to wait until we're older to really change anything, but what *jobs* do you think we should be trying to get so that we can make the greatest difference to things? We've obviously discussed it with Mum and Dad, but I told Grace that you were the first people I ever talked to about it, and we're both interested in what you think!' Grace nodded in agreement. Their grandparents thought long and hard before answering.

'It's often best,' said Grandpa, 'to become good at something before you start trying to influence others. If you achieve knowledge and respect in a particular field, people know that you can compete and succeed in open competition and know that you have some experience of real life.' Grandma nodded in agreement and added:

'Then, if you still want to, you can move into those areas of life or institutions in which you wish to bring about changes.'

'So what you're saying,' said Grace, 'is that we should just get back to school and try to pass all our exams and get a job or profession, same as anyone else.'

'Exactly!' said Grandpa. They all laughed.

Epilogue

BBC News, Friday 27th April 2040

'... and now, after that quite extraordinary news, we go over to our special correspondents in Westminster and New York. First to Sally at Westminster:'

'Thank you, John. As you say, today has been one of the most extraordinary days in the history of politics and, indeed, the history of this country. Earlier today Dr Grace Bonaventure was received at Buckingham Palace by His Majesty the King and invited to form a government as the new Prime Minister of the United Kingdom of Great Britain and Northern Ireland. Dr Bonaventure qualified in medicine in 2020 and worked for several years for the International Red Cross in trouble spots and deprived areas across the globe, receiving widespread recognition for her astonishing results in improving healthcare in remote areas lacking in infrastructure and resources. She settled in England after marrying a fellow doctor and went into what was to prove a brilliant career in politics. She was rapidly acknowledged by politicians on both sides of the house to be unsurpassed in her knowledge of matters relating to the environment and energy resources and after a brief spell as Minister for the Environment she has now, on her forty-second birthday, become the youngest Prime Minister since William Pitt in 1783 and only the second woman Prime Minister in British history. I must leave you now, John, for the new Prime Minister has kindly agreed to spare me a few moments. I will come back to you with that interview as soon as it is over.'

'Thank you, Sally. We look forward to hearing from you with that report. Well, for most families, having a daughter as Prime Minister would be success enough in itself but we go over now to our New York correspondent to hear the background to today's other big news, the astonishing appointment of Dr Bonaventure's twin sister as Director General of the United Nations."

'Thank you, John. Yes, here at the UN the media are in what can only be described as a feeding frenzy. There has simply never been anything like it. For the youngest-ever Secretary General to be appointed on the very same day that her identical twin is made the Prime Minister of Great Britain is nothing short of mind-blowing. Dr Bonaventure – Dr *Lucy* Bonaventure that is – first qualified as a vet in England and obtained her doctorate in the diseases of Cretaceous Period Animals at the recently established University of Prehistory in Manaus, Brazil. She then started on her brilliant career with the United Nations Organization, first out in the field and, more recently, at the central organization in New York. Her knowledge of the world's fauna is reported to be unequalled even by leading international zoological experts and she is unquestionably the most erudite person, notwithstanding her relative youth, ever to be appointed to this prestigious position. She is, of course, the first-ever woman in the post. I must apologize for the background noise to this recording. I am standing in the main foyer of the UN and the level of excitement here exceeds anything I have ever experienced in a long career in journalism. Now back to you, John, in London.'

'Thank you, Michael. Well, there it is: identical twin sisters appointed on the same day to two of the most influential jobs on the planet. Both are married with children. Both are interested in, and extremely knowledgeable about, the great environmental issues that now dominate our thoughts and our future.

'Between them they wield enormous power and influence. The question now on everyone's lips is: "How they are going to use it?" Only time will tell.'

Lucy's Lexicon

(the suffix –kin is both singular and plural)

animanet	animal communication network
arborikin	monkey
arborimane	baboon
bonobokin	pygmy chimpanzee
Brilliant One	the Sun
cacklekin	hyena
carrionquill	vulture
clovenkin	antelope, gazelle, etc.
common tongue	universal animal language
cornukin	rhinoceros
Dreadful One	crocodile, alligator
fellfang	any species of venomous snake
fledgibane	hawk
fledgiquill	any species of bird
fleetfang	cheetah
giant greypod	large herbivore: elephant, rhino
gilliquill	fish eagle

Great Flitterkin	pterodactyl
Great Salt	the ocean
Greater World	the rainforest
greathorn	giant unicorn (Mokèlé-Mbèmbé)
greatkine	buffalo
Hairy Tailless One	any species of great ape
hipposnort	hippopotamus
house that floats	boat
house that moves	any vehicle: car, lorry, etc.
junglekin	all the animals of the rainforest
Lesser World	all the world outside the rainforest
Little Tailless One	forest pygmy
malevobane	mongoose
Malevolent One	any species of snake
manefang	lion
mimicquill	parrot
raptoquill	eagle
scurripod	rat, mouse, vole, etc.
shieldkin	tortoise, turtle
spotfang	leopard
Tailless One	human being
The Special One	Neema
thunderstick	rifle
tuskikin	elephant
wolfkin	wild dog, jackal, wolf, etc.

Notes on the names in the book

These notes give some information about the people and places referred to in the book, and cite the chapter or section in which their name first appears. Some of the names are real and the information given is simply factual. Many of the names, however, are fictitious, or used in a fictitious manner, and these tell you something about the character to whom they belong. Some are very obvious, others much less so; some are in Portuguese, the language of Brazil, and some in Swahili, the main language of East Africa. See how many hidden meanings or associations you spotted as you read the story.

Unusual words or abbreviations used in this section are explained in the glossary.

Alan Cutcliff *Chapter 7* This man is a curator of minerals. *Alan* comes from the Breton name meaning "little rock" and *Cutcliff* is an appropriate name for one who obtains stones from cliffs.

Angstrom *Chapter 5* The angstrom is a unit of length equivalent to 0.1 nanometre. It is used to express wavelengths in the electromagnetic spectrum and is a very appropriate name for a scientist researching the physics of light.

Biggles *Chapter 8* Biggles happens to have the same name as the famous fictional pilot hero who appears in the books by W E Johns. Major James Bigglesworth, known always as *Biggles*, was a fighter ace who featured in numerous flying adventures.

Bonaventure *Preface* Bonaventure is Lucy's surname. Saint Bonaventure (1221–74) was a mystic and philosopher who was the author of '*Life of St. Francis.*' Saint Francis, like Lucy, was said to be able to communicate with animals.

Boyoma Falls *Chapter 11* Formerly known as the Stanley Falls, the Boyoma Falls are a series of seven cataracts that extend for 60 miles (100 kilometres) along the Lualaba River between Ubundu and Kisangani. Below the seventh cataract the river becomes the Congo River.

Chakula *Chapter 4* Chakula means food in Swahili and is a good name for Neema's cook.

Colarinho *Chapter 5* Captain Colarinho is one of the Brazilian policemen. *Colarinho* is a Portuguese word for a person who catches someone.

Ferret *Chapter 21* Ferret is an investigative journalist with a very suitable name (see glossary).

Fossfinder *Preface* Helen and Julian Fossfinder are palaeontologists who look for *fossils*.

Haggard *Chapter 21* Sir Henry Rider Haggard (1856–1925) was a writer of adventure stories, mostly set in Africa. *King Solomon's Mines* is one of his most famous books. *(see Solomon)*

Hakimu *Chapter 3* This is a Swahili word meaning chief. It is a suitable name for the chief ranger at the reserve!

Hans *Chapter 8* Hans is a variant of Johannes, the German name equivalent to John in English.

Hogwarts *Chapter 13* Hogwarts is the school of witchcraft and wizardry in J K Rowling's best-selling *Harry Potter* series. The mail is delivered to and from Hogwarts by owls and Sarah thinks this is similar to the use of hawks and eagles for the same purpose by Lucy.

Jambo *Chapter 3* Jambo means "hello" in Swahili and is the name of the first bonobo to greet Neema in the forest.

Jangili *Chapter 9* As you might have guessed, *Jangili* is a Swahili word meaning poacher or rogue.

Johannes *Chapter 21 see Hans.*

Kasai Craton *Chapter 7* A famous diamond-bearing seam that extends from Angola into Kasai in the DCR.

Kilimanjaro *Chapter 6* Mount Kilimanjaro is an inactive volcano in north-eastern Tanzania. It is 5892 metres high (19,331 feet), and is the highest point in Africa.

King Solomon *Chapter 21 see Solomon*

Kinshasa *Chapter 3* Kinshasa, formerly known as Léopoldville, is the capital city of the Democratic Republic of Congo. With a population of approximately 10 million people it is the third largest city on the African continent and the second largest Francophone city in the world, after Paris.

Kongamato *Chapter 4* This is a cryptid (*qv*) that has been the subject of numerous sightings over the last hundred years in Zambia and the DCR, including a report from a British Museum expedition in 1932. It is supposedly a living species of pterodactyl.

Kuficha *Chapter 10* This is a Swahili word meaning to hide or conceal. It is a suitable name for someone with an invisibility robe!

Kukamata *Chapter 10* This is a Swahili word meaning to detain or restrain and is an appropriate name for an anti-poaching officer.

Littleporkton *Chapter 24* A seaside town which must be somewhere similar to Little*ham*pton.

Livingstone *Chapter 13* Dr David Livingstone(1813–73) was a Scottish missionary doctor who was one of the greatest European explorers of Africa. He publicised the horrors of the slave trade. He died on an expedition to expose further information about slavery and to discover the source of the Nile.

Loch Ness Monster *Chapter 4* A cryptid, also called 'Nessie' (Scottish Gaelic: *Niseag*). Its (disputed) scientific name is *Nessiteras rhombopteryx,* meaning *The wonder of Ness with the diamond-shaped fin.* The name was given by the late Sir Peter Scott and sceptics point out that this 'scientific' name is an anagram of '*monster hoax by Sir Peter S.*' Loch Ness is the largest body of fresh water in Britain (by volume) and the monster is claimed to be one of a colony of lake creatures similar in appearance to the (long-extinct) plesiosaurs. The first reported sighting of the creature was said to have been by St. Colomba on 22 August 565 AD.

Lucinda *Prologue* The name Lucinda means 'bringer of light', an appropriate name for this scientist. The Roman goddess of childbirth, Lucine, gave first light to the newborn.

Lucius *Chapter 7* The name Lucius comes from the Latin word, *lux*, meaning light.

Lukwata *Chapter 22* A cryptid water monster that has been the subject of several reported sightings in the swamps of eastern and central Africa.

Luz *Chapter 9* This is the Portuguese word for light, the subject studied by the professor.

Masai Mara *Chapter 9* A large park reserve in south-western Kenya, famous for its abundance of game. It is adjacent to the Serengeti reserve in neighbouring Tanzania.

Mgosa *Chapter 10* This is a Swahili word meaning "thief or "criminal." It is a very suitable name for Sid's henchman!

Mlezi *Chapter 2* This is a Swahili word meaning "nurse" or "children's governess." It is an appropriate name for Mzuri.

Mlinzi *Chapter 2* This is a Swahili word meaning "watchman" or "protector." It is a suitable name for Mzuri's father who is a ranger guarding the game reserve.

Mokèlé-Mbèmbé *Chapter 4* A large cryptid that has been the subject of numerous sightings along the Congo river. Some reports describe it as having a giant single horn.

Moriarty *Chapter 8* Professor James Moriarty appears in the famous fictional detective stories about Sherlock Holmes by Sir Arthur Conan Doyle. Moriarty is Holmes's arch enemy and is commonly regarded as being the first 'supervillain' in literature. In the present book *Moriarty* is the maiden name of Prof. Strahlung's mother so, appropriately, the two evil professors are presumably related.

Mzuri *Chapter 1* This is a Swahili word meaning good.

Ndoki *Chapter 4* A remote jungle area in the north of the republic of Congo, famous for its wildlife.

Ndugu shetani *Chapter 10* Ndugu is a Swahili word meaning *brother* and shetani means *devil* or *evil spirit*.

Neema *Chapter 2* This is a Swahili word meaning good fortune or *grace*.

Ngorongoro crater *Chapter 6* The Ngorongoro crater is the world's largest unflooded volcanic caldera, having an approximate diameter of 12 miles (20 km). It is situated in a conservation area in Tanzania and contains a wide variety of wild life. It is a popular tourist attraction.

Peter Flint *Chapter 5* Lucinda's fiancé. He is a geologist with very appropriate names. *Peter* comes from the Greek word petros meaning stone, and *Flint* is a type of rock called quartz

Photogyraspar *Chapter 5* This is not a real substance but is the name Lucinda coined for the ore discovered by Biggles. *Photo* comes from the Greek word 'phos' meaning light. *Gyrate* means to rotate or spiral from the Greek word 'guros' a circle. *Spar* is a transparent or translucent microcrystalline mineral. Thus *photogyraspar* is a crystalline mineral that twists or distorts light

Poirot *Chapter 5* Hercule *Poirot* is a famous Belgian detective who appears in many of the detective stories written by Agatha Christie.

Pterodactyl *Chapter 4* Meaning: *Winged finger*. Any of a large variety of flying reptiles belonging to the order *Pterosauria*. The

wings were covered in thin membranes of skin, like a bat, and the animals ranged in size from that of a small bird to monsters with a wing span of 14 metres. Pterodactyl species existed over an immense span of time: 228–65mya.

Queen of Sheba *Chapter 21 see Sheba*

Rider Haggard *Chapter 21 see Haggard.*

Sabedoria *Chapter 7* This is the Portuguese word for *wisdom*. A suitable name for the university.

Salonga National Park *Chapter 1* This is the largest tropical · rainforest reserve in Africa. It is situated at the heart of the Congo river basin and is only accessible by water. It is home to many rare and endangered species, including the bonobo.

Schadenfreude *Chapter 8* This is a German word meaning to take pleasure in another's misfortune.

Serengeti *Chapter 6* The Serengeti National Park is a large conservation area in Tanzania, established in 1951. It is famous for its variety and quantity of game, including all of the "big five"– lion, elephant, buffalo, leopard and rhinoceros. It is the site of immense natural migrations of wildebeeste and zebra.

Shangazi *Chapter 3* This is a Swahili word meaning paternal aunt – the relationship Shangazi bears to Mzuri.

Sheba *Chapter 21* The queen of Sheba is mentioned as visiting Solomon in the biblical book of *1Kings*. Sheba was a nation spanning parts of both Africa and Asia across the Red Sea.

Solomon *Chapter 21* King Solomon was a king of Israel. He was the son of David and mentioned in the biblical book of *1Kings*. He was

credited with great wisdom and was visited by the Queen of Sheba. Popular legend has it that he possessed fabulously wealthy mines somewhere in Africa, but this is not a proved historical fact. *(see Haggard)*

Stanley *Chapter 11* Sir Henry Morton Stanley (1841–1904) was a famous explorer and journalist. He was asked by the New York Herald to try and find David Livingstone (qv) who had not been heard of for years since setting off in 1864 on a journey to find the origin of the Nile. After a series of adventures and misfortunes Stanley eventually found Livingstone in the village of Ujiji near the shores of Lake Victoria. He walked up to him and uttered the famous words: "Doctor Livingstone I presume?".

Strahlung *Chapter 7 Strahlung* is the German word for radiation. The professor studies light, which is a form of electromagnetic radiation.

Tsavo National Park *Chapter 2* The Tsavo National Park is in Kenya. Established in 1948, it is the largest national park in Africa (22,000 sq.km.) and, despite immense losses from poaching, still contains a spectacular quantity and variety of game.

Ulindaji *Chapter 2* This is a Swahili word meaning security or protection It is a suitable name for a ranger at the reserve!

Glossary

The explanations in this glossary give only the meanings of words as they are used in the book. Many of the words have other meanings as well, and if a full description of a word is required the interested reader should consult a dictionary.

(abbrev. – abbreviation, adj. – adjective, adv. – adverb, conj. – conjunction, interj. – interjection, n. – noun, pl.n. – plural noun, prep. – preposition, v. – verb)

abbreviation *n.* a shortened word or phrase

abduction *n.* the removal of someone by force; kidnap

abruptly *adv.* suddenly; unexpectedly

abysmal *adj.* very bad; terrible *(modern informal usage)*

access *n.* the right or ability to enter, use or approach something

acknowledge *v.* to recognize the truth of something; to admit a reality

acquire *v.* to get something; to obtain; to gain possession

acrid *adj.* unpleasantly sharp; pungent; having an irritant smell or taste

acronym *n.* a pronounceable word made up from some or all of the initial letters of a longer title

adjacent *adj.* next to; near; adjoining

adopt *v.* Chapters 2, 3, 4: to take responsibility for; to take into the family; *v.* Chapters 16, 20: to take on or use

adrenaline *n.* a hormone associated with excitement, stress or activity

advocate *n.* one who pleads a cause; one who speaks on behalf of another

affluent *adj.* wealthy; rich

affront *v.* to insult; to offend; to upset the dignity of

aforementioned *adj.* someone or something that has been referred to previously

aftermath *n.* the results of a previous event; the period after an event

aggro *n.* *(slang)* an abbreviation of *aggravation* meaning annoyance or nuisance

aghast *adj.* filled or overcome with horror; appalled

agog *adj.* very curious; intensely attentive

akin *adj.* like; similar to; having the same characteristics

alcove *n.* a recess in a wall; a niche

alert *adj.* attentive; vigilant

alleged *adj.* described as such; presumed to be; said but not proved to be

allocate *v.* to give to; to assign; to allot

aloof *adj.* distant; having a superior attitude; supercilious

amateur *n.* a non-professional person; one who engages in an interest for enjoyment or sport, rather than for remuneration

ambition *n.* a strong desire for success or power

ambush *n.* a trap, usually involving people waiting in hiding to catch or attack others

ammo *n. (slang)* an abbreviation for ammunition

ammunition *n.* projectiles that can be fired from a weapon e.g. bullets

anagram *n.* a word or phrase the letters of which can be rearranged to form another meaningful word or phrase

analyse *v.* to study in detail; to examine to discover specific information, meaning or composition

analysis *n.* the results obtained from examining something, or determining its composition

anguish *n.* severe pain; misery; intense grief

animanet *n. see Lucy's Lexicon*

anon *adv. (poetic or archaic)* soon; in a short time

aperture *n.* an opening

appal *v.* to horrify; to shock; to dismay

apprehension *n.* a state of fear or anxiety about something that might happen

approbation *n.* praise; approval

appropriate *adj.* suitable; fitting

archaic *adj.* out of date; ancient; antiquated

arduous *adj.* strenuous; difficult; requiring great effort

arrogant *adj.* conceited; boastful; proud

artefact *n.* a man-made article

ashen *adj.* pallid; drained of colour; like ashes

aspiration *n.* the hope or desire to achieve something

assemble *v.* to gather together

assent *n.* agreement; compliance

assets *pl. n.* possessions; property

assignment *n.* task; mission

assuage *v.* to calm; to soothe

assume *v.* to suppose; to take for granted; to accept without proof

audit *n.* the process of inspection and verification, e.g. of accounts

Auf Wiedersehen! *German phrase* Goodbye!; See you again!

auspices (under the auspices of) *phrase* under the authority of;
    under the guidance or patronage of

avaricious *adj.* greedy for riches

aversion *n.* repugnance; extreme dislike for something or someone

avert *v.* to turn aside (one's gaze)

awesome *adj.* very impressive; amazing; outstanding

balcony *n.* a projecting platform on the wall of a building, having a
    rail or balustrade

ballast *n.* heavy material providing stability or weight

BAOR *abbrev.* British Army On the Rhine

barrel *n.* the metal tube in a firearm from which the bullet or
    projectile emerges

bayonet *n.* a blade for stabbing that can be attached to a firearm

beacon *n.* a signal; a light or fire to attract attention

beak *n. (slang)* magistrate, judge, headmaster, or similar authority figure

benign *adj.* kindly

bewildered *adj.* confused; puzzled

binoculars *n.* optical instrument with a telescope for each eye which magnifies distant objects

bird *n.* *(slang)* an informal term for a girl or young woman

bite one's tongue *phrase* to try very hard to stop oneself from saying something

bizarre *adj.* very unusual; odd; extraordinary

blab *v.* to give away a secret (in speech)

black panther *n.* a melanistic (black) variant of a big cat such as a leopard, cougar or jaguar

blackmail *n.* the use of threats (usually of disclosure) to obtain money or, as in Chapter 21, to influence the actions of another

bleeper *n.* a portable radio receiver

blighter *n.* an old-fashioned slang word meaning an annoying or irritating person or thing

bloody *adj.* *(slang; swearword)* a strong imprecation used to lend particular emphasis to a phrase or statement

boisterous *adj.* lively; unruly; unrestrained

bond *v.* to create a close relationship with another; to befriend

boon *n.* a favour

booty *n.* stolen valuables; plunder

booze *n.* *(slang)* any kind of alcoholic drink

botanist *n.* one who studies plants

bowdlerize *v.* to remove unwanted words or passages from an article or account; to edit; to redact

brand *v.* an identifying mark made on the skin, usually with a hot iron

breakthrough *n.* a significant discovery; a ground-breaking development

bribe *n.* a gift of money or goods in exchange for a favour

brood *n.* the young in a family; offspring

brunch *n.* a late morning meal, combining *br*eakfast with l*unch*

bureaucracy *n.* a system of administration, particularly one that is rigid or impedes progress

bush *n.* uncultivated, wild countryside (especially in Africa and Australia)

bush meat *n.* the flesh of wild animals killed for food (often illegally)

butt *n.* the end of the stock of a rifle that is placed against the shoulder

cacophony *n.* an unpleasant mixture of different sounds or notes

cahoots *pl.n.* "in cahoots with" means in league with; in collusion

cairn *n.* a mound of stones, usually erected as a memorial

calamity *n.* a disastrous event

caldera *n.* the basin-like crater within a volcano

canape *n.* a small piece of bread, biscuit or toast covered with a tasty topping

canopy *n.* the highest general level of foliage in a forest, formed by the crowns of trees and penetrated by only the tallest species

captor *n.* one who captures and holds another captive

carburettor *n.* engine part that controls the air–fuel mixture

carcass *n.* a dead body

caricature *n.* an inaccurate representation of some person or thing, often exaggerating certain characteristics

carnage *n.* slaughter; massacre

carpe diem *phrase (Latin)* seize the day; take action; go for it

cassava *n.* a tropical plant, also called manioc, with an edible starchy root

cataract *n.* a rough waterfall, often across rocks; rapids

causeway *n.* a raised road or path crossing water, mud, swamp, etc

cavort *v.* to jump around; to caper; to prance

cf. *abbrev. (Latin)* confer; compare; see. Used to guide the reader to another source of information

chassis *n.* the steel frame of a vehicle

cite *v.* to refer to; to mention; to quote

cliché *n.* a word or expression that has lost its force through overuse

cluster *v.* to gather round in a close group

coarse *adj.* Chapters 2, 18: vulgar; indelicate; ribald; *adj.* Chapters 4, 15: rough; unrefined

cock-a-hoop *adj.* boastful; crowing; in high spirits

cocktail *n.* a drink mixed from different elements, usually alcoholic and usually drunk before meals

coincidence *n.* the simultaneous chance occurrence of events that are apparently connected

commonplace *n.* ordinary; everyday; common

commune *v.* to communicate closely

compass *n.* an instrument used to find direction by means of a magnetized needle that points north

comply *v.* to agree with or submit to rules, conditions or requirements; to be obedient

composure *n.* calmness; serenity; tranquillity

comprehension *n.* understanding

compromise *n.* a settlement arrived at by choosing something
between two extremes

compunction *n.* mercy; regret; remorse

concession *n.* a right to land, or to conduct a certain activity,
granted by a government or other authority

concierge *n.* a caretaker or attendant

concur *v.* to agree

condone *v.* to pardon; to overlook; to forgive

condor *n.* a species of large vulture found (principally) in the South
American Andes

confer *v.* to bestow upon; to endow; to grant

confidential *adj.* secret; private

conscience *n.* the feeling of what is right or wrong; a sense of
morality

conscript *v.* to enrol for military service

conservateur *n. (French)* warden; guardian; custodian

console *v.* to comfort; to bring solace

consternation *n.* worry; concern; anxiety

contorted *adj.* twisted

contrive *v.* to arrange; to manage

convalescence *n.* a period of recovery from illness

conviction *n.* a state of feeling convinced; feeling sure or certain
about something

coordinates *n.* sets of numbers that define an exact location

cope *v.* to manage; to deal with a situation; to succeed (often in the face of difficulty)

coy *adj.* shy; demure, usually in a provocative manner

crackdown *n.* a policy of strict enforcement; the imposition of severe measures

craton *n.* a part of the earth's crust that has been geologically stable for many millions of years

credence *n.* belief (in); acceptance

Cretaceous Period *n.* the last period of the Mesosoic era, between the Jurassic and Tertiary periods, 144–65 million years ago

crucial *adj.* decisive; critically important

crustacean *n.* one of a class of animals having a carapace or shell

cryptid *n.* a cryptozoological term for a creature rumoured to exist but not recognized by mainstream science

crystal *n.* a substance with a characteristic regular shape that results from the specific internal arrangement of its atoms or molecules

culminate *v.* to end; to bring to a final stage

curator *n.* person in charge of a museum, department, etc.

dastardly *adj.* cowardly; sneaky; mean; contemptible

data *pl.n.* facts; measurements; observations; recordings

daunting *adj.* frightening; disheartening; intimidating

dejected *adj.* downcast; despondent; miserable

demise *n.* death

denizen *n.* a person or animal living in a place; an inhabitant; a resident

desperado *n.* a desperate or reckless person

destination *n.* the place where a journey is planned to end

deterrent *n.* something that deters or puts off; something that prevents or restrains

devour *v.* to eat greedily or voraciously; to consume

diplomatic *adj.* Chapter 12: sensitive; delicate; tactful; *adj.* Chapter 20: pertaining to diplomacy or affairs of state

disable *v.* to put out of action; to make ineffective

disarming *adj.* reducing or counteracting suspicion; reassuring

disembodied *adj.* without a body; lacking a body

disparaging *adj.* contemptuous; insulting; belittling

dispel *v.* to drive away; to disperse

disperse *v.* to leave a gathering; to break up; to scatter

distort *v.* to twist out of shape; to deform; to contort

distraught *adj.* very upset; agitated; distracted

divert *v.* to change the direction of someone or something; to turn aside

DNA *n.* deoxyribonucleic acid. The substance in cells of which genes are made and which can be used to identify species and individuals

dock *v.* to subtract or remove

domain *n.* land or area owned or dominated by a person, family or group

double take *n.* a repeated, delayed, or exaggerated reaction to a given event or situation

dough *n.* *(slang)* money

down a peg *phrase* "to take down a peg" means to diminish another's self-esteem or importance

DRC *abbrev.* Democratic Republic of Congo

dugout canoe *n.* a boat made by hollowing out a log

dung *n.* droppings; excrement; faeces; 'poo'

duo *n.* a pair; a twosome

duplicity *n.* deception; doubledealing

e.g. *abbrev. exempli gratia (Latin).* This means 'for example'. Now frequently simplified to e.g.

ebb *v.* to fall away; to recede; to decline

ebony *adj.* a hard, black wood

edible *adj.* eatable

eerie *adj.* mysteriously frightening; spooky

elaborate *v.* to give more detail in a story or account; to expand upon

elation *n.* extreme happiness; joy

elevated *adj.* high up

eloquent *adj.* fluent and persuasive

emanate (from) *v.* to come from; to originate from

embarrass *v.* to cause to feel self-conscious; to disconcert; to fluster

embed *v.* to fix in firmly; to stick into

embellishment *n.* an improving detail or adornment

ember *n.* glowing fragment of wood (etc.) in a dying fire

emphatic *adj.* forceful; definite

en route *adv. (French)* on the journey; along the way

encounter *n.* a meeting, especially one that is unexpected

encroach *v.* to intrude or spread gradually

endeavour *v.* to try; to attempt to attain something

energize *v.* to provide with energy; to stimulate

engulf *v.* to completely surround; to overwhelm; to swallow up

enigmatic *adj.* puzzling; mysterious

enlist *v.* to engage support or service for a task or venture

enmity *n.* hostility; discord; ill will; antagonism

enthral *v.* to enchant; to spellbind

entice *v.* to attract with a reward; to allure

entreaties *pl.n.* pleas; earnest requests; supplications

epilogue *n.* a short postscript

equator *n.* an imaginary circle around the middle of the Earth at 0 degrees latitude. It divides the Earth into the Northern and Southern Hemispheres

erode *v.* to wear away

erstwhile *adj.* former. In Chapter 9 *his erstwhile companions* means the people who used to be his companions

erudite *adj.* learned; scholarly

escarpment *n.* a long, broad, very steep slope

espionage *n.* spying

esteem *n.* respect; high regard

etc. *abbrev. et cetera (Latin).* This means 'and the rest'; 'and so forth'; 'and the others'

eventuality *n.* a possible event or outcome; a contingency

eviscerate *v.* to remove all internal organs; to disembowel

excavate *v.* to dig out; to remove (earth, etc.); to make a hole or cavity

exile *v.* to expel from home or country; to banish

exotic *adj.* possessing strange beauty or quality; having unusual allure

expansively *adv.* extravagantly; all-inclusively; widely

explore *v.* to travel into unknown territory

expostulation *n.* argument; reasoning

exquisite *adj.* particularly beautiful; attractive with delicate, refined qualities

extort *v.* to obtain money (or favours) by threats, intimidation or violence

extraction *n.* taking out; removal; withdrawal

extra-curricular *adj.* taking plavce outside the normal course of duties or activities

fabulous *adj.* based upon fable or myth

facilities *pl.n.* the equipment and buildings required for the conduct of some activity

faculty *n.* a university department

fading *adj.* slowly disappearing; diminishing

fag *n.* *(slang)* cigarette

fake *adj.* false; not genuine; spurious

falter *v.* to speak hesitantly, haltingly, or with uncertainty; to stammer or stutter

fauna *n.* all the animals living at a particular time, or in a particular place

FCO *n.* The Foreign and Commonwealth Office

feasible *adj.* possible

feral *adj.* wild or savage, especially after being previously tame or domesticated

ferret *n.* a variety of polecat used for hunting rabbits and rats, renowned for its ability to seek out hidden creatures. We use the phrase "ferret out" to mean the discovery of hidden information by persistent investigation

feverishly *adv.* desperately; energetically; restlessly

fiancée *n.* a female to whom one is engaged to be married (male: fiancé)

fictitious *adj.* not real; made up; imaginary

fiddle *v.* Chapter 8: to falsify; to cheat; *v.* Chapter 11: to rearrange; to experiment with the controls

fitful *adj.* occurring in irregular spells. A *fitful* sleep (Chapters 1&2) is broken and restless

flawless *adj.* without any defect or imperfection

flora *n.* all the plant life living in a particular place or at a particular time

flog v. *(slang)* to sell

fogey *n.* an old-fashioned, fussy, "uncool" person

foment *v.* to instigate; to stir up; to cause trouble

foolhardy *adj.* rash; heedlessly adventurous

forage *v.* to search for food

ford *v.* to cross a river

fortitude *n.* courage; endurance

fortuitously *adv.* by happy circumstance; by accidental good fortune

foster *v.* to bring up and care for another's child

fragment *n.* a portion of something larger; a broken-off piece

Francophone *n.* one who speaks French

fraternity *n.* brotherhood

Frau *n.* a German title equivalent to Mrs.

fray *n.* a disturbance; a fight or brawl

freak *n.* an abnormal or deformed creature; a monstrosity

frenzy *n.* wild excitement; frantic activity

fret *v.* to worry; to be distressed

frisk *v.* to feel or pat to check for concealed weapons

frustrate *v.* to stop; to prevent; to hinder; to thwart; to annoy

fuselage *n.* the main body of an aircraft

gem *n.* a precious stone

geology *n.* the study of the history, structure and composition of the Earth

gesticulate *v.* to send a message or signal by using body movements (usually of the hands or head)

gesture *n.* something done or said to make a point or to emphasize something

get out of jail free card *phrase* a passport to freedom (derived from the name of a card in a popular board game)

ghastly *adj.* horrible; hideous

gig *n.* *(informal)* an event or performance

gingerly *adv.* in a timid or cautious manner

glade *n.* a clearing or open space in a wood

glean *v.* to obtain in small pieces; to gather gradually; to garner

gleeful *adj.* merry; happy, particularly because of another's misfortune

glimpse *v.* to catch sight of briefly or incompletely

glitch *n.* a malfunction, often of unknown cause

glossary *n.* an alphabetical list of terms relating to a particular
  subject, topic or field, with explanations and definitions

glow *v.* to emit a steady light; to shine evenly

gorge n. a deep ravine

gouge *v.* to dig out; to scoop; to make a hole

GPS *n.* global positioning system. A worldwide location and
  navigation system based upon satellite signals

grapple *v.* to struggle in close combat; to come to grips with
  somcone or something

greypod *see Lucy's Lexicon*

grille *n.* a grating of metal bars that admits cooling air

ground-breaking *adj.* novel; making a new advance

gruesome *adj.* horrible; ghastly; repugnant

guerrilla *n.* a member of an irregular group fighting against some
  official force

gully *n.* a small valley; a channel; a fissure between rocks

gung-ho *adj.* keen to engage in activity, often to excess

guts *pl.n.* Chapter 10: intestines; bowels; entrails; *pl.n. (slang)*
  Chapter 19: courage; pluck; daring

hack *v.* to gain unauthorized entry to a computer system

hark *v. (archaic)* to listen

harmony *n.* agreement; accord

hassle *n.* trouble; worry; nuisance

haughty *adj.* arrogant; exalted

hazardous *adj.* dangerous; involving risk

hearken *v. (archaic)* to listen; to pay attention

heftier *adj.* bigger; stronger; bulkier

henceforth *adv. (archaic)* from now on

henchman *n.* a supporter; an attendant or servant

hero-worship *v.* to feel intense admiration for; to adulate

herpetological *adj.* relating to reptiles and amphibians

hesitant *adj.* uncertain; irresolute; wavering

hijack *v.* to take by force; to steal (particularly a vehicle)

hinder *v.* to hamper; to prevent; to get in the way

hist *interj. (archaic)* an exclamation attracting attention, or warning others to be silent

hither *adv. (archaic)* towards this place; to here

Hogwarts *see notes on the names in the book*

Holy Grail *n.* the bowl or chalice used by Jesus Christ at the Last Supper. The phrase is now often used to describe something that is very highly sought after or aspired to

homage *n.* an act or display of respect or allegiance to one of superior status

Homo sapiens *n.* the scientific name of modern mankind

hostage *n.* a person held captive as a security for a ransom or the fulfilment of stated conditions

hot-wire *v. (slang)* to start an engine without a key by bypassing the ignition switch

huddle *v.* to nestle closely together

hue *n.* a colour or a shade of colour

hue and cry *n.* the public pursuit of a suspected criminal

huffily *adv.* resentfully; angrily

hulk *n.* the abandoned body or frame of a vessel or vehicle.

hunch *v.* Chapter 18: to crouch or bend; *n.* Chapter 21: an intuition; a guess

hypnotism *n.* the process of inducing sleep or an altered state of mind

immemorial *adj.* very ancient; from a time too long ago to be remembered

impart *v.* to give to; to bestow upon

impassive *adj.* not revealing any emotion

impenetrable *adj.* not possible to get through

imperial units *pl.n.* standards or definitions legally established in Great Britain for distances, weights, measures, etc.

implicate *v.* to show to be involved

implications *pl.n.* effects or results that might not at first be obvious

import *n.* significance

impregnable *adj.* unable to be broken into

impunity *n.* immunity from unpleasant consequences

inaccessible *adj.* not reachable; unapproachable

inaudible *adj.* unable to be heard

incessant *adj.* never stopping; continual

incinerate *v.* to burn; to reduce to ashes

inconspicuous *adj.* not easily seen

incorporate *v.* to include

incriminating *adj.* suggestive of guilt

indigenous *adj.* belonging to a particular region or country; native to that part

indisposed *adj.* sick, but usually not seriously so. In Chapter 7 the word is used in a slightly ironic sense

initiate *v.* to start; to begin

inexplicable *adj.* not possible to explain

infamous *adj.* notorious

inferiority complex *n.* a disorder in which a desire to be noticed conflicts with a fear of humiliation

ingestion *n.* eating or drinking

innocuous *adj.* harmless

insurance policy *n.* a protection against a possible contingency

insurgency *n.* uprising; rebellion

insurrection *n.* insurgency; uprising

intently *adv.* very attentively

interminable *adj.* endless

intervening *adj.* between

interwoven *adj.* interlaced; entwined

intravenous *adj.* into a vein; within the venous system

intrepid *adj.* fearless; bold; daring

intrusive *adj.* encroaching in an unpleasant manner

intuitively *adv.* instinctively

irksome *adj.* annoying; bothersome

ironic *adj.* surprising or incongruous in a slightly amusing or sarcastic way

IT *abbrev.* information technology

ivory *n.* the hard, creamy dentine in the tusks of elephants, rhinos, walruses etc. Its value makes it highly sought after by poachers

jail-bird *n.* one who has spent time in prison, especially repeatedly

jeopardy *n.* danger; peril; risk

jet lag *n.* the fatigue experienced after rapidly crossing several time zones

kaleidoscope *n.* an optical toy which produces complex symmetrical patterns of frequently changing shapes and colours

kidnap *v.* to abduct someone and keep them captive

kimberlite *n.* an igneous rock often containing diamonds

kin *n.* relatives; kindred; a group related by blood ties

landline *n.* a wire or cable for telecommunications. It is usually more reliable than a mobile network

lavish *adj.* extravagant; luxurious; prodigal

league *n.* an old unit of distance equal to 3 miles (4.8 kilometres)

legacy *n.* money, property or possessions, handed down as an inheritance from a deceased relative or predecessor

legend *n.* a traditional story from long ago that may or may not be true

lest *conj.* in case; for fear that

liana *n.* a tropical climbing plant; a woody vine

liberation *n.* freedom

Lingala *n.* the common vernacular (qv) language of Kinshasa and much of the Congo

locality *n.* an area or neighbourhood

location *n.* situation; position; site

Loch Ness Monster *see notes on the names in the book*

lode *n.* a vein of ore in a rock stratum

lope *v.* to walk or run with a long, easy movement

lore *n.* accumulated knowledge on a specialised subject or topic

lucidity *n.* clarity; normality

lumber *v.* to move in an awkward or ungainly fashion

lurch *v.* to pitch suddenly forwards or to one side

mahogany *n.* a hard, reddish-brown wood

maiden name *n.* a woman's surname before marriage

makeshift *adj.* something found or put together to use when a
proper tool is unavailable

malevolent *adj.* wishing evil on others, or appearing to do so

malignant *adj.* causing harm or evil

manipulate *v.* to handle or control, often skilfully

manoeuvre *v.* to move into a suitable position

maraud *v.* to roam or wander in search of spoils; to raid; to harry

maroon *v.* Chapters 5,7,8: to abandon; to leave isolated; *adj.*
Chapter 22: a dark, purplish-red colour

masquerade *n.* disguise; pretence

massacre *n.* the indiscriminate killing of a large number of people

melanistic *adj.* black

Memsahib *n.* a term of respect for a married woman, especially one
who is an employer.

metamaterial *n.* a material with properties that depend upon
its structure rather than on its composition. The term is used
particularly to describe artificial materials with properties not
found in naturally occurring substances

metric units *n.* the decimal units used in measurement systems based upon the metre

midwife *n.* a person who assists in the delivery of a baby

militia *n.* a group of citizen soldiers (not a professional army)

millennium *n.* a period of one thousand years (plural: *millennia*)

mobilize *v.* to organize and marshal in preparation for war

modest *adj.* self-disparaging; unpretentious; understating one's achievements or ability. The word is used in its true sense in Chapters 18 & 20, and in an ironic sense in Chapter 17; Chapter 22: small; not large

momentous *adj.* of great significance

monotonous *adj.* boring; tedious; dull

morsel *n.* a small piece; a little bit (usually of food)

motley *adj.* made up of disparate elements; mixed

mph *abbrev.* miles per hour

mucus *n.* the slimy secretion from a mucous membrane

muse *v.* to think; to ponder

musings *pl.n.* contemplative thoughts

muslin *n.* a finely-woven cotton fabric

mya *abbrev.* million years ago

myriad *adj.* very many; innumerable

myth *n.* someone or thing whose existence is unproven

naïve *adj.* innocent; credulous; ingenuous

naught *n. (archaic)* nothing

navigate *v.* to plot the position and direct the path taken, during a journey

neologism *n.* a new word

nick *v. (slang)* to steal

nigh *adv. (archaic)* near

nihil nisi bonum de mortuis *phrase (Latin)* speak nothing but good of the dead

nil desperandum *phrase (Latin)* don't despair!

Nobel prize *n.* a famous international prize named after the Swedish scientist and philanthropist, Alfred Nobel. It is awarded for outstanding contributions in a number of fields, including physics – Lucinda's subject

nonchalant *adj.* casual; unconcerned

notwithstanding *prep.* despite; in spite of

nudge *n.* to give a gentle poke or push to attract attention; to jog someone

nuzzle *v.* to rub or push gently with the snout

obstetric *adj.* to do with childbirth

opt *v.* to choose; to show preference (for)

optical *adj.* to do with light or the eye

optics *n.* the study of light and vision

optimistic *adj.* hopeful; confident; expecting a good outcome

option *n.* choice; decision

orb *n.* something spherical; in Chapter 11 this means the hawk's eyeball

ore *n.* a mineral or mixture of minerals from which useful materials such as metals, gems, salts, etc. can be extracted

oresome *adj.* there is no such word in the English language! It is a neologism (qv) used as a pun in the title of Chapter 7. The chapter is about ore and the developments are *awesome*

ostensibly *adv.* to all outward appearances; apparently; seemingly

outcrop *n.* a protruding section of rock

PA *n.* abbreviation for *p*ersonal *a*ssistant

pact *n.* an agreement, usually bringing mutual benefit to the parties making it

palpable *adj.* capable of being touched; tangible

pang *n.* a sudden, sharp, brief sensation, usually unpleasant (such as of pain or hunger)

paracetamol *n.* a pain-relieving drug; an analgesic

patio *n.* a paved area adjoining a house

pendant *n.* an ornament hanging from a necklace

pensive *adj.* deeply thoughtful, often with an element of sadness

perfidious *adj.* treacherous; deceitful; faithless

perilous *adj.* very dangerous; extremely hazardous

perplex *v.* to puzzle; to confuse; to bewilder

peruse *v.* to study; to read carefully; to scrutinize

pestilential *adj.* troublesome; annoying; harmful

peter out *v.* to diminish and finally cease; to gradually die out

photogyraspar *see notes on the names in the book*

pick-up *n.* a truck with an open rear body and low sides

pillage *v.* to rob, especially during a war

placate *v.* to pacify; to calm; to appease

plesiosaur *n.* an extinct marine reptile

plod *n. (slang)* a disparaging term for a policeman

plumage *n.* a bird's feathers

plummet *v.* to descend rapidly; to drop down; to plunge

poacher *n.* one who hunts illegally

pockmark *n.* a pitted scar; a small depression in a surface

ponder *v.* to think thoroughly and deeply about something; to give careful consideration to something

pot *v.* to shoot

potentate *n.* a ruler; one with power

potential *n.* unrealised capacity; latent possibility

potentially *adv.* possibly

pothole *n.* a deep hole in a road

precambrian *adj.* relating to the earliest geological period, which lasted for 4 billion years, ending roughly 600 million years ago

preceding *adj.* foregoing; former; coming before

precipice *n.* a sheer, steep cliff face

predator *n.* a carnivorous (meat-eating) animal; a hunter–killer

predominant *adj.* principal; prevailing; most important or obvious

preface *n.* foreword; introductory statement

preoccupied *adj.* absorbed in one's thoughts; engrossed

preserve *v.* to save; to protect

prestigious *adj.* having status or importance; impressive

primitive *adj.* early; crude; undeveloped

proclaim *v.* to announce in public

prodigious *adj.* very great; vast

profusely *adv.* abundantly; copiously

prologue *n.* an introductory section to a story, play, speech, etc.

prospector *n.* one who searches for valuable minerals

prototype *n.* a preliminary or experimental version of something

provenance *n.* place of origin

psychological *adj.* to do with the mind

pterodactyl *n.* any of a large variety of extinct flying reptiles belonging to the order *Pterosauria*. Pterodactyl species existed over an immense span of time: 228–65mya

pterosaur (see pterodactyl)

pugmark *n.* pawprint of an animal; spoor

pun *n.* a joke that relies on a play on words; usually words that sound the same but have different meanings

punctuate *v.* to interrupt frequently

purportedly *adv.* supposedly; allegedly

pursuit *n.* a chase; the act of following

quagmire *n.* bog; mire; marsh; swamp

quaver *v.* to tremble; to quiver

query *n.* a question

qv *abbrev. quod vide (Latin)*. This means 'which see' and is used to denote a cross-reference

RAC *abbrev.* Royal Automobile Club. An organization that gives assistance to car drivers

radioactive *adj.* emitting radiation spontaneously from atomic nuclei (includes alpha-, beta- and gamma-radiation)

rampage *n.* destructive or violent behaviour

randomly *adv.* haphazardly

ransack *v.* to plunder and pillage; to take apart

ransom *n.* the price demanded for someone's release

rapprochement *n. (French)* the resumption of peaceful relations

raptor *n.* a bird of prey

raucous *adj.* hoarse; loud; harsh

ravage *v.* to destroy; to damage

ravenously *adv.* very hungrily; voraciously

ravine *n.* a deep, narrow valley

reagent *n.* a substance used in chemical tests or reactions

realm *n.* field or area of interest

realm *n.* kingdom; domain

rebel *v.* to rise up against authority or an established institution

recess *n.* a space that is set back; an alcove; a niche

recipient *n.* one who receives

recollections *pl.n.* memories

reconciliation *n.* the settlement of a quarrel; the re-establishment of
   friendly relations

reconnoitre *v.* to inspect; to survey; to examine; to explore

recount *v.* to tell; to describe; to narrate

recumbent *adj.* lying down; reclining

reflection *n.* careful thought or consideration

refuge *n.* a place of safety; somewhere providing shelter or
   protection

regale *v.* to give pleasure or amusement

rehabilitation *n.* restoration

reminiscences *pl.n.* memories; recollections

remnant *n.* vestige; surviving trace

remorse *n.* sorrow; regret; compunction

remote *adj.* far away; distant; out-of-the-way

rendezvous *n.* (*from French*) a pre-arranged meeting

renegade *n.* outlaw; rebel

repercussion *n.* consequence; result

replenish *v.* to restore that which has been used up; to replace

repressive *adj.* restraining; suppressing; subjugating

research *v.* to obtain information or collect facts about a subject; to study in detail

reserve *n.* an area of land set aside for the conservation of animals, plants, etc.

respiratory *adj.* to do with breathing

respite *n.* a pause; a rest interval

rest my case your honour *phrase* a legal phrase indicating that one has finished presenting evidence to a judge. In Chapter 9 Clare uses the phrase to indicate that she thinks she has delivered a powerful argument

retch *v.* to heave as if to vomit; to vomit ineffectually

retract *v.* to draw in; to be drawn in

retribution *n.* punishment, especially as vengeance

retrieve *v.* to recover something; to get something back

rev up *v.* to increase the speed of an engine (from *rev*olutions per minute)

revel *v.* to take pleasure or delight in

revelation *n.* something revealed or disclosed, usually in a surprising way

roam *v.* to wander; to move about with no fixed objective

Rolex *adj.* (*trade name*) an expensive brand of wristwatch

rottweiler *n.* a species of robust dog with a reputation for being fierce

round the corner *adj. phrase* soon; imminent

rueful *adj.* sorrowful; repentant

ruffian *n.* a villain; a violent person

rummage *v.* to search carelessly or untidily

ruthless *adj.* hardhearted; merciless

sack *v. (slang)* to dismiss from employment

safari *n.* an expedition into the bush or wilderness, often in search of animals and especially in Africa

sarcastic *adj.* mocking; ironic; stating the opposite of what is really intended

sardonic *adj.* derisive; mocking

saunter *v.* to stroll at a leisurely pace

savannah *n.* open grassland, studded with trees and bushes

saved my bacon *phrase* an expression indicating great relief at having been rescued from a difficult situation

scam *n. (slang)* a swindle; a method of cheating

sceptical *adj.* disbelieving; doubtful; mistrustful

scree *n.* a heap of rock fragments

scrutiny *n.* close observation

seam *n.* a linear deposit or stratum of rock, ore, etc.

secure *adj.* safe; free from danger; carefree

seduce *v.* to entice; to attract; to lure

senhor *n.* a Portuguese courtesy title equivalent to Mr or Sir

serpentine *adj.* snake-like

shades *pl.n.* suggestions; memories

shale *n.* fine-grained sedimentary rock deposit

shudder *v.* to shake violently in fear or horror

SI units *n.* The *Système International D'Unités* is an international system of units used in science and technology

sibling *n.* brother or sister

slander *n.* defamatory statement; falsehood; calumny

slang *n.* a word or phrase that is not standard language but is used informally; jargon

sojourn *n.* a period of temporary residence; a limited stay

specimen *n.* an object of interest, collected and kept for future study or display

spectacle *n.* an unusual or interesting sight; a phenomenon

spellbound *adj.* fascinated; enthralled

spiral *v.* to move along a helical course

spit *n.* a long rod on which meat or a carcass is skewered for roasting over an open fire

spooky *adj.* eerie; ghostly; supernaturally frightening

sporadic *adj.* intermittent; every now and then

sprawl *v.* to spread out; to straggle

stalk *v.* to prowl stealthily towards prey

stammer *v.* to speak hesitantly

static *adj.* stationary; unmoving

steed *n.* a horse upon which one rides. In Chapter 15 Neema's 'steed' is an elephant

stifle *v.* to cover up or suppress a sound

stifling *adj.* oppressive; stuffy

stimulate *v.* to arouse; to generate activity

stipulation *n.* a condition, usually one upon which an agreement depends

straddle *v.* to stretch across something with gaps or intervals between the supporting structures

strand *v.* to leave helpless; to maroon

strata *n.* the plural of stratum (qv)

strategic *adj.* relating to the conduct of a project or mission, especially one to do with war

strategy *n.* a plan of action

stratum *n.* a layer (especially of rock)

stunning *adj. (slang)* amazing; astonishing; very impressive

stupefaction *n.* bewildered amazement; astonishment

stupor *n.* unconscious state; torpor

subdued *adj.* not harsh or bright; dimmed

subside *v.* to settle down; to sink to a lower level

subtle *adj.* not very obvious; difficult to detect. Clare's use of the word in Chapter 21 is, of course, sarcastic

suburb *n.* a district on the outskirts of a town or city, usually residential (where people live)

succulent *adj.* juicy

sullenly *adv.* morosely; gloomily

suppress *v.* to hold back; to keep in check; to restrain

surmise *v.* to conjecture; to infer

surmount *v.* to rise above

surveillance *n.* the act of watching; observation; scrutiny

sustained *adj.* suffered; undergone

Swahili *n.* a language used in Kenya, Tanzania and many other East African countries

swamp *n.* an area of ground that is permanently waterlogged; marsh; quag

swarm *n.* a large group of small animals, especially bees and other insects

sympathy *n.* emotional feelings for others (compassion, anguish, etc.)

syndicate *n.* a business group undertaking a project

synopsis *n.* summary; condensed review

talent *n.* ability; aptitude

talons *pl.n.* the hooked claws of a bird, especially a raptor

tan *n.* a yellowish-brown colour

tangle *v.* to twist together; to mix up; to snarl; to make confused

tarpaulin *n.* a sheet of tough, waterproof fabric used as a cover

temporarily *adv.* for a short period; transiently

tentatively *adv.* hesitantly; cautiously; uncertainly

terrain *n.* ground (when describing the geography or topography of an area)

tersely *adv.* shortly; curtly; abruptly

thee *pronoun (archaic)* you, the objective form of thou

thermal *n.* Chapter 11: a column of rising air produced by uneven heating of the ground and local area, often used by birds or gliders to gain height with minimum effort; *adj.* Chapters 13, 19: relating to heat or temperature

thicket *n.* an area of dense vegetation composed of small trees, bushes, shrubs, brambles,etc.

thine *adj. (archaic)* belonging to you; yours

thou *pronoun (archaic)* you; the one addressed

throng *n.* a large crowd gathered closely together

thug *n.* a violent individual

thumbs-up *phrase* a gesture indicating success; pleasure; approval; etc.

tidings *pl.n.* news; information

to and fro *adv.* back and forth

toerag *n.* (slang) an unpleasant, despicable or contemptible person

tormented *adj.* anguished; tortured

torso *n.* the trunk of the body

transcript *n.* a reproduction or copy of a document

transfixed *adv.* rendered motionless by shock, fear or horror

transversely *adv.* crossways

traverse *v.* to cross; to go over

trek *v.* to make a journey, often a long and difficult one

tributary *n.* a river or stream that joins a larger one

trilogy *n.* a series of three associated works

trio *n.* a group of three

trivial *adj.* unimportant; petty

truculently *adv.* aggressively; obstreperously

trudge *v.* to plod wearily and heavily

trumps *pl.n.* the cards that outrank all others

turmoil *n.* confusion; tumult

tussock *n.* a dense tuft of grass, reeds or other vegetation

twig *v. (slang)* to understand suddenly; to work out what is going on; to catch on

ultrasound *n.* high-frequency sound waves used in medical diagnosis

unaccosted *adj.* unchallenged; not confronted or stopped

unassailable *adj.* irrefutable; undeniable

unblemished *adj.* without any flaw or imperfection

undergrowth *n.* the vegetation growing beneath tall trees, consisting of small trees, bushes, shrubs, brambles, etc.

unique *adj.* without equal; sole; singular; only

unison *n.* complete harmony; complete coordination

unprecedented *adj.* unparalleled; not having occurred or been observed previously

unpredictable *adj.* changeable; capable of behaving in a surprising way

unscathed *adj.* unharmed

unsurpassed *adj.* not exceeded in achievement or excellence

upshot *n.* outcome; result; conclusion

uranium *n.* a radioactive, metallic element used as a source of nuclear energy

UN *abbrev.* United Nations. An international organization set up in 1945 to bring about cooperation in international law. international security, economic development, social progress, human rights and the establishment of world peace.

UNESCO *acronym (qv)* The United Nations Educational Scientific and Cultural Organization. One of 18 specialized agencies within the UN

USB *abbrev.* Universal Serial Bus. A USB memory stick is an electronic device for the storage and easy transport of large data sets

usher *v.* to show in or out; to escort

vacate *v.* to leave empty; to quit

valid *adj.* true; having foundation

vantage point *n.* a position giving a favourable view of a scene or situation

vaporize *v.* to cause to evaporate or disappear; to destroy by turning into gas

Velcro *n.* *(trademark)* a fastening made out of two strips of adherent nylon fabric

velociraptor *n.* *a* turkey-sized, bipedal, theropod dinosaur. Scientific name: *Velociraptor mongoliensis,* meaning: *swift thief.* Velociraptors achieved popular awareness through the 1990 novel *Jurassic Park* by Michael Crichton, and the 1993 film of the same name.

vendor *n.* one who sells something

venomous *adj.* poisonous

verandah *n.* a porch or balcony on the outside of a building

verge *n.* a grassy border along the roadside

vernacular *n.* the commonly spoken language or dialect of a particular country or region

vertical *adj.* perpendicular; upright

vibrate *v.* to shake; to quiver; to oscillate

vice-chancellor *n.* a senior official in a university

vigorously *adv.* energetically; robustly

villa *n.* a large and often luxurious residence

villain *n.* a wicked person

visa *n.* a document, or an endorsement in a passport, permitting the owner to enter or travel through a particular country

void *n.* an empty space

vulnerable *adj.* capable of being hurt or wounded; weak

waste *v. (slang)* to murder someone

whence *adv. (poetic)* from; from what place

whereabouts *adv.* approximate position; location

white lie *n.* a fib; a minor untruth

whither *adv. (poetic)* to what place; where

wily *adj.* crafty; sly; cunning

wimp *n. (slang)* a feeble, ineffectual individual

wisp *n.* a thin, insubstantial streak

withhold *v.* to keep back

wrath *n.* extreme anger; rage leading to retribution or vengeance

wry *adj.* twisted; contorted (facial expression) as an indication of quiet amusement

WW 2 *abbrev.* World War Two. The second world war (1939–45).

ye *pronoun (archaic)* form of address to two or more people

yonder *adv. (poetic)* over there – often far away

Unit conversion table

1 inch = 2.54 centimetres
1 foot = 12 inches = 0.3 metres
1 yard = 3 feet = 0.91 metres
1 mile = 1760 yards = 1.61 kilometres
1 league = 3 miles *(archaic)*
1 pound = 16 ounces = 0.45 kilograms
1 ton = 2240 pounds (1016 kilograms)

1 centimetre = 0.39 inches
1 metre = 3.28 feet = 1.09 yards
1 kilometre = 0.62 miles
1 kilogram = 2.2 pounds
1 tonne (metric ton) = 1000 kilograms (2204.6 pounds)